THE UNSEEN

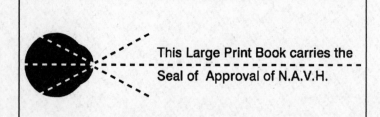

THE UNSEEN

HEATHER GRAHAM

THORNDIKE PRESS

A part of Gale, Cengage Learning

Detroit • New York • San Francisco • New Haven, Conn • Waterville, Maine • London

Copyright © 2012 by Slush Pile Productions, LLC.
Thorndike Press, a part of Gale, Cengage Learning.

Thorndike Press® Large Print Core.
The text of this Large Print edition is unabridged.
Other aspects of the book may vary from the original edition.
Set in 16 pt. Plantin.

LIBRARY OF CONGRESS CATALOGING-IN-PUBLICATION DATA

Graham, Heather.
   The unseen / by Heather Graham. — Large print ed.
     p. cm. — (Thorndike Press large print core)
   ISBN-13: 978-1-4104-4816-3 (hardcover)
   ISBN-10: 1-4104-4816-9 (hardcover)
   1. Women—Crimes against—Fiction. 2. Murder—Investigation—Fiction.
3. Paranormal fiction. 4. San Antonio (Tex.)—Fiction. 5. Large type
books. I. Title.
PS3557.R198U57 2012
813'.54—dc23
                              2012005713

Published in 2012 by arrangement with Harlequin Books S.A.

Printed in the United States of America
1 2 3 4 5 6 7 16 15 14 13 12

For Kathryn Falk, Ken Rubin, Jo Carol
Jones, Sharon Murphy, Lisa and Chris,
Barney, and the Cumbess family
in memory of "Maw."

And to all the great friends I've made
who live in and love the
Great State of Texas!

PROLOGUE

Galveston Island, Texas
Spring, 1835

The moon that night was enchanting. Rose Langley walked barefoot on the beach, looking up at the splendor in the sky. She had no idea what had caused this beautiful spectacle; she just knew she'd never seen anything like it. It was a large and shimmering half crescent, and behind it, like a silent and glowing echo, was a second half crescent. Once upon a time, she might have gone to her tutor, Mr. Moreno — so old, soft-spoken and wise — and asked him where such an intriguing sky had come from. He would have studied it and perhaps told her that one of the other planets was aligned with the moon. Or, perhaps, he might have said it was an illusion created by cloud cover or by tiny dewdrops in the air that didn't quite become rain.

But, of course, she couldn't ask Mr.

Moreno anything. She'd given him up, along with anything that resembled decency and a respectable life when she'd become convinced that her father was cruel and unreasonable, incapable of seeing what a wonderful, illustrious man Taylor Grant would prove to be.

She'd run away from the gentility of her home in New Orleans, certain that Taylor loved her and that her world with him would be wonderful.

She tried to think only of the moon and feel its enchantment. But she could hear the men back at the saloon. Pirate's Cove — an apt name for a saloon, since Galveston Island had first been settled by the pirate Lafitte. Lafitte was long gone. Older men, remnants of the pirate's day, still sat in the bar, where they drank and cursed and spoke of the days of Spanish rule and French rule, Spanish rule again and the coming independence of Texas. It was all talk. Galveston was a rising port city, and there were plenty of ill-gotten gains to be found here. Maybe a few of the men would be leaving to take up arms for Texas, but for the most part, they were lecherous miscreants who seemed to sit around all day drinking, smelling worse and worse by the hour. And they'd get Taylor drinking, and he'd have no money, and he'd convince them to pay for her services — and convince her that they'd pass out as soon as they were alone with her. They generally did, though not always quickly enough. . . . She winced, staring up at the moon. She would feel sweaty and horrid, and the stench of them would stay with her long after they'd passed out, and even walking into the waters of the bay would not erase that stench.

She could hear the laughter and the curses and the bawdy remarks. And sometimes, she could hear the feigned laughter of one of the saloon whores — women who were mostly old and used up, who poured on the perfume and accepted small amounts of money and whiskey or rum for their quick services.

Taylor had turned her into one of them.

Tears stung her eyes. She tried to pretend she'd never left home and she was just a young woman walking on a beach beneath a whimsical moon. But it didn't change a thing. And it couldn't ease the pain that suddenly filled her.

She still loved Taylor. After everything he had done to her. She was such a fool!

"Rose!"

The sound of his excited cry made her turn. Taylor had come out of the saloon, and he was running toward her. She saw, as he breathlessly reached her, that his eyes were glittering.

His excitement, however, was no longer contagious to her.

"What is it, Taylor?" she asked him.

"Finally! Finally, I've made the play that will get us out of here. Rose, my darling Rose, look at this!"

He produced a ring.

She remembered jewelry. She remembered *good* jewelry, like the cross her father had bought on a business trip to Italy, and the beautiful little pearl-drop earrings her mother had given her on her fourteenth birthday. She'd never owned magnificent pieces, just the gold and semiprecious gems that were the cherished items of a young girl on a working plantation.

Still, she *knew* good jewelry.

And this piece was far more than simply *good.* It was probably worth her father's entire plantation. The glowing illumination of the strange moon picked up on the brilliance of the diamond in the delicate gold setting. The diamond was multifaceted, shimmering with an assortment of colors; it had to be five carats, if not more.

And it seemed to have a life of its own. It was almost as if the fiery brilliance of the gem burned in her hand.

Rose stared at Taylor. He'd been drinking, but he was sober. His beautiful blue eyes were on her with tenderness, and his lips — weak lips, in a beautiful but weak jaw — were curved into a loving and tremulous smile.

Yes, despite all that he had done to her, he loved her, really loved her.

"Where did you get this?" she asked.

"I started playing poker, and the other fellows had taken their winnings and moved on, and I was still playing with old Marley — you remember, the decrepit old man who says he sailed with Lafitte. He put this on the table, and he said Lafitte himself had called it the Galveston diamond. Once upon a time, it belonged to the Habsburg kings! It came off a Spanish ship Lafitte took in the days before the War of 1812. Rose! Marley swears Lafitte gave him the diamond, although he likely stole it. But that doesn't matter. He had it — and we have it now. It's the key to our salvation. We can go anywhere. You never have to be with those old bastards again, and we don't have to sleep on a beach. We can get married, buy horses, join the Texans, make a land claim —"

"Taylor, Texas is going to war! We have to

get out of here. And we've got to do it tonight — before someone realizes you have this." Rose felt his excitement, but despite its beauty, there was something about the gem she didn't like. She wanted to go — right then. And she wanted them to sell the stone — at whatever price. They'd have to be paid enough to get by, but after that . . . The most important thing was that they escape now. Quickly. She was willing to leave what paltry items they had in the tiny room that was all they could afford and just run down the beach. Along with her own growing excitement, she felt a growing sense of danger.

Was it the diamond? Was it warning her — or was it causing her fear?

"Oh, the others don't know about it, and even if they did, the thing is supposed to be cursed," Taylor said. "It seems the princesses or whoever had it died young. I've got a bit more in winnings. We're going to buy horses and get out of here. We'll leave at first light. And if we can't buy land, we'll go back east. We'll go to Virginia or maybe all the way to New York!"

For a moment, the curious moon appeared to be luminescent, shining down on them with the sweetest of blessings.

And then she heard a commotion, coming

from the saloon.

"Taylor, what's happening?" she whispered.

There were men running toward them. She started to back away, but there was nowhere to run. This was an island. The beach stretched on for miles here and headed into bracken.

Nowhere to run.

"There he is. Get the bastard!" one of the men shouted.

She felt pressure on her hand. Taylor was thrusting the ring into her grasp. She took it. And she knew that if these men were after the diamond, they would strip her down and search her on the beach. She pretended to push back a stray lock of hair and stuck the diamond in her chignon.

Her heart thundered. Five men had come out; one was Matt Meyer, known for scalping Indians in Tennessee. He was surrounded by his henchmen — rough frontiersmen who'd seen better days, but who had never lost their talent for brutality.

She stepped forward. "Gentlemen, what is the problem?" she demanded. She moved past Taylor, praying they'd hesitate before actually offering physical violence.

She was forgetting herself. And them.

Meyer grabbed her by the shoulders and

13

threw her on the sand. "Cheater!" he said to Taylor. "Where the hell is my watch and fob?"

"What?" Taylor shrieked. "I didn't cheat, and I don't have your watch and fob! I swear, I swear on all that's holy, I —"

"Men," Meyer said quietly.

They descended on Taylor. They beat him as they stripped him naked and left him half-dead in the sand. Rose cried out in horror, but her one attempt to stop them was quickly diverted as one of the men backhanded her in the face and sent her down again, her mind reeling.

"He ain't got it," another of the men finally said to Meyer.

And then, of course, they looked at Rose.

"He was telling the truth!" Rose screamed in fury and despair. She staggered to her feet and stood as proudly as she could, with all the old disdain she could summon. "He doesn't have your watch or fob, never had it, and neither do I." She knew, however, that her protest would be in vain. And she was worried sick about Taylor. He lay bleeding and naked in the sand. She'd heard him groan once; now he was silent.

"You've murdered him," she accused Meyer.

There was more commotion coming from

14

the tavern. Others, hearing the fracas on the beach, were spilling out of the saloon.

"Take the whore," Meyer said to his men. "Let's move out of here."

"Wait! You can't just leave him!" Rose sobbed. "He could be alive!"

Meyer, who was a big man, perhaps forty, and strongly muscled, walked over to her and jerked her toward him. "How did you wind up with such a pathetic excuse for a man?" Suddenly he smiled. "All those airs, my dear Miss Southern Belle! Well, well. I'll find out later if you've got my property. Come on, boys, time to leave this island and move inward. If there's going to be a war, I think we'll be part of it. Hmm. And, Miss Southern Belle Rose, I guess you're going to be *my* whore now!"

"Let go of me, you bastard!" She had to play for time. People were streaming out of the saloon and she had to tell them Taylor was innocent and that these men had half-way killed him. It was one thing to have a fight, or even shoot at a man, but to do *this,* to gang up on someone and beat him so badly . . .

Meyer hauled back and hit her again with such force that she would've fallen if he hadn't grabbed her. The world around her was whirling as Meyer tossed her over his

15

shoulder. She tried to free herself, tried to protest, but his voice grated in her ears. "You want your boy to have a chance to live? Then shut up! You're with me now, Rose. Ah, yes, Miss Rose, you're with me. Think of the glory! We're on to fight for Texas!"

He started to laugh.

For Texas . . .

She fought against his hold. She raised herself, clutching his shoulders, and for one moment, she saw the moon again. Or moons. Now there seemed to be ten of them swimming in the sky, still absurdly beautiful crescents.

Then the moons all disappeared. Yet as her world faded to black, Rose could feel the gem somehow burning against her skin through the tight knot of hair.

Meyer, these men, didn't even know she had the diamond, but it had already destroyed her life.

CHAPTER 1

San Antonio, Texas
April

Logan Raintree had just left his house and was walking toward his car when the massive black *thing* swept before him with a fury and might that seemed to fill the air. He stopped short, not knowing what the hell he was seeing at first.

Then he saw it. The *thing* was a bird, and he quickly noted that it was a massive bird, a peregrine falcon. Its wingspan must have been a good three feet.

It had taken down a pigeon.

The pigeon was far beyond help. The falcon had already ripped the left wing from the creature and, mercifully, had broken the smaller bird's neck, as well.

As Logan stood there, the falcon stared at him. He stared back at the falcon.

He'd seen attacks by such birds before; they had the tenacity of jays and the power

17

of a bobcat.

They also had the beaks and talons of their distant ancestors — the raptors, who'd once ravaged land and sea. This kind of bird could blind a man or, at the least, rip his face to shreds.

Logan stood dead still, maintaining his position as he continued to return the bird's cold, speculative stare. There seemed to be something in its eyes. Something that might exist in the eyes of the most brutal general, the most ruthless ruler. *Touch my kill, and you die!* the bird seemed to warn.

Logan didn't back away; he didn't move at all.

He knew birds, as he knew the temperament of most animals. If he ran away, the bird would think he should be attacked, just to make sure he did get away from the kill. Come forward and, of course, the bird would fight to protect it. He had to stay still, calm, assured, and not give ground. The falcon would respect that stance, take its prey and leave.

But the bird didn't leave. It watched Logan for another minute, then cast its head back and let out a shrieking cry. It took a step toward him.

Even feeling intimidated, Logan decided his best move was *not* to move. . . .

18

"I have no fight with you, brother," he said quietly.

The bird let out another cry. It hopped back to the pigeon, looked at Logan and willfully ripped the second wing off, then spat it out and stared at Logan again.

This was ridiculous, he thought. He'd never seen a peregrine falcon so much as land in his driveway, much less pick a fight with him.

He reached with slow, nonthreatening movements for his gun belt and the Colt .45 holstered there; he had no desire to harm any creature, but neither would he be blinded by a bird that seemed to be harboring an overabundance of testosterone.

As if the bird had known what the gun was, it leaped back.

Logan had the gun aimed. "I don't want to hurt you, brother bird," he said. "But if you force my hand, I will."

The bird seemed to understand him — and to know he meant his words. It gave yet another raucous cry, jumped on the pigeon and soared into flight, taking its prey. Logan watched as the bird disappeared into the western sky.

Curious about the encounter and very surprised by it, he shook his head and turned toward his car again.

He took one step and paused, frowning.

It suddenly looked as if he'd stepped into an Alfred Hitchcock movie.

The Birds.

They were everywhere. They covered the eaves of his house, the trees and the ground, everything around him. They sat on the hood and the roof of his car. Every bird native to the state of Texas seemed to be there, all of them just staring at him. Jays, doves, grackles, blackbirds, crows and even seabirds — a pelican stood in the center of his lawn.

It was bizarre. He was being watched . . . stalked . . . by birds!

None made a move toward him.

As he started to walk, a sparrow flapped its wings, moving aside. He continued to his car, wings fluttering around him as the smaller birds made way. When he reached his car door, he opened it slowly, carefully, and then sat behind the wheel, closing the door. He revved the engine and heard scratching noises as the birds atop his car took flight.

Logan eased out of the driveway. As he did so, a whir of black rose with a furious flapping of wings. He blinked, and when he opened his eyes again, they were gone.

Every last bird was gone.

He looked back at his old mission-style house, wondering if he'd somehow blacked out, had a vision, and yet managed to get into his car. But that was not the case. He didn't black out. For him, visions were dreams. They occurred only when he slept, and he usually laughed them away. His father's people believed that all dreams were omens, while his mother's father — psychiatrist and philosopher William Douglas — believed that dreams or "visions" were arguments within the human psyche. In William's view, fears and anxiety created alternate worlds seen only in the mind; their role was to help resolve emotional conflicts.

Whichever approach was correct didn't matter much. He'd seen what he had seen. This hadn't been a vision or a dream.

But it was odd that it had happened when he was on his way to meet with Jackson Crow, FBI agent and head of the mysterious Krewe of Hunters — a unit both infamous and renowned.

San Antonio. It was different, that was all. *Different.*

Kelsey O'Brien looked out the Longhorn Inn's kitchen window. From here, she could see the walls of the old chapel at the Alamo. The city was bustling, pleasantly warm now

21

that it was spring, and the people she'd met so far were friendly and welcoming.

She still felt like a fish out of water.

That's what she was missing — the water.

She'd been in San Antonio almost three days and they'd been nice days. San Antonio was a beautiful city. Kelsey actually had a cousin living here, Sean Cameron, but he worked for a special-effects company, and they were currently out in the desert somewhere, trying to reproduce the Alamo as it had once been for a documentary. She was grateful that her old camp friend, Sandy Holly, had bought the historic inn and one-time saloon where she was staying. Sandy made her feel a bit less like a fish out of water, but it was strange not to be within steps of both the Atlantic Ocean and the Gulf of Mexico. Her life — except for summer camp and college upstate — had been spent in the Florida Keys. Where there was water. Lots and lots of water. Of course, they had the river here, and she loved the Riverwalk area, with its interesting places to go and dine and shop. The history of the city appealed to her, too.

It was just . . . different. And it was going to take some getting used to. Of course, she still had no idea what she was doing here, or if she was going to stay. She might not be in San Antonio long; on the other hand, she could be transferring here. And she might be taking on a different job.

She was a United States Marshal, which meant she worked for a service that might require her to go anywhere. She'd certainly traveled in her life, but the concept that she could be moving here, making a life here, seemed unlikely — not something she would have chosen. Now that it might be happening, she had to remind herself that she'd always known she could be transferred. But her training had been in Miami, and because of her familiarity with Key West, where she had grown up, she'd been assigned, as one of only two Marshals, to the office there. She'd been doing the job for two years now, enjoying an easy camaraderie with Trent Fisher, her coworker. They reported in to the Miami office when required, and occasionally their Miami supervisor came down. Key West was small, and despite the friction that could exist between law enforcement agencies, she'd quickly established excellent working relations with the police and the Coast Guard and the other state and federal agencies with which the two Marshals worked. And then . . .

Then she'd suddenly ended up here. She was still wondering why, because Archie

Lawrence, her supervisor, had been so vague.

"You're going to love the situation," Archie had assured her. "You go to this meeting, and then you'll have a two-week hiatus to decide what you feel about an offer you're going to receive. So, nothing is definite yet."

"I'm being given a vacation so I can get an offer and think about it?" That hardly seemed typical of the government. "What's the offer?" she'd demanded.

"That's what your meeting is about," he'd said.

And no amount of indignant questioning or wheedling would convince him to share the details. If he even knew them . . . "Look, your meeting is with an FBI agent and you may be transferring services," Archie had told her. "That's all I'm at liberty to say."

"Why?" she'd asked him. "I don't want to change agencies!"

"Hey, it's come down from the brass, kiddo, and it sounds unusual — two federal agencies getting together on a friendly basis. Hallelujah!" Archie rolled his eyes. "No one's going to *force* you to change. You're being presented with an opportunity. You can say no. I mean it. If you don't like this offer, you have the option to pack up and come home, with no harm done to your status here. So quit asking me questions. Go away. Don't darken my door — for the time being, anyway. You have things to do, arrangements to make." He'd sent her one of his lopsided grins. She liked Archie and considered him a great boss. He was always easygoing until he went into "situation" mode and then he could spew out orders faster and with more precision than the toughest drill sergeant.

Sometimes, of course, she wondered what Archie really thought of her. She was good at her job, although some of her methods were a bit unexpected. Luckily, a lot of criminals were still sexist. They didn't realize that a woman could and would hold them to task, shoot with uncanny aim and manage handcuffs with ease. But she'd felt Archie's eyes on her a few times when she hadn't really been able to explain the intuition that had led to her discovery of a cache of drugs, a hiding place — or a dead body. She even wondered if he was *hoping* she'd take another position.

Today, soon, she'd attend a meeting with a man from the FBI: He had an offer for her that presumably had to do with the unique abilities she'd shown during her two years with the government, and due to the status of this particular branch of service, various government offices were cooperating. On the one hand, she felt like telling someone that if she'd wanted to work for the FBI, she would have applied to the FBI. But she was curious, and she wasn't prone to be difficult; it was just the mystery of the situation.

Law enforcement agencies were not known for their cooperation — rather sad, really, since they were all working toward the same goal. That was one of the reasons she'd loved working in Key West; they had plenty to deal with, but they were smaller, and thus got along fairly well. Drugs were constantly out on the waterways. The Coast Guard was overworked, ditto the state police and the county police. The cops in Key West loved the Marshals. It had all been pretty good. State police, Monroe County police, the Coast Guard and the U.S. Marshal's Office, all getting along, most of them meeting for a beer here and there on Duval Street or some off-the-tourist track location. In her case, it had probably helped that she'd gone to the University of Miami and done an internship with the U.S. Marshal's Office. She'd zeroed in on her chosen profession early. And she'd expected to stay in south Florida.

To contemplate a life here, in Texas, was just . . . strange.

Nothing wrong with Texas, of course.

But she had it all figured out. It was the water. In San Antonio, there was no coast. There was the river, though.

She glanced at her watch. Two hours until her meeting.

When she looked out the window again, she nearly jumped. In those few seconds, a massive crow had landed on the outer sill. The damned thing seemed to be staring at her. She waved a hand at it.

The bird didn't fly away. It continued to stare.

Then it pecked the window.

She almost stepped back, then didn't. She scowled at the bird. "I'm a United States Marshal, and I will not be intimidated by a bird!" she said aloud.

"What's that?"

Kelsey swung around. Sandy Holly had come breezing into the kitchen.

"You have really big, aggressive birds around here," Kelsey said.

"We do?"

"Yeah, look!"

When she turned to the window again, the crow was gone. It bothered Kelsey to realize that the bird disturbed her. Ah, well,

27

she had discovered earlier that one of the men she'd be meeting was Agent *Crow*. Maybe that knowledge had made the bird's appearance seem like something more — like some kind of omen, for good or . . .

Sandy smiled, raising her eyebrows. "Anyone would think you were trying not to like Texas," she said.

"No, no, I *love* Texas. Texas is great," Kelsey told her.

"Maybe you're just a little nervous. This is the big day, right?"

"This is it," Kelsey agreed. Sandy Holly was proving to be a true friend. Kelsey had gotten to know her almost twenty years ago, when they'd been a pair of awkward eight-year-olds at the West Texas dude ranch Kelsey's parents had been sure she'd want to attend. But she'd been terrified of horses, while Sandy was terrified of being alone. Sandy had ridden before, even at five, because . . . because she was a Texan from San Antonio. Texans rode horses and wore big hats. So, at eight, Kelsey had toughened up enough to tell Sandy she didn't need to be homesick, and Sandy had promised Kelsey she'd learn to love horses. She did, Kelsey mused. Thanks to Sandy, she'd become an excellent rider. And, thanks to Sandy, she'd known where she wanted to stay when she came to San Antonio. The Longhorn Inn and Saloon.

It wasn't as if they'd seen each other frequently. After a few years, they had skipped camps of any kind. But they'd met with other friends in Vegas to celebrate their respective twenty-first birthdays and kept up with each other through Facebook and email. When she'd first talked about applying to be a U.S. Marshal, Sandy had encouraged her.

Kelsey was particularly glad to be here because Sandy wasn't in great shape at the moment — taking over the old inn had proven to be a monumental task, and there were problems Sandy had hinted about that Kelsey didn't entirely understand. They hadn't really had a chance to sit down and talk, since Sandy was running a business, which meant her time was limited. It was even more limited because she'd lost a manager the week before — the young man simply hadn't shown up for work — and while Sandy had a great housekeeping staff of three, the organizational and hostessing duties had all fallen to her. Of course, as Kelsey well knew, Sandy could be high-strung, and she wondered if working for her friend wasn't a little stressful. On the plus side, Sandy did like to hire college guys who needed a break on a résumé. None of them seemed to last too long, however.

Sandy walked over to some controls on the kitchen wall and squinted as she looked at them. "Hmm. I'm going to hope this turns on the music and doesn't open the storm windows," she said, twisting the dial.

Country rock filled the air.

"I think you got it," Kelsey told her.

"How about some coffee?"

"You can actually sit for a few minutes?" Kelsey asked. "And tell me what's up?"

Sandy poured coffee into cups and set them on the table, shrugging. "There's nothing really wrong. The past few days around here have been tense, that's all. People are so ridiculous!"

"Okay, explain, will you?"

Sandy let out a long sigh. "It's just this *haunted* thing about the inn. I sometimes wonder if I was crazy or what to get involved with it, even though I like a ghost story as much as anyone. Well, you know I've wanted this place for years. I've always been fascinated by the history — especially what happened to Rose Langley."

"The poor girl who was killed right before the fall of the Alamo?" Kelsey asked.

Sandy nodded. "Rose was killed by her lover — or pimp, depending on how you

30

want to look at it — in Room 207. It's a sad story about a good girl gone wrong. She took off from her parents' home because she was madly in love with Taylor Grant, and when they were in Galveston, she ended up being more or less kidnapped by a notorious bad guy named Matt Meyer, who wounded Grant. She might have fought Meyer and gained time for help, but she seems to have been afraid he'd finish Grant off if she didn't go with him. So, the revolution was about to begin, and Meyer wanted to fight for Texas. They came here, and apparently, Rose and Matt Meyer got into a terrible fight, and he murdered her. He'd been known to kill, so it wasn't a surprise. We wouldn't just consider him a criminal today, we'd consider him to be as sick and perverted as the most heinous killer out there. Oh — and, of course, he took off before the battle of the Alamo, or before anything resembling the law could catch up with him. But . . ."

"But?"

"I don't know how much of this you remember from my emails," Sandy said. "I had just bought the place — money down, no way out — when all of a sudden there were problems. I was already in here, deciding what to do about renovating a week or so before the closing, when a girl named Sierra Monte disappeared."

"Of course I remember. But remind me what she was doing here, when the inn was in the middle of changing owners," Kelsey said.

"Peter Ghent, the last owner, still had the place until closing. That's how it works. I'd gotten a deal because there was no return on the down payment if anything went wrong. *Anything.* Ghent had some of the rooms rented, but he was like an absentee landlord. Sierra came here, apparently, because she wanted Room 207. Go figure. The rooms were super-cheap, even though it was a historic property, because Ghent wasn't running it well. The bar sucked! It was all falling apart and I'd just started to renovate. But Sierra Monte insisted on staying. Anyway, she disappeared. A maid found blood everywhere and then the cops came in — but there was no body. And, of course, she disappeared from Room 207, so the legend continued to grow. I closed down for a bit when I took over to get the renovations finished. And then I didn't rent out the room at all afterward but the mystery of the place encourages people to come in. You know how that goes. Now people are *clamoring* for 207. I'm careful who I give it to, though, because I'm afraid of some idiot freaking out in the middle of the night and jumping out the window or something! It's hard to read people over the phone or through the internet, but, like I said, I'm careful. It's rented out now — only because I have a big ol' rodeo cowboy staying in it."

Kelsey winced. "I know what you're saying. At the Hard Rock in Hollywood, Florida, people vie for the room where Anna Nicole Smith died. And people book way ahead for the 'murder room' at the Lizzie Borden house in Fall River, Massachusetts."

"Exactly!" Sandy said. "But now, the stories about Room 207 are scaring people away from the inn, not bringing them in!"

As if to confirm Sandy's words, a high-pitched scream pierced the hum of easy-listening music. Kelsey had just picked up her mug, but the earsplitting cry of terror startled her so badly that coffee sloshed over the brim. She leaped to her feet, staring at Sandy.

Sandy stared back at her, stricken, shaking her head. Kelsey set her mug on the table and went flying out to the inn's grand salon — now its lobby — looking around for the source of the scream.

It came again, stretching long and loud, and Kelsey raced toward it.

■ ■ ■ ■

When he reached the riverfront area and parked, Logan was still mulling over the strange behavior of the birds. He knew that the Native American half of the family — no matter how "modern" or forward-thinking they might be — would see omens in the situation. He couldn't help wondering about it himself.

But he had to put it out of his mind.

Logan had been told by his captain that this meeting was important. In that case, he wasn't quite sure why he was meeting an FBI agent beneath a brightly colored umbrella on the Riverwalk. It wasn't that he had anything against the Riverwalk; it just didn't seem like the place for an important meeting. Tourists thronged the area, along with locals. The shopping included both high-end boutiques and Texas souvenir shops, and the restaurants were varied as well as plentiful. He loved the river; watching water always seemed to improve anything. Still, this was unusual.

He wasn't surprised that he was noticed — and hailed — by many people. He'd spent his life in San Antonio, and he'd been called on during many a "situation" at the riverfront, so he knew a number of bartenders, shopkeepers and restaurant owners. Of course, the tourists and visitors were something else entirely. One teenage boy called out, "Look! It's Chuck Norris! Hey, Walker, Texas Ranger!"

He tipped his hat to the kid. No need to make their visitors think Texans weren't hospitable and friendly.

He was dressed in standard departmental wear — boots, white hat and gun belt. He was carrying a Colt .45, his weapon of choice, and a popular gun among Rangers. He guessed that, in a way, he did look like Chuck Norris — or the character he'd played on a long-running TV show. Except, of course, that Norris was blond and light-skinned and he had dead-black hair and hazel eyes. People did stare. There weren't even two hundred Rangers in the whole state, so he supposed that made his appearance especially interesting for tourists.

Another reason *not* to carry out an important meeting in a public place.

He did, however, recognize the man he was supposed to see, despite never having previously met him. Agent Jackson Crow was seated at one of the tables lining an iron fence that arced right out over the water, a cup of coffee in front of him. He was dressed in a black suit that seemed to scream FBI, to Logan's mind at least. He wore dark glasses and seemed perfectly comfortable, sitting at ease while he waited for the meeting. Whatever people thought of him, he obviously didn't give a damn.

Logan walked straight to the table. Crow was aware of him; he stood.

"Raintree, I presume," he said, smiling as he offered his hand.

Logan shook hands, studying Crow. Yep, Indian blood. He assumed Crow was staring back at him, thinking the same thing.

"Yes. I'm Logan Raintree."

"Comanche?" Crow asked.

"All-American mutt in every way," Logan told him. "One ancestor was Comanche, one was Apache — and two were European. Norwegian and English. You?"

"Cheyenne and all-American mutt, as well," Crow said. "I like the concept of that. Sit, please. Thank you for meeting with me."

"You're welcome, but I wasn't really given a choice — I was given an order."

Crow didn't respond to that. "Coffee?"

"Coffee sounds good," Logan said, pulling out a chair. He noted that the table had been set for three. "Someone's joining us?" he asked.

"Yes — a U.S. Marshal," Crow said.

"We'll eat when she gets here."

Logan slowly arched his brows. "All right, what kind of felon, madman or serial killer do we have running around San Antonio?"

"We don't know much about him as yet. That's where you come in," Crow explained. "And I'm meeting with you first. Marshal O'Brien isn't due for another half hour or so."

"Doesn't that mean you have to go through all of this twice?"

Crow gave him a grim half smile and shrugged. Logan had the feeling that there was always method to his madness, though at the moment, he sure couldn't tell what it was.

A leather briefcase lay on the table. Crow reached into it and produced a sheaf of papers — photos, Logan saw.

He didn't immediately recognize what he was looking at. At first glance it appeared to be a trash pile, but then, peering closer, he saw human bones beneath the branches, boxes and other refuse.

He looked back at Jackson Crow. "I wish I could say that a dead body was something unusual," he said.

"It's the circumstances that are unusual," Jackson murmured. "Here's another."

The next picture was of a half-decayed

body on a gurney in an autopsy room. This was a far more gruesome sight, resembling a creature imagined by a special-effects wizard; the flesh was ripped from most of the jaw and the cadaver seemed to be grinning in a macabre manner.

"Where was this body discovered? He? She?" Logan asked.

"She. Both sets of remains belong to women. Both disappeared from the San Antonio area, one a year and a half ago, one about a year ago. Both had made it to San Antonio and were never seen again. Or not alive, anyway," he added.

"I'm assuming traces were done on their credit cards, and the usual procedures carried out."

Jackson nodded. "Neither actually checked into a hotel. The bones in the first picture belonged to a young woman named Chelsea Martin — schoolteacher, part-time gemologist. The cadaver on the gurney was once a dancer named Tara Grissom. She worked out of New Orleans."

"Dancer? As in stripper?" Logan asked.

Jackson shook his head. "She was with a modern dance company. The show she was in closed down and they weren't due to cast the next show for a few months. She headed out to Texas. According to friends, she was fascinated with the Alamo. She flew from New Orleans to Houston and on to San Antonio, and she was never heard from again after she waved goodbye to the fellow who'd been sitting next to her on the plane."

"What about the other girl?"

"Similar story. She was a new teacher, and when budget cuts came down, she lost her job. Chelsea Martin left New York City for San Antonio, took a cab straight to the Alamo and wasn't seen again."

Logan frowned. "I should've heard about this by now."

"You probably did. Think about all the missing-persons reports," Crow said with a shrug. "There are hundreds of them — thousands. Some people go missing on purpose. You have to remember that. Thing is, until you really start digging, you don't always know if someone's disappeared on purpose or not." He pulled out more sets of pictures. They were all of bodies in various stages of decay. Female bodies.

Logan frowned at Jackson Crow. "All these corpses — they're from here?"

Crow nodded. "Most of these women have yet to be identified. A number of them might have been prostitutes or women living on the edge. When someone doesn't have family or close friends, there's no one to hold law enforcement to task once the case has gone cold. We wouldn't have known about this if an enterprising young officer hadn't stumbled on the first body in a trash pile — just a block from the Alamo. Don't look so appalled. No unit of Texas law enforcement has been neglectful in this case. First off, we still don't know if the cases are related, although studying the way the killer disposed of the bodies, it seems likely." He grimaced. "There may be a few who were killed by someone else — someone who happened upon a body-disposal system that has eluded the law — but I believe most of these women met the same killer. They all just disappeared. And of all the corpses and skeletal remains we've discovered so far, we've only been able to match two of the women to missing-persons reports."

"Are you putting together a task force?" Logan asked him.

"More or less. I'm putting together a team."

Logan began to feel uneasy. He'd looked up Jackson Crow. He had a reputation for being a crack behavioral profiler; he also had a reputation for running a crew of — for lack of a better term — ghost hunters. Hired by a somewhat reclusive government bigwig, Adam Harrison, he investigated the unusual. To the man's credit, it seemed that his team generally found real human beings who'd perpetrated the crimes and brought them to justice.

Still . . .

Somehow, he felt Crow knew something about him. It wasn't a comfortable feeling.

"And you want me to be on this team?" Logan asked.

"We have one special unit working now — a team of six, and six seems to be the optimal number. I'm starting a second team. I don't just want you to *be* on the team — I want you to head the team."

"Why?"

"You've had incredible success finding missing people," Jackson said smoothly.

Logan didn't blink. "Logic," he told Crow. And a little luck . . .

"Logic is the most important tool we have," Crow agreed. "I'm a man of logic myself."

Logan winced, then said flatly, "You look for ghosts."

"I look for killers," Crow said, correcting him. He indicated the briefcase. "I have a lot of info on you, too, of course. I know you're *exceptionally* talented." Crow hesitated, thoughtful for a minute. When he

41

spoke again, it was with both respect and empathy. "And I know that your wife was kidnapped by the brother of a drug runner you put in jail. I know you found her — buried in a pine box. The killer had been playing a game with you, but he screwed up. He didn't provide enough oxygen. You were able to find her, although no one ever really knew how. You just found her too late."

Logan felt tension seep into his bones. Alana had been gone nearly three years, yet he still couldn't think about her without a sense of loss and rage burning in his gut. She'd died because he was who he was. She'd been a shimmering spirit of laughter and giving, and she had died because of him. His *exceptional* talents had been useless.

Her death had sent him into the hills on a long leave; only a return to the land far from the city had somehow kept him halfway sane.

Maybe that was why he hadn't been aware of what had gone on with these missing women. And maybe everyone had overlooked the real and horrendous danger for the reason Jackson Crow had just given him. Sad, but true. Those on the fringes of life were often simply not missed.

"You have what we need," Crow told him.

No, I don't, Logan thought. *I failed the woman I loved.*

"I'm a Texas Ranger," Logan said, startled by the sound of his own voice, which was almost a growl.

"Yes. You returned to being a Ranger," Crow said. "Because you can't help yourself. You have to work in law enforcement. But, even as a Ranger, you have limitations. I can provide unlimited resources for you."

"Thanks. I like being a Ranger. I'm not so sure about being a fed."

"It's a matter of choice. Texas pride aside, there are a few things you might want to keep in mind, such as the fact that federal services have jurisdiction everywhere. In our case, of course, we work where we're invited in, except when we're talking about criminals and situations that cross state lines. That's always our jurisdiction. Crossing state lines is something killers do often enough. It's as if they know they can throw law enforcement into confusion and break chains of evidence when they do, and that's one reason the FBI is so important. Of course, your superiors know about this offer, and although they'd be sorry to lose you, they understand the unique possibilities of the position I'm offering you."

Logan shook his head. "Thank you. No. You've got a serial killer on your hands. Or — since one way or another, I'll get involved — we've got a serial killer on *our* hands. We'll dig in, too, work with the FBI. But I think I'll stay right where I am. I don't see any reason to change."

Crow nodded. "As I've been saying, it is your choice. But there's something different about this case that does require an extra ability to *see*."

"See what?"

"Beneath the obvious."

"And what's that?"

"Chelsea Martin called a friend just before she disappeared," Jackson Crow said.

"From the Alamo?"

"Yes."

"And?"

"She said she saw a ghost. She thought it had to be the ghost of a Texas hero. He was trying to urge her to get away."

"You've lost me."

"She phoned Nancy McCall, a friend in New York, when she reached the Alamo. At first, according to Nancy, she was laughing, telling her that a reenactor was playing a game with her. Then she was concerned, saying that the 'performer' was getting very dramatic, insisting she leave the Alamo, go

44

and hide somewhere. At the end of the conversation, Chelsea seemed to believe she'd seen a ghost. She sounded frightened, and said this ghost or whatever he was had just disappeared."

"And then?"

"Nothing. The line went dead. Her phone was never used again, and it was never found — and I've shown you what was left of Chelsea Martin."

CHAPTER 2

The Longhorn had been built at a time when men were men and . . . men were men. The saloon had a long curving bar, a piano and a large space for gaming tables. Near the front entry, which came complete with swinging doors, a staircase led to the balcony above and to the rooms on the second floor. When Kelsey sped into the main saloon area from the kitchen, she was stunned to see a man running down the stairs as if he were being chased by every demon in hell.

A big, tough-looking man. Leanly muscled, he stood a good six foot two — and he was wearing an expression of sheer horror.

He had to be the "big ol' rodeo cowboy" Sandy had told her about.

As Kelsey ran to the foot of the stairs to discover the cause of his terror, he nearly knocked her over in his haste to reach the door.

"Sir! What is it? What's happened?"

Luckily, it seemed that the few other guests currently checked in to the Longhorn were already out or still asleep, and that the staff was either busy or not at work yet. No one else had appeared at the sound of the screams.

"Let me out of here! Let me out of here now!" he yelled. He seemed like a decent man. Even in his near hysteria, he wasn't going to mow her down or pick her up bodily to toss her out of the way.

She hadn't realized that Sandy had come behind her until she heard her speak. "Mr. Simmons, what's wrong?" she asked.

Simmons was perhaps thirty; he had the ruggedly handsome look of a modern-day cowboy, and Kelsey assumed he was in town for the upcoming rodeo trials. The man might have been ready to brave the meanest bronco, but he pointed up the stairs with a trembling hand. "Blood . . . blood . . . blood. Oh, God, blood everywhere, all over the room!" he said. "Let me out. For the love of God, let me out of here!"

Kelsey arched a brow at Sandy and placed a hand on Simmons's shoulder. "Sir, it's all right. Sandy will help you," she said.

Sandy looked back at Kelsey, her eyes

47

filled with a silent plea. *See? I've been trying to tell you. It's happening again, and it's getting worse and worse. Do something!*

Kelsey stepped past Mr. Simmons and hurried up the stairs to the gallery. She paused, gazing down over the rail of the landing. Sandy held her guest by the arm and was urging him to calm down. But Simmons seemed adamant about leaving.

"If you'll just show us, Mr. Simmons," Sandy said.

"What, are you insane?" he shouted. He stared up at Kelsey. "Don't . . . oh, God, don't go in there! Get the police!" he cried.

"Mr. Simmons," Kelsey called down. "I am a law enforcement agent. I'm a United States Marshal."

"Room 207," Sandy said gravely.

Kelsey nodded, turned and hurried down the hallway. It was a straightforward numbering system; the second floor had ten rooms, 201 through 210. Room 207 was to her left along the gallery. Her own room was 201, but she didn't really have to check at the numbers; the door to 207 was wide open, just as Simmons had left it.

She stepped inside and paused, biting her lip. There was nothing there. Certainly no blood.

The room was handsomely appointed. In

fact, Sandy had done a beautiful job restoring the whole place. She'd renovated it with authenticity, studying historic documents and outfitting it with period pieces. Kelsey knew something about all of this, because Sandy had been in love with the inn — longing to buy it — for years. The Longhorn was one of the oldest original wooden structures of a bygone era. It had opened in 1833 as the Longhorn Saloon and Gentleman's Palace, and through its history, it had been *the* place where travelers to San Antonio, especially "gentlemen," had come to enjoy the liquor, poker, ambiance and female entertainment provided here. Every now and then, Sandy arranged a night with old-time entertainment; it was no longer a house of prostitution, of course, but she held poker games for charity, and hired period singers, actors and dancers to evoke the feel of the old west.

Needless to say, any building as old as this one held its share of ghost stories. Room 207 had come with the Rose Langley legend, and much more recently, Sierra Monte had disappeared from it.

Kelsey considered what Sandy had told her about the Sierra Monte case.

Blood spray and spatter had covered the room. There had never been any sign of her body, and there had never been an arrest. DNA testing proved that the blood was hers, and the medical examiner had claimed it was highly unlikely that anyone could have lost that much blood and survived. How her remains had been removed from the room was a mystery, just like the identity of her killer.

It had been a horrible story. But in law enforcement, officers and agents heard a lot of horrible stories. And if every hotel in the world closed when something bad happened, they'd be tearing down buildings right and left.

Afterward, Sandy had hired special crews to come in and clean up.

There wasn't a drop of blood to be seen anywhere.

Kelsey walked into the bathroom, once a dressing room for the "girls" who had entertained at the Longhorn. She hadn't been in on the investigation, although she'd researched it, primarily because of her friendship with Sandy. She knew that blood had been found in the bathroom, as well, a great deal of it. Detectives and forensic crews had determined that Sierra was most likely killed in the bedroom and possibly dismembered in the bathroom.

When the police had finished and Sandy

had taken over the place, she'd had the bathroom in 207 completely remodeled. The old tub was still taking up a lot of space in the evidence room at the police station.

The bathroom looked completely ordinary. Shaving equipment and toiletries were on the counter by the sink, and the old claw-foot tub Sandy had bought to replace the original one was damp. Sandy's guest had obviously had a bath or a shower before finding himself mesmerized by the blood his imagination had conjured up.

When Kelsey left the room and walked down the stairs, she saw that neither Sandy nor Mr. Simmons was in the main saloon area. She wasn't sure if they'd run outside — or if Sandy had managed to calm him down. She pushed open the swinging doors and looked out at the street. No one there. Kelsey quickly returned to the kitchen and the table where she'd been about to drink her now-cold coffee.

Simmons and Sandy were sitting there, but Simmons wasn't drinking coffee. A shot glass and a bottle of whiskey stood in front of him. He'd apparently downed several shots already.

Sandy and Simmons both turned to Kelsey. She shook her head. "There's nothing there, Mr. Simmons. Nothing at all."

He gaped at her, disbelief in his eyes.

"I swear to you," she added quietly, "there's nothing."

He groaned, lowering his head, pressing his temples between his palms. "Well, that's just great. I'm going crazy."

Kelsey drew up a chair next to him, setting a reassuring hand on his shoulder. "Mr. Simmons —"

"Corey. Call me Corey, please," he interrupted gruffly.

"Corey," she said. "You're not going crazy. You're merely human, which makes you susceptible to the history of places like this. Everyone knows the stories about the Longhorn. You *know* the room was covered in blood at one time, and not that long ago, either. So, in your mind, you saw it covered in blood. You're not crazy. What happened wasn't a fun ghost story. It was reality."

"I should just not rent out that room," Sandy murmured.

Corey waved a hand in the air. "Not your fault," he said. He gave them both a rueful grimace. "I asked for that room. I told the boys going to the rodeo that I'd be sleeping with the ghosts. I was a real hotshot. I didn't know I had a crazy susceptible mind. At least . . . that's what I'm going to believe, Miss . . . ?"

"O'Brien. Actually, Marshal O'Brien," Kelsey said.

"Kelsey's been working with the U.S. Marshal's Office in Key West," Sandy explained.

"A U.S. Marshal," he repeated, looking at her as if she were some kind of alien life form.

She smiled at him.

"You don't look like a cop," he said.

"Technically, I'm not a cop."

"But you . . . you do cop things." He still seemed confused.

"More or less."

"Can a U.S. Marshal get my stuff out of that room?" he asked.

"I can do that for you, Mr. Simmons. And I'll help you find another location to stay, too," Sandy told him.

"Um, can you just put me in another room?" he asked.

Sandy was clearly surprised by his request. "Of course I can. But you were pretty desperate to get out the door, Mr. Simmons."

"Corey," he said again, smiling. He flushed. "Ladies, I'm going to ask you to do me a massive favor. Never repeat the fact that a six-foot-three two-hundred-and-thirty-pound bronco buster ran out of his

53

room screaming like a baby."

Sandy laughed softly. Kelsey shrugged.

"Please," he murmured, looking at Kelsey.

"Don't worry. I don't really have anyone to tell," Kelsey said. She checked her watch. "You two will have to excuse me. I have a meeting this morning. That is, if you're sure you're all right now, um, Corey?"

"I'm feeling like the biggest fool in Texas, and that's some mean space," Corey said. "I'll be fine."

"Good." Kelsey glanced at Sandy. "You call me if you need anything. And, Corey, as soon as I'm back, we'll see to it that all your things are moved to your new room."

"Thanks, Kelsey," Sandy said. "But I'm sure I can manage." She hesitated. "Uh, Kelsey? Are you interested in switching rooms with Corey? That would save me a lot of bother."

Kelsey thought about it for a moment, then said, "Sure. Why not?" She wondered whether she'd been too rash, but Sandy's gratitude confirmed that she'd made the right decision.

Kelsey took another look at the half-empty bottle of whiskey. Corey Simmons was either going to lie down and pass out soon, or he'd be seeing more ghosts. But Sandy smiled at her with confidence, and Kelsey figured she'd manage, just as she'd said. Sandy had supported both her parents through protracted deaths due to cancer, and Kelsey believed that was one reason she'd been so caught up in the restoration of the Longhorn. She'd pulled herself out of mourning and she'd done it by throwing herself into this massive project. She could be tough as nails when she chose. Not only that, her livelihood now depended on the inn.

"I don't even know what this meeting is," she said. "So don't worry about phoning if you need me."

Sandy nodded. As she started out, Corey Simmons called her back. "Miss — I'm sorry, Marshal! Miss O'Brien, thank you."

She gave him a tiny salute of acknowledgment. Leaving the kitchen, Kelsey hurried back up to her room to grab her handbag. She paused to study herself in the freestanding Victorian swivel mirror. She felt she looked professional — something she hadn't worried about in ages. She was five-nine, decked out in a black suit and simple white cotton tailored blouse. Her hair was a deep auburn, secured in a band at her nape. She had what she hoped were steady green eyes, and a lean sculpted face that lent her a look of maturity — at least in her own opinion.

Despite Corey Simmons's surprise that she was a woman who did "cop things," she made the proper appearance for a U.S. Marshal. That seemed important in light of today's meeting.

She hurried out of her room, then walked down the hall to 207 again. Stepping inside, she held very still and closed her eyes. She'd come up here before because of Corey's hysteria; now, she decided to take a moment to see what her intuition would show.

She opened her eyes, but didn't focus on the room as it was now. What she saw looked similar, but . . . different. Out of kilter. There was a wardrobe in the corner, but it was a slightly different wardrobe. Where the bathroom should have been, she saw a slatted Oriental divider: The bed was smaller, and a white chemise lay at the foot of it.

There were two people in the room, a man and a woman. The woman was beautiful, dark curly hair piled atop her head, long legs clad in old-fashioned stockings and garters. She wore a white shirt and corset. Her dress had been thrown on a nearby chair. The man was wearing a dark suit, a tall hat and appeared to have stepped out of an 1850s fashion ad for gentlemen. He was tall and, despite his apparel, had the rugged look of a cowhand. He strode angrily across the room and grasped the woman by the shoulders. "You won't hold out on me!" he shouted at her. "I want it, and I want it now."

"I don't have it," she said.

"You're a liar! I know what happened in Galveston that night, and I know your pretty-boy lover won it. I want it!"

"No, it's mine!" she responded.

"You think you'll get back to that no-good weakling? Well, give up that dream. He moved on the moment you were gone."

"I hate you," she told him, shaking herself free. "I hate you, Matt. I *loathe* you. You forced me here, and you've used me enough. Even if I had it, I'd never let you have it!"

"You're an old whore already, Rose," he said. "I want it, and I'll get it."

"I will *never* give it to you!"

He didn't respond. Instead, he wrenched her to him again; his fingers curled around her neck. He squeezed his hands together; he shook her hard. She grabbed desperately at his arms, trying to break his hold on her.

"Please, Matt!"

"I'll kill you, and I'll rip this place to shreds — and find it."

"Please!"

That one word escaped her lips, more

breath than word, as her face became red and mottled and she began to flail at him helplessly. Kelsey was so horrified by the vision that she ran to the man and woman, but of course they weren't there, not in this time and space. As she reached them, the woman went limp, and the man picked her up and tossed her onto the bed as if she were refuse.

Then they both disappeared.

Kelsey blinked. She wanted to cry for the woman who seemed to have fallen in love so foolishly, been abused and then murdered. There'd been no future for her; she had died still a beauty.

What was the *it* they'd been talking about?

However, that wasn't a concern right now.

She hurried out of the room, curious about the meeting her superior had insisted she attend.

She found herself remembering the bird on the window ledge that morning and, once again, couldn't shake the strange feeling it had given her.

She was about to meet men named Crow and Raintree. She wondered if this meeting had something to do with the Bureau of Indian Affairs.

And yet, somehow, she had the feeling it didn't.

She suspected it would have to do with her so-called "special" abilities. Abilities she usually kept to herself, but in the recent situation . . .

In all honesty, she knew why she'd been called.

This had to be connected to the body she'd found three weeks ago in Key West. That was when Archie had really begun to look at her strangely.

Body? No . . . she hadn't actually discovered a body.

Just bones. Broken and disarticulated bones. They might've all wound up in the garbage heap or a landfill if the trucks had come through a few more times. But Kelsey had seen the woman standing there, sobbing over the heap. And when she'd looked again, there had been no woman, but . . .

But there'd been the bones.

Logan shook his head, staring at Jackson Crow. "I don't understand."

"Don't understand what? The gravity of the situation?" Crow inquired.

"No. I don't understand what setting up a team with the FBI will accomplish that various law enforcement agencies working together won't," Logan said. "I don't believe a ghost killed her."

"I don't, either," Jackson said. "There are two possibilities, and since you're a Texan, I should think either one would bother you. One, a killer is dressing up as a Texas hero to attack innocent women."

"Or?"

"Dead Texas heroes remain . . . heroes. They're still trying to save the lives of others, and warn them away. Because they recognize a killer when they see one."

Logan wanted to argue with him; he even raised a hand to do so, but didn't find the right words. He was suddenly reminded of the very strange experience with the birds that morning.

Strange, but certainly natural. A physical phenomenon.

And, of course, he knew that things could happen, things that didn't always fall into the realm of natural physical phenomena.

"You don't have to answer me now. My people are working on it. But," Crow added wryly, "we're being stretched far too thin."

"I'm glad you're not expecting an answer yet," Logan said. "Because if you were, I'd have to say no."

Crow shrugged. "We don't expect anyone to just say, 'Hey, I'll jump on it.' But I've studied law enforcement profiles, and I'd like to begin with you and Marshal

O'Brien." He sent Logan a quick smile. "I wasn't keen on this when it first came up, either. I assumed I was receiving a major demotion. But you'd be astonished by what can be accomplished when you put the right network of people together."

"When you have a good team, yes, it can work exceptionally well. But you don't *really* know someone until you've met him. Or her. So, you study profiles. What happens if you meet someone you don't like?" Logan asked.

"Then I don't make the offer. Just so you know, I don't work alone. A man named Adam Harrison started this . . . experiment, shall we say. He had friends, and he identified people around the country who had abilities. Instincts, if you prefer. He put my team together. Adam's an interesting man, not particularly talented in this area, but he's developed a sense for people with these uncanny skills. So far, he's zeroed in perfectly every time."

"Adam Harrison. The name's familiar."

"He's done a great deal of good. He and his team have uncovered many charlatans, and found the truth behind their mist and mirrors. He watches people carefully. He knows who to approach for the Krewe."

"I'm not trying to be argumentative,"

Logan muttered, "but a lot of what you hear about Texans is true. We were our own country for a short while, and we're still dedicated to being Texans."

"Dedication is a good thing. But, like I said, you can think about it. And regardless of what you decide, you're now apprised of this situation." Crow indicated the pictures, then got to his feet. "I believe Marshal O'Brien has arrived." He smiled, glancing at his watch. "Precisely on time."

Logan stood, too. He saw a woman coming toward them. He noted first that she had a thick head of auburn hair that fell to her shoulders, and then he went on with his assessment. She moved with fluid confidence, and she was tall, about five-ten. Slim and well-built. She wasn't wearing a badge, but there was a quality about her that spoke of law enforcement. He was pretty certain the bulge on her hip was a Glock.

As she came nearer, he realized that she had exceptionally fine features and might have graced a model's runway rather than a crime scene. But before she reached them and offered each man a firm handshake as introductions were exchanged, he could tell that she wasn't some kind of delicate hothouse flower. Her walk, her movements, the way she'd looked for them and found them instantly — they all registered authority and determination. Maybe she'd perfected her manner to offset her beauty, which was vivid and startling. When she removed her sunglasses, he saw that she had green eyes, their color almost as deep as a forest.

He also realized that she was as curious as he had been about the meeting. "Shall we order?" he suggested. "We're all here now."

He lifted his hand to summon their waitress. Crow was polite and friendly as he ordered his meal, and despite the fact that Kelsey O'Brien couldn't have done more than glance at the menu, she ordered quickly. He did, as well, although he wasn't hungry. Something about this meeting was causing his stomach to knot.

Jackson Crow began the new conversation casually. "How are you enjoying Texas, Marshal O'Brien?"

"It's great," she said. "San Antonio is beautiful."

"Have you been able to see or do much yet?" Crow asked.

"I'm staying at the Longhorn, a historic saloon. I can see the Alamo from my window. Very poignant, really."

"The Longhorn has quite a reputation," Logan commented. *Ridiculous!* he told himself. For some reason, he'd just had to

63

throw that out.

He was irritated at his own pleasure in thinking he might know something Agent Crow didn't. This meeting was confusing him. He was usually willing to do whatever it took to stop crime, especially murder. But this . . .

It felt as if once he took a step, he'd fall into a pit, and he wasn't sure he'd know how to maneuver his way out.

Maybe because he hadn't known that there seemed to be a pattern of disappearances. It was true that the FBI could recognize the similarities between these crimes.

Maybe he was still off his stride because of what had happened on his way here — the scene with the birds.

Logan began to explain. "A murder took place there around the time of the Texas Revolution," he said. "And about a year ago, a young woman disappeared from the 'murder room.' Local homicide detectives tore the room and half the hotel apart, and she was never discovered. The room looked like there'd been a bloodbath. I'm not sure if that fits with the cases you've been showing me."

"Sounds like it does," Jackson said. "What do you think, Marshal O'Brien?"

Logan studied the young woman he had

so recently met.

She smiled awkwardly and looked around before answering. "We seem to be pretty casual here. Please call me Kelsey. And I'm sorry but I'm not up to speed. What cases?" she asked.

"One moment," Crow murmured. "Our food is coming."

Kelsey O'Brien had ordered salmon. Logan wondered if she avoided red meat and realized he'd ordered fish that afternoon, too. When their waitress left the table, Jackson launched into the story he'd already told Logan.

Logan sat back, listening, while Jackson Crow explained the FBI involvement. He waited until they had finished eating and then spread out the pictures to show her.

"Horrible," she whispered.

"I do believe we're looking for one killer. Although, as I told Raintree, it is possible that these murders and the unknown remains we've discovered aren't *all* connected. We're talking about a huge population here and, obviously, the larger the population, the easier it is for people to get lost in the crowd," Crow said.

Logan saw that Marshal Kelsey O'Brien wasn't turning away from the pictures, but neither was her expression devoid of empathy and distress. She raised her eyes. "I'm sorry," she said. "I've seen the dead before, but . . . in my area, it's often a drug runner shot and down. Nothing like . . . this."

Jackson Crow scooped up the pictures as the waitress came to clear the table and bring them more coffee. When it had been poured and they were alone once again, Logan found that he was intrigued to discover what Kelsey knew about the Longhorn Inn.

"What have you learned about the murder?" he asked her.

She looked at him, and he gazed into her clear green eyes. "You mean Sierra Monte? Very little, I'm afraid. The owner, Sandy Holly, is an old friend of mine. That's why I'm staying at the Longhorn. So I only know what Sandy's told me and a few things I read online. I also know it was incredibly complicated when she purchased the place, because she had a nonrefundable deposit down, with access to begin the renovations, and then Sierra Monte disappeared. Sandy still had to pay on the closing date and everything was put on hold while the police finished their investigation and then the people hired to do the crime-scene cleanup were brought in. She was devastated about the young woman, of course, but she was also in a predicament herself."

"It's up and running now, and doing well, right?" Logan asked.

Kelsey nodded. "She did a stunning job with it. There are parts of the inn that make you feel as if you've been transported almost two hundred years back in time. And, of course, Room 207 was gutted, and yet there've been people clamoring to get into it — and people claiming they've seen ghosts and blood. . . ." She paused. "Some people are fascinated by this stuff. Sandy was worried about it, naturally. And now . . ."

She stopped speaking. There was a lot more to the *"and now . . ."* but she didn't seem sure she should be talking about it.

Kelsey was aware that both men were watching her, waiting. She shrugged. "It's odd — just before I left today, a big bruiser of a cowboy came running out of that room, screaming. He was convinced that the entire room was covered in blood. Of course it wasn't." She grinned. "Eventually, he calmed down and I went up to the room and looked around."

"And?" Jackson asked her.

"It was just as the cowboy had left it," Kelsey O'Brien said slowly.

Logan noticed that she'd hesitated before

she spoke. Her words were smooth enough, but there was something she wasn't saying. She didn't fully trust them; however, that was okay. He wasn't sure of his own feelings about Jackson Crow or Marshal O'Brien yet, either.

"Impressionable minds can create ghosts," Crow said.

"Very true," Kelsey O'Brien agreed.

But Crow homed in on her words. "What about you? What did *your* mind see in that room?"

She leaned back, startled, but composing herself as she returned Jackson Crow's gaze.

"Anyone could get impressions in that room — once you know what happened there," she replied. "And, of course, I know."

"Does it ever distress your friend?" Crow asked her.

"Definitely. She's sunk a lot of money into the Longhorn, especially since she bought it in bad condition — and under bad circumstances. Sandy's wanted to own it for ages, though."

"Anything unusual occur during your nights at the inn?" Crow asked next.

"In my room? Not a thing," Kelsey said.

She didn't share easily, Logan thought.

"But you do feel the saloon *is* haunted?" Crow persisted.

She hesitated again, frowning, and then answered with "What exactly do you consider haunted, Agent Crow? When I walk through places that are steeped in history, there's always an air about them. The Alamo? I feel like I'm walking on hallowed ground. I get that same feeling at the Tower of London and the battlegrounds at Gettysburg. I think many people feel this way in certain places. The Longhorn Inn is no different. It witnessed history. I suppose many people imagine they see the past when they're going through places like that."

Crow listened, nodding, a small smile curving his lips. "Nice reply. And not an answer to my question."

"Well, what do you want?" Kelsey asked him, clearly irritated. "Do I pass ghosts walking up and down the stairs or in the saloon? No."

"Have you seen them at all?"

She looked as if she'd been trapped. Obviously, she had to be competent and able to stand on her own, but Logan suddenly felt that he wanted to step in; he hated being cornered himself, and he didn't like to watch it being done to someone else.

"What kind of haunting are you talking about, Agent Crow?" he asked. "*Residual* haunting, where the same traumatic event occurs over and over again? Or are you referring to *intelligent* or *active* haunting, where the ghosts actually partake in life?"

"Either," Crow said, shrugging. "I'm curious." He leaned across the table, his casual manner gone. "Kelsey, I know damned well that you see what others don't. What did you see in Room 207?"

She frowned. "What did I see? A murder." She looked over at Logan, and he couldn't tell whether she saw anger or appreciation in his eyes. "Absolutely nothing that could help us with the here and now. I saw a murder that took place over a hundred and fifty years ago, and the murderer himself is long gone. I guess what I saw was a *residual* haunting. No blood — the poor woman was strangled. So, perhaps we should get back to what we're actually dealing with. Dead women. Corpses dumped here, there and everywhere in San Antonio. I'm assuming you have more to work with than just photos, Agent Crow?"

He nodded. "I'm set up at the police station, about a mile away. I'll pay for our meal, then we'll go there and you can see how far we've gotten. Tomorrow, I'll be briefing local law enforcement, but for now, you can come over and get started."

"Whoa, Agent Crow. I haven't agreed to

be part of this team," Logan reminded him.

Crow raised one shoulder. "You don't want to see what we have?" he asked.

Logan let out a deep breath.

Of course he did. This was happening in *his* city, and Jackson Crow had been right about one thing — he *had* to be in law enforcement.

He had to be involved.

And since he'd seen the pictures of the remains . . .

He turned to face Kelsey O'Brien. She was watching him with her intent green eyes, and he wondered if she felt the same sense of urgency he did. The same need to know, despite the risks.

"Ready when you are," he said quietly.

CHAPTER 3

This is not going to work! Kelsey thought.

Jackson Crow seemed pleasant enough, like a man who could be a team player. But Logan Raintree seemed almost hostile. Except that he'd pitched in with information about the Longhorn and he'd also risen to her defense when Crow had been hammering away about what she'd *seen* at the inn. Still, it was pretty obvious that he didn't want to be a member of any team, and if he wasn't part of the team — was there a team? There would be a task force, she supposed. Now that the FBI had become aware of the number of corpses, there'd have to be. The fact that a serial killer was suspected of targeting the area was bound to become known, and the public would demand it.

But did *she* want to be part of it?

Something inside her wanted to recoil. And something else wanted to go with the two men, go and look at the available evidence.

So she went. She had certainly seen violence and death as a U.S. Marshal. Gun battles happened on the open sea when drug traffickers found themselves under siege. Bodies were dragged out of the Gulf and the Atlantic. She'd seen the ugly side of human nature. Despite that, the murders of the women seemed far more horrific than the cold and impersonal violence she most frequently witnessed. Cocaine dealers shot their rivals and their enemies — people who worked for the law.

True, she'd found those bones in Key West. . . . And because she had, the victim had been identified, and a family had learned the sad truth.

She forced herself to appear cool, professional, stoic as they reached the police station and passed through the outer areas, where petty offenders were being booked. San Antonio was not without its share of prostitutes and thieves, and a number of them were being interviewed, along with traffic offenders and others brought in by the police for their various misdeeds. But Jackson Crow barely noticed them. With a brief word to the desk sergeant, he led her and Logan through a hallway to a large room enclosed by smoked glass. Within that room were several desks, a free-standing, forty-inch computer screen, a small lab area, a board with marker notes and a private snack station with a large coffeepot and a small refrigerator and microwave oven. It was almost its own little fortress.

This could be her place. For now at least.

A man sat at one of the desks, but rose when they all entered. He was tall and striking in a lanky, easy way, and was quick to shake their hands when Jackson introduced him as Jake Mallory. On Jackson's own team, he was adept with cameras, recorders and, he admitted dryly, a guitar.

"Only one member of your team's here," Logan pointed out.

"I told you," Jackson Crow said. "We're stretched too thin. There's been a murder at an old hotel in D.C. Some of my people are there."

Logan Raintree merely nodded.

"So what do you have?" Kelsey asked Jake Mallory.

"You've given them the information about Chelsea Martin and Tara Grissom?" Jake asked Crow.

Again, Crow nodded. Jake sat at his computer and hit a key. The large screen against the far wall came to life. "That's

74

Chelsea Martin on the left, Tara Grissom on the right," he said. "Both photos were taken a few months before they disappeared."

No matter how long a person worked in law enforcement, Kelsey thought, it was heartbreaking to see the image of a young woman in life — and to know how that life had ended. Chelsea Martin had huge blue eyes and dark brown hair. Tara Grissom was a blonde, with green eyes. Chelsea's face had been round, while Tara's was slim with high cheekbones. Chelsea peered out at them, smiling. The close-up had been cropped, and it looked as if her face had been taken from a picture with kids in it. She'd presumably had her arms around some of them. They must've been children she'd taught. Tara's picture had probably been a publicity photo, because it had a neutral background and she smiled at them from a posed angle.

"These are the young women we know, and they're at the morgue, along with six we have yet to identify," Jake said. "The killer isn't going for a particular look, or not that we can pin down from these two, at any rate. One's a brunette, the other a blonde. One was plump, and one was lean. And although we haven't identified the other remains, there's hair on most of them, or remnants of hair, and the colors vary." He cleared his throat. "I was listening to Chelsea's last phone conversation when you arrived."

"Her phone conversation? How was it recorded?" Logan asked. "If her friend answered the phone, there wouldn't be a recording."

"Apparently, she answered right when the recording began. We got lucky. Nancy Mc-Call had an old-fashioned answering machine," Jake said. "It's strange — I've been isolating sounds on the tape, but . . . well, you want to listen to the original recording first?"

Crow nodded.

"This is the conversation," Jake said, hitting another key.

Chelsea Martin, with her wide cheeks and big eyes, smiled at them from the screen as they listened. "Nancy! Hey!" said her voice, sweet and excited.

"You were supposed to call me when you landed," came the reply.

"I'm sorry. I went straight to the Alamo, which is crazy, 'cause I'm dragging around a bag and all. But I *had* to come here! I've read so much about it, so many stories about the siege and the battle and the people who were here . . . oh! Too funny! There's a man in costume. I've been flirting with him. He's pretty cute, too!"

Before her friend could respond, another voice broke in. It was deep and husky, and had a rattling sound, almost as if someone were speaking through a mouthful of dust.

"Come away, come away, now. You're in danger!"

They heard Chelsea giggle. "The battle's over," she said.

"You're in danger," the rattling voice said again, *"Please, listen to me."*

That voice. Kelsey had been in dire situations several times, but she couldn't remember when any sound had caused such a chill to suddenly sweep through her.

"Nancy, I think a ghost is playing with me," Chelsea said, and she laughed again.

"Chelsea, what's going on?" her friend asked.

"I —"

And that was it. Silence. For a moment, those in the room were silent, as well.

"And just how do you figure the third voice got on the phone?" Logan Raintree asked. His voice was hard and cold. "For it to be that clear, he had to have his mouth right next to the phone. What did the friend say when you questioned her about it?"

"I called Nancy McCall earlier this afternoon," Jake said. "She didn't hear the other voice when she spoke to Chelsea, and she has no idea how it can be so clear on the recording — or even how it managed to record at all. I told you, I've been isolating sounds, but I can't separate this voice from Chelsea's when I try to bring them onto different frequencies. I just played you the original. I can isolate Chelsea's voice, and you'll hear that it's still in there."

He played the recording again.

Afterward, Jackson walked over to Jake's desk, which held a pile of folders. He picked up two of them. "Take these," he said, handing one to Logan and one to Kelsey. "They have all the information we've got on Chelsea and Tara, and the times and dates the six unidentified bodies were discovered. Please take a look at the folders. If you decide to join the team, I'd like you to come to the morgue with me tomorrow."

"Have those bodies been there all this time?" Logan asked.

"No. We've exhumed them," Jackson told him. "They were buried by the city as unknowns."

Logan shook his head, eyes narrowed. His expression was impassive, and yet Kelsey felt that some kind of emotion was seething inside him. "Why now?" he asked. If he exploded, he'd be frightening.

Yet she was equally certain that he never just exploded. He controlled himself at all times.

"It's in the folder," Jackson said.

Next, Jake passed out pages he'd obviously printed for them. "I was looking up information on another case when I found out that a young woman, Vanessa Johnston, has recently disappeared — on her way here," he told them. "Right now, she's a missing person. She was driving in. Neither she nor her Honda has been seen since she stopped at a gas station near the county line. I brought the problem to Jackson's attention. Everything's on those sheets I gave you."

Kelsey slipped hers inside the folder.

"I spoke with your captain about this case, Raintree," Jackson was saying. "And he invited us in."

Kelsey watched as Logan Raintree nodded curtly and headed toward the door.

He paused and turned to face them. "What time are we going to the morgue?" he asked.

"9:00 a.m."

"I'll meet you there."

He left the room.

"I'd like to hear the recording again, please," Kelsey said.

She found a chair at one of the empty desks and sat, listening as Jake replayed it. Once more she felt the strange chill, but along with the sense of fear and dread, she felt . . .

A sense of something being oddly right. Not about the recording. About *her.* She might miss the water, miss home, miss being a Marshal, but she knew she could help on this case. And she wanted to.

She held her folder with hands that seemed to freeze around it. When the recording finished, both men were watching her.

"Nine?" she asked. She'd heard Jackson the first time. She'd just needed to say something.

"Yes," Jackson said. "I'll pick you up at the Longhorn."

"One more thing." Jake touched a key. The picture on the large computer screen changed.

Another young woman of about twenty-five smiled out at her. She was wearing a tiara on sandy-colored hair.

"That's our missing girl," he said. "Vanessa Johnston. Last year's Miss Maple Queen of Montpelier, Vermont."

Kelsey rose. "I'll have these read by tomorrow and be completely up to speed," she told Crow. "I'm in, provided you still want this team to exist if Raintree opts out."

She was surprised when Crow smiled grimly. "He'll be at the morgue tomorrow, and he won't opt out."

Kelsey decided not to answer. Raintree hadn't looked as if he planned to agree. Not in her opinion, anyway.

But then, maybe she was better at understanding the dead than the living.

"Good afternoon," she said. And she left the two men, still feeling the same sense of dread.

And the same sense of purpose.

Logan drove straight to his own office. Others greeted him as he walked through the main room, both those sworn in as Texas Rangers and civilians busy at other tasks. The world hadn't changed for any of them; they waved at him, smiled, chatted. He went to Captain Aaron Bentley's office, tapped on the door, but walked in without waiting for an answer. Bentley was on the phone. He was a big man with snow-white hair, as rugged-looking as any man who'd ever run a Texas Ranger division.

Bentley seemed to be expecting him. He

lifted a hand in greeting and ended his conversation.

"What the hell did you send me into, sir?" Logan demanded.

"Sit down," Bentley told him. Logan stood there stiffly for a minute, then sighed and took the chair in front of Bentley's desk. "Sir —"

"Oh, don't 'sir' me," Bentley said. "We've been together too long for that."

"I've been good at my job," Logan said.

"You have."

"So . . ."

"So, I'm trying to get you onto a team where you can really be of service. Is that going to be on the Texas level or on the national level?" Bentley murmured. "I had to ask myself where you could do the most good, Logan. And if I'm honest, it's with this new team. Your instincts have helped us in hundreds of cases. You have the sort of mind that reads others, and you've predicted the course of a perp's actions a dozen times. I thought we'd lost you after Alana died, but you headed out to that rock you love so much and your grandfather's place, and you came back stronger. I'd like to keep you, but when the request comes down from the top of the food chain, you do what you need to do."

"I'm told I have a choice."

"You do. You have time to think about this."

"*What* time? Captain, do you know what's been going on? And if I'm so damned good at this kind of thing, why the hell didn't I know?"

"The FBI has just shared its information," Bentley said. "We're in the process of analyzing it, and supplying them with whatever info we can find. Every law enforcement agency in the area will be on the hunt now. But, Logan, you . . ."

Bentley's voice trailed off. Bentley's voice never trailed off. Logan knew they were both thinking about the same thing — what had happened with Alana.

"The Rangers have changed over the years, Raintree," Bentley said, recovering his voice. "We're a true law enforcement agency under the Texas Department of Safety. You know as well as I do that we're actually older than Texas as a republic, a state, a Confederate state and a U.S. state again. Hell, when Stephen Austin organized Rangers to protect the frontier while the Anglos were first moving in, we were frontier guards, and that was our business for a long time. Then we battled the Mexican government, and the Native American tribes, and the outlaws. We kept peace on the frontier until there was no more frontier. We had our valiant moments in the sun, and we were some of Zachary Taylor's finest troops in the Mexican-American war. At times we also acted like a law unto ourselves. Those days are over — for all their brilliance. We're a respected law enforcement agency. We serve a higher god, you might say. And that's the thing, Logan. No matter how you look at it, we're part of the greater good."

He had neatly sidestepped the real conversation.

Alana.

Logan remained silent.

"Logan, the feds have way more power than I can ever have or give," he said in a resigned voice. "And this team the government wants to set up — it has a direct connection to the most powerful law enforcement men in the country. Anything that can be done within constitutional limits will be done. Warrants achieved at all hours of the day or night. In any city, any state of the Union. The right to cross geographical boundaries to chase the truth. I've heard that the man responsible for creating these teams has the White House on speed dial. But more than that, Logan, they have what you need, and you have what they need."

He had what they needed.

Sitting there, he suddenly felt defeated. Nothing seemed real. He'd been pretending that his life could return to normal. Playing at being a good Ranger, following the clues, investigating leads. If he didn't think about Alana, he could look back on his life as if it were history, as distant as the events at the Alamo.

"It's a unique opportunity," Bentley said.

Logan didn't have anything more to say to Bentley. Except this, "I still have time," he said as he rose from his chair.

"Yes."

He exited the office, pausing at the door to turn around. "Thanks, Captain."

"Raintree, you're a great officer. I'll be sorry to lose you."

Logan didn't deny that Bentley had lost him. But he wasn't sure yet. He'd know in the morning.

Kelsey couldn't decide where to go.

Her mind was spinning. She should get back to the Longhorn, log on to her computer and look up everything she could find on Jackson Crow and Adam Harrison and the Krewe of Hunters. But she wasn't ready to go back yet; she wasn't ready for questions or even for Corey Simmons and the ghosts of a century gone.

She needed to mull over the meeting.

She parked her rental car by the Alamo. She'd taken the tour several days ago. But there was something special about the place, an aura of a certain time, the acts of men who'd changed history.

And she couldn't forget the recording she'd just heard. Chelsea Martin at the Alamo, laughing at first, happy as she talked to a friend. Then . . . gone.

And now . . .

Dead.

She wandered aimlessly for a while, watching as a group worked with schoolchildren, reenacting what had occurred at the fort. She gathered that one man was playing the role of Davy Crockett, and another, that of twenty-six-year-old Lieutenant Colonel Travis, who'd run the battle — since his co-commander, Jim Bowie, was in bed, probably dying, and probably of tuberculosis. A few men were playing other defenders, those who hadn't gone down in history with such giant names and reputations, but who had died there nonetheless.

She listened to them, impressed. The actors were doing a brilliant job, bringing the situation to life. The men they portrayed were tired. They spoke of day-to-day things

— their meals, scouting expeditions, their exhaustion, their desire for more comfortable beds.

She was so busy watching them that she hardly noticed when a man sat next to her. Then she caught sight of him in her peripheral vision, and became instantly aware. Perhaps she shouldn't have been surprised, but she was.

There was no mistaking Logan Raintree. The best of many cultures had mixed in his face, a face as cleanly sculpted as a marble bust, with high broad cheekbones and a determined chin. He wasn't beautiful, but he was one of the most imposing men she'd ever met. The ever-simmering energy within him added a vitality and heat that made him even more intriguing, more attractive.

Seductive. She immediately tried to wipe that thought from her mind.

She didn't speak but gazed at him solemnly. He'd known she was there. He hadn't walked away when he saw her. Quite the opposite — he'd joined her.

She was almost shocked when he smiled at her. "I'd like to apologize, Marshal O'Brien. I've been an ass."

She smiled in response. "Um, apology accepted. Except . . . you weren't *that* bad," she said with a laugh.

"What made you come here?" he asked her.

She shrugged. "It's not that far from the Longhorn, where I'm staying. I wasn't ready to go back and answer a bunch of questions about the meeting. I needed time."

He nodded, looking toward the chapel. "I wondered if you'd come here because this is where Chelsea Martin was last seen."

"It might've had something to do with that."

"You going to accept Jackson Crow's offer?" he asked her.

"I . . . don't know. Maybe. You?"

"This morning, I would've given him a definite *no.* Now . . . I'm not sure. Either way, I want to find out what there is to see at the morgue tomorrow."

She felt a tightening inside. Yes. The morgue.

They were both silent for a minute. Then he began to speak, his tone relaxed.

"The Alamo's a shrine," he said softly. "Of course, it's different than it was at the time of the battle. The chapel and this area — including the long barracks — was just a small part of the original Alamo," Logan explained. "The walls extended for a quarter of a mile. In fact, that was one of the problems for the defenders once Santa

Anna's men breached the walls — the place was too big to protect easily. The men who fought here fought hard, and they fought knowing they were likely to die." He glanced at her. "Courage is being afraid — and going ahead, anyway."

Kelsey nodded in agreement.

"Santa Anna had his men raise a red flag in a nearby church tower, and that blood-red flag indicated there'd be no quarter given. But, of course, the Alamo was part of a bigger story, and like most history, it depends on who is doing the telling. The Spanish had been in control. They'd signed a treaty ceding Florida to the U.S. and creating a boundary between the United States and Spanish America. But before that, men called *impresarios,* Stephen Austin among them, had been luring Americans into Texas with land grants that required no down payment. Then the Mexicans fought the Spanish for independence and won. Santa Anna become president, or more accurately, dictator. Texians or Anglo-Americans, and Tejanos, Mexican-Texans, had been living under the Constitution of 1824 until Santa Anna rescinded it and pretty much pissed them all off."

"Which led to what happened here," she said, absorbed in what he was telling her.

"Right. But a lot of movies about the Alamo forgot to depict the Tejanos who were part of the effort — *and* part of the effort to create an independent Texas. Some of the early books and movies about the Alamo were downright racist. The good old Anglo-Americans were the heroes, while the Tejanos who fought just as hard were ignored. I'm glad to say we're moving past that." He smiled slightly. "But it's also true that regardless of background, these men weren't on some idealistic mission for freedom and honor. They were like most of us — looking for a way to make a better life for themselves."

"And there would've been no Texas without both groups," Kelsey remarked.

His smile deepened. "Santa Anna miscalculated. He thought that his 'no quarter given' policy would scare off the revolutionaries. Instead, 'Remember the Alamo!' became a battle cry. Soon after, the massacre at Goliad occurred. Santa Anna had everyone there executed, and the war became one of revenge as well as Texan independence. Of course, if they'd lost, the whole thing would've been described as the Mexicans putting down an uprising by a group of rebels."

"But Texas did gain its independence and

then became part of the United States," Kelsey said. "I appreciate what you've told me. I'm really interested in history."

"Me, too. I just want it to be *history* and not fiction."

"You're a Ranger and obviously Native American," she said. "What's *your* history?"

"Very typical of Texas — a real mix. My father's a quarter Apache and three-fourths Anglo. My mother's half Norwegian and half Comanche. They're both all-Texan. And all-American. And they're alive and well and living happily in Montana now."

"Didn't the Texas Rangers spend a lot of years battling the Comanches?" she asked.

"Yes," he said. "But they also learned from them." He eased back a little as he spoke, leaning against the bench as he watched the young people around him seek to learn about the past. "A Comanche warrior could ride at breakneck speed — while clinging to the side of his horse with his shield, bow and quiver. He could fire off twelve arrows while a Ranger was trying to reload his rifle. To fight the Comanche, the Rangers had to learn how to do the same — or something equivalent and their fights led to some real renovations in weapons." He turned to face her. "I like to think I've learned from all my ancestors, including the Vikings," he added with a grin.

"Why not?" she said, shrugging comically.

"O'Brien. Are you Irish?" he asked.

"Like you, I'm mostly all-American mutt, but yes, my dad's family immigrated from Ireland."

"And you come from the Sunshine State. Do you miss it?"

"No," she said. "Okay, a little. But I'm at the Longhorn, as you know, and Sandy's an old friend. I have a cousin here, too. Sean Cameron. But he's —"

He straightened. "Sean Cameron is your cousin?" he asked.

"Well, *a* Sean Cameron is my cousin."

"He works for a company called Magic on Demand?"

"Yes. You know him?"

He nodded, staring at her.

"How?"

"He's been a consultant for us a few times. I haven't seen him in quite a while, but one Halloween we had a murder in a haunted house, and he was brought in. He helped the crime-scene people dig through the fake gore and get down to the real evidence." Logan was quiet for a minute.

"Oh," she murmured. "Did you always want to be a Texas Ranger?" she asked, changing the subject.

He nodded. "My dad was a Ranger," he said. "What about you?"

"I always wanted to be a Marshal," she told him. "I knew it from when I was in high school."

He slouched down on the bench, thoughtful as he studied the tourists coming and going. "Most people would say you don't look the part," he said.

"What am I supposed to look like?"

"John Wayne, maybe."

She laughed. "Didn't he play a Texas Ranger once? He was definitely here at the Alamo in one of his movies."

He turned to her, but as he did, he saw someone behind her and frowned.

She turned around, as well, and saw a man. He was the only person in their vicinity and he was dressed in costume, a big wide-brimmed hat, buckskins and boots. She assumed he had to be a member of the little group who'd just reenacted the scene between the men at the Alamo. He obviously knew Logan Raintree and wanted to speak to him, while Raintree looked as if he wanted the man to disappear.

What was his problem? Logan Raintree was being downright rude, and in her opinion, there was no excuse for that kind of behavior.

"Hello." She smiled, hoping to compensate for her companion's lack of courtesy.

She was startled when Raintree stood abruptly and even the costumed stranger took a step back.

"Who are you talking to?" Raintree asked suspiciously.

Kelsey stared at him as if he'd lost his mind. She stood, too, and said pointedly, "The gentleman you're ignoring." She turned back to look at the man in costume, but he was gone.

When she turned toward Logan Raintree again, his expression had hardened, and he seemed to have withdrawn from her.

"You *saw* a man?" he demanded.

"Of course I saw him," she said. "He wanted to talk to you, and you acted like he was a martian or something."

As she frowned at him, both of them standing near the chapel of the Alamo, she heard an intense whirring sound.

Birds.

Black birds . . . crows. Settling down, all around them.

"I'll see you at the morgue tomorrow," Logan Raintree said, and he began to walk away, his footsteps moving through the sudden sea of birds, scattering them in all directions.

CHAPTER 4

A murder could be easier to solve than the case of a missing person, Kelsey reflected. When a body was discovered, there was a chance to collect evidence and — usually — a trail to follow. When a person had simply disappeared, you had to assume *someone* must have seen *something,* but finding that someone was often next to impossible.

The files they'd been given contained all the known information about Vanessa Johnston, who was last seen purchasing gas at a station near the county line.

She'd spoken briefly with a young cashier when she had gone in to buy coffee, saying she was excited about going to San Antonio, and then she'd gotten back into her Honda and driven off. Neither she nor the car had been seen since.

Her cell phone records indicated that she'd made no calls. Nor had she used her charge card again.

"A car has to show up somewhere," Kelsey murmured aloud to herself.

There was a tap on her door. She was in bed — having moved into Room 207 — and she rose up, leaning against her pillow.

"Kelsey?" Sandy called.

"Come on in," Kelsey said.

She hadn't had a chance to speak with Sandy since she'd gotten back; the inn was now full, and there'd been a number of bartenders and waitresses in the busy downstairs area, along with the singer who was reprising old tunes with a piano player. The saloon had been bustling. She'd been glad, since she wasn't ready to share anything about her day. Yet.

When she'd returned, however, Corey Simmons had been waiting for her, hoping to buy her a drink. She'd declined. Sandy had packed up his belongings, brought them to Kelsey's room, then packed up Kelsey's stuff. He wanted to thank her, he'd said rather sheepishly, for moving into Room 207.

"Hey, just wanted to make sure you're okay in here," Sandy told her, stepping inside. Sandy was wearing an apron, since she'd pitched in with the serving downstairs.

Kelsey smiled. "I'm fine, absolutely fine.

Nothing's going to happen to me in this room," she assured Sandy.

Sandy let out a soft sigh. "Well, thank you. You were wonderful. I can hardly believe Corey decided to stay here."

"Well, you know, if the inn's filling up and someone else wants this room, I can always go to another hotel," Kelsey told her.

"No! You're staying right here. I'm not renting this room to macho men, cowboys or hunters. I'm keeping things calm. I have to make a living on this place!"

"Okay, then, not to worry. I'll stay, and I'll be just fine," Kelsey said again.

"So, how did your day go? What's up? What was the big meeting about?"

"Well . . . I've been asked to join the FBI," Kelsey said.

"Really? Wow! I didn't know the FBI went out and asked people to join it! Don't they have an application process and training, and all that?"

"I imagine that's the usual case."

"Wow. You must be special!"

Kelsey shrugged one shoulder. "I don't know about that."

"Why?"

"Pardon?"

"Why you? I mean, honestly, I think that's amazing!" Sandy said.

"I *am* a United States Marshal," Kelsey reminded her. "I have all the training that went along with that, and they're both federal agencies."

Even with Sandy, she didn't want to talk about the reasons. And, in fact, those reasons hadn't actually been discussed. Oddly enough, it hadn't been necessary. They'd all understood.

"I don't really know," she lied.

Sandy came in and perched on the foot of her bed. "What are you going to do?" she asked.

"I'm not sure yet," she said evasively. "Sandy, forgive me, but I'm not at liberty to discuss any of this yet."

"Oh, I'm sorry! Of course not. I'd just love it, though, if you moved to Texas. I mean, I know you love your home and all, but Texas is a great state."

Kelsey made a point of casually closing the folder she'd been reading, then sat up straighter in bed. "I'll make a decision by tomorrow."

"And you can live right here!" Sandy said excitedly.

Kelsey laughed. "Don't worry, the scuttle-butt about the room will die out. Or you can bring in one of those ghost expedition groups. Either way, you'll get lots of business. But I'll probably stay for a while. So, thank you."

"This is great," Sandy said happily, as if it was all settled. "I know Sean is off working now, but you have a cousin here. And you have me. It'll be like home."

"I'm sure it will." Despite herself, Kelsey yawned.

Sandy stood quickly. "Okay, well, I'll let you get some sleep. But I'm so thrilled you're going to be here! Yay!" She walked to the door. "Good night."

"Good night. Thanks, Sandy."

When Sandy had gone, Kelsey got out of bed and went to the door. She hadn't thought to lock it earlier; now she did.

She looked at the files again, but she really was tired. Facts, figures and faces were beginning to swim before her eyes. She left the bathroom light on, but turned off the others, set the files on the bedside table and slipped back into bed.

She should've realized she wasn't going to sleep well that night. . . .

At first she felt as if she'd been disturbed by the sound of someone whispering. It was annoying, but not enough to completely wake her. Then she began to see it all again. The room changing, ever so slightly. The Oriental divider by the bathroom door.

She noticed something different about the darkness with the glow of just the bathroom light.

No, there was a gas lamp burning.

Kelsey saw the two people in the room, the man and the woman. She, so beautiful with her dark curling hair piled atop her head and tumbling around her face with a few stray dark locks. The dress lay on the floor, and the woman wore old-fashioned stockings and garters. The man stood in his dark suit.

As he'd done in her earlier vision, he strode across the room and grabbed the woman. "You won't hold out on me!" he shouted. "I want it, and I want it now."

"I don't have it," she said.

"You're a liar! I know what happened in Galveston that night, and I know that your pretty-boy lover won it. I want it, and I want it now!"

"No, it's mine," she responded.

The rest of the scene played itself out, just as it had earlier that day.

When the man squeezed the life out of the woman, she went limp. He picked her up and threw her down, the same way he had before.

Then they both disappeared into the darkness. Seconds later, light began to show from the bathroom and the room resumed its earlier appearance. She'd been unable to move; she'd really never wakened.

A tiny light seemed to hover directly in front of her. She realized she was seeing a woman's face. In dream, in vision, in half sleep, in the tormented corners of her mind, she saw a face. She thought it would be Rose Langley, the pathetic creature murdered in this room.

But it wasn't. It was a face she'd seen in a picture that day.

The face of the missing girl, Vanessa Johnston. She wasn't smiling now. She was sad. She looked at Kelsey and whispered, "Too late."

Too late, too late, too late . . .

There was a whir of flapping black wings in the room, and the sound they made seemed to mock the words that had been spoken.

Too late, too late, too late . . .

The flapping stopped, and the wings seemed to merge and create a shape.

A man.

She saw him only as a silhouette at first. Then he turned to her, his expression grave. It was Logan Raintree, so tall and lean and solid, his face like chiseled marble, his hazel eyes alive and burning.

"You *saw* a man?" he asked her.

She heard wings again, and now she seemed to be outside. The black birds, the crows, settling all around them, on the ground, the benches and the nearby power lines and poles.

And then he was gone, and the darkness swept around her.

When she woke in the morning, she remembered her dream about the murder of Rose Langley, her vision of Vanessa Johnston.

And the appearance of Logan Raintree in her room.

Surrounded by crows.

The Bexar County morgue was large, and a special room had been set aside for the victims who might have been associated with a single killer.

Jackson Crow did have all the right connections. Logan had been at the morgue often enough in years gone by, and he was familiar with various members of the staff. But he'd never seen anything like the way people scurried for Jackson Crow, nor had he been there when an entire facility was dedicated to one pursuit.

There were eight gurneys in the room.

Each had a sheet draped over the length of a body.

One sheet was almost flat. He assumed it covered a victim who was little more than bones.

One of the bodies had already been in the morgue, along with those of Chelsea Martin and Tara Grissom. Five others had been exhumed. They walked from gurney to gurney with Dr. Frazier Gaylord, medical examiner. He carried a clipboard with his notes on the remains of Chelsea and Tara — and the unknowns. The unknowns, of course, had been buried by the county and exhumed by the county, but they had numbers rather than names. Gaylord was thorough in his discussion of each one. Logan kept silent as he followed Jackson and Kelsey. The first body was skeletal and the second had no discernible features. Medical reports indicated that all the women had been between twenty-two and thirty-five; none had borne children. Hair proved to be of every color. Five had been Caucasian and two were Hispanic. One, according to Gaylord, was Asian — Logan didn't ask what had given him that impression. The girl still had a pretty face beneath the damage and decay. "Or possibly American Indian?" he suggested.

"No, I believe she was Chinese," Gaylord told him. "Based on the set of the skull and the cast of the eyes. There's enough left . . . as you can see."

Kelsey O'Brien hadn't said a word. He liked that about her. If she had a question, she asked it. If she didn't, she listened. Absorbed.

"I'm puzzled as to why you've put these deaths together," Gaylord mused, looking at Jackson Crow, "since the cause of death isn't consistent." He glanced at his notes. "There are nicks on this woman's skeletal remains, suggesting that she was stabbed to death. Broken hyoid bone in the next one suggests strangulation. The young woman over there —" he pointed to the farthest gurney "— was drowned. So, we have, in our collection of Jane Does, two strangulations, three stabbings and a drowning. And, then, of course, we get to the bodies of the two young women who have been identified, Chelsea Martin and Tara Grissom. This is a big city, and that means big-city crime. These poor souls might have encountered any member of the criminal element. Or they might have been murdered by someone in a fit of anger."

"We don't know yet, Doctor," Crow said. "Let's move on, shall we?"

They walked to the last two gurneys, those holding the remains of Chelsea Martin and Tara Grissom. "We're facing the same inconsistency of method." Gaylord paused to pull back one of the sheets. "Chelsea Martin," he said quietly, "identified from dental records. As you can see, there wasn't much left when she was discovered."

Chelsea Martin had been found in a trash heap in almost skeletal form. There were still bits of flesh adhering to the bone here and there, and strands of pretty brown hair attached to the scalp that remained. Dr. Gaylord pointed to her throat. "Hyoid bone broken. My guess is that this young woman, too, was strangled."

They paused for a moment, looking at the gurneys with their sad burdens. Logan found himself thinking of a pirate slogan: *Dead men tell no tales!*

Except that the dead *could* tell tales — when something of the killer stayed behind. When there was a shred of physical evidence. A hair, fiber, skin cells caught in the fingernails of a murder victim. And the dead could tell many tales when they left clues about where they'd been going, who they'd been with. . . .

Or when they could actually come back.

The others were moving on. Logan trailed

after them.

Gaylord removed the last sheet. The remains of Tara Grissom were so gruesome they appeared to be something created by a special-effects master for a horror movie. "Half-covered. Half in the ground, half out," Gaylord said. He indicated areas of the body. "But you'll see here that a knife was used on her. It was thrust into the abdomen several times, once in the throat, and the fatal blow chipped a rib — here — and pierced the heart. Death couldn't have been easy for this poor girl."

Tara Grissom had half a decaying face.

Gaylord went on talking to Jackson Crow, telling him they'd been thorough with the autopsy. Scraping had been done under the nails, the crime-scene units had considered every conceivable clue or chance of DNA evidence. He launched into an explanation of their procedures, but Logan had ceased to hear him. He was vaguely aware that Kelsey O'Brien was giving him, rather than Crow or Gaylord, her attention. She was still, silent, as she gazed at him, standing a few feet back.

Logan didn't care that she was watching him. He stepped closer to the gurney.

He closed his eyes briefly, then touched the remains.

Speak to me.

He looked down. For a moment, he saw her as she'd been in life. Young, beautiful, vivacious, a dancer with a dancer's grace of movement. She opened her eyes, and they were both there, lime-green eyes that were striking with the lovely blond hair. She tried to offer him a wistful smile. Her lips moved.

"I barely saw him," she seemed to say. "He came out of the darkness, and he was in darkness. I fought so hard, but I was bleeding. . . . I just kept thinking that I'd never dance again. I didn't even realize at first that I'd never breathe again."

Her voice was real to him. He could hear her as plainly as if Gaylord were saying the words.

Where were you? he asked in silence.

But she didn't reply.

Back at the station, in the dedicated room, Logan sat contemplatively, watching Kelsey O'Brien as she worked. Besides the computer screen, she used a board and markers, attaching photos of the victims' remains. By each of them, she made notes. They were alone in the room.

"All right," she said, "we know that we're looking at one woman who disappeared a year and a half ago, and one who disappeared a year ago. Because of the deterioration, Dr. Gaylord can't precisely pin down the time of death, but . . ." She paused, pointing at one of the pictures. He'd already learned that Kelsey couldn't think of the unidentified victims as Jane Doe I, II, III and so on, and she'd given them names. They were Jane Doe, Jenny Doe, Judy Doe, Jodie Doe, Julie Doe and, finally, Josie Doe. He'd seen that she had tremendous empathy for all their victims, although she was professional as she handled photos that could churn any stomach. She indicated Julie Doe. "But! Dr. Gaylord believes Julie is the most recent victim, and that she's been dead around a month." She went back to the photo of Tara Grissom. "As you know, Tara was found half-hidden by a tarp in a boatyard on the river, one that had been closed down for a year. Chelsea was found at the bottom of a compost heap at a nursery. There was no known connection between her and anyone there, and all the employees checked out when the police investigated. Let's get to our other women. Jane, discovered by a rock pile near a pond at a public park. Strangled. Jenny was found by garbage men at a trash dump — stabbed to death. Judy in another park, again by some rocks, half in and half out of the water, strangled. Jodie was dragged out of the river. Cause of death, drowning. Julie was found when divers were cleaning out a park pond. She was strangled. And Josie was in a compost heap, too. She'd been stabbed. The killer is incredibly lucky. He keeps disposing of the bodies in almost public ways, and yet he's never seen, and he doesn't leave anything behind. Not a fiber, a hair . . . nothing. To the best of Gaylord's ability to discern, considering the amount of decomposition, the women weren't sexually molested. But . . . it appears that our killer is escalating his activities. Say his first murder was a year and a half ago, then a year ago . . . and then every couple of months, and now every month. We have another missing woman at the moment, who may or may not be his ninth victim." She stopped speaking and looked at him. He'd heard her voice and her words, but he realized he'd been concentrating on the woman herself more than anything she had to say. Kelsey was young, but she was grave. Mature. Only when he'd seen her really smile, while they talked at the Alamo, had it occurred to him that she was probably in her mid-to-late twenties. When she smiled, her face lit up, and her emerald-green eyes became enchanting.

She was the same age as their victims.

"I don't think the drowning victim was attacked by the same killer," he said. "The rest, I believe, were. And he's local. He knows exactly where people will and won't look. But why? And how has he managed to kill them without anyone seeing a thing?"

She was pensive. "At the Alamo," she said quietly, meeting his eyes.

He admitted that he was glad they were by themselves. Jackson Crow had stayed at the morgue where Jake had joined him to take photographs; they were going to work with artists to reconstruct the faces of the dead.

He studied her a moment longer. He winced, staring down at the floor. He felt strangely close to her, although he had no idea why. And he felt guilty. He'd loved his wife with his whole heart. He'd been responsible for her death, not directly but responsible nonetheless. It wasn't that he hadn't found another woman attractive since her death. He'd dated casually in the past year, and even gone home with a woman from a bar a time or two. There was something different about that, something that, for good or ill, spoke of a lack of feeling.

But he had a connection with Kelsey

O'Brien, and before he'd recognized that, he'd noted how beautiful she was, how conscientious, competent, bright and . . . appealing.

And so now, although they'd scarcely touched, he felt that he'd become too *involved* with her. *Intimate* in an unfamiliar way.

He steeled himself; this was a professional matter. Women were dead. More women could die. A killer had gotten away with heinous acts for a long time.

"Don't shut me out, please," she said, and he had to look away again. He wasn't shutting her out — not deliberately, and not on a professional level.

"You saw Zachary at the Alamo yesterday," he said, his voice louder than he'd intended.

"Zachary? The guy in costume?" she asked.

He smiled, amused despite himself. The question was so innocent.

"He wasn't in costume. He's dead," Logan told her.

He'd taken her by surprise. That was certain. Eyes wide, she groped for a chair, then sat down across from him.

"Dead."

"Long dead," Logan went on, feeling a bit

incredulous. "Come on, you must be aware that you're a wind-spirit."

"Wind-spirit?" she repeated, like an automaton.

"That term came from my dad's family," he said. "It means you speak with the dead. You see ghosts. You hear them and see them, and you can actually carry on conversations with them."

Kelsey swallowed hard. She set her hands on the table, and they were trembling.

"That's why we're here," she murmured.

"Yes. But you knew that."

"Yes, I guess I did," she said. "And so did you."

"Yes." He drummed his fingers on the table. "I suppose I didn't want to admit it. I thought it was a part of my life that I just kept quiet, and used when I needed to. When it didn't fail me," he added, and he could hear the rasp in his voice. He cleared his throat; there was no reason to make Kelsey think he hated *her* for what had been his own shortcoming. "I know all about Adam Harrison, his early links to the government and various strange cases, and his decision to start Jackson Crow's Krewe of Hunters team. I even know about the cases they've solved, and some of their considerable accomplishments."

She regarded him with her beautiful gem-like eyes. They reminded him of emeralds, they were such a deep, true green.

"Then why are you so determined to be against Jackson Crow?"

"Because I've failed, miserably, upon occasion," he told her flatly.

"But people fail in many situations, and maybe this kind of force can make a difference," she said.

"Maybe." He shrugged. "For the moment, I'm in. I am a Texas Ranger, this is my state and I'm appalled that these poor women are dead and we weren't even aware of a connection. And now there's another missing girl."

He saw an expression of shock on her face. "What's wrong?"

"She's dead," Kelsey whispered.

He frowned. "How do you know that?"

"Last night . . . well, it could just be a dream." He looked at her steadily and she blinked, then explained. "I'm not sure — maybe I simply have a cinematic imagination. But I see what I suppose they call *residual* haunting. I see the murder in Room 207, the one that took place in the nineteenth century. When Rose Langley was killed. The first time I saw it was yesterday, right before we met for lunch. I really didn't have any experiences at the inn before that. But last night I moved into Room 207. The Longhorn is filling up — there's a rodeo here next week, and Sandy asked me to stay in 207, as a favor to her. When I went to sleep, the same scene played out before me. Then there was a tremendous flapping of wings —"

"Wings?" he interrupted.

"Yes, as though birds were whirling around." She paused. "Like they did yesterday, at the Alamo."

He was silent.

"Hmm, wait. I saw the first haunting, the residual one, and then, when that faded away, I saw her face."

"How did you know it was hers?"

"Because Jake Mallory showed it to me on the screen before I left yesterday."

"But if you'd seen her face, maybe you were just recalling it."

"Maybe."

"But?"

"She said, 'Too late.' Then the birds seemed to take up the cry. Over and over again. *Too late, too late, too late.*"

He watched her as she spoke. She never took her eyes from his, and he sensed how hard it was for her to say all this to him. He didn't speak for a moment. "You figure . . .

I'm a little on the unbalanced side?" she finally asked. She tried to smile.

He shook his head slowly and offered her a wry smile. "I have Apache in me. The Apache believe in the dream state. They're very religious people. Spirits take on the form of humans, and there's an afterlife, in which everyone lives in happiness and abundance."

"Does that mean you *do* think it's possible that the dead speak to us in dreams?"

He laughed suddenly. "Well, you already know that I speak to a dead man at the Alamo."

"No, I hadn't known he was dead until you told me. He died at the Alamo?"

"Yes, but not the way you probably think. He'd been a courier — he was sent out by Travis during the siege. Travis kept sending out letters, because he was desperate for more men. Zachary Chase rode out on March 5, and Santa Anna's troops attacked in full strength before dawn the next morning. So Zachary survived the Alamo and went on to fight at San Jacinto — the battle that won independence for Texas. He survived it, too, but returned to live in San Antonio. He died near the bench where we were sitting, a heart attack most likely brought on by the wounds he'd received fighting."

"So, he's real. I mean, as real as a ghost can be. Maybe he can help us?"

"I doubt it."

"Why?"

"If he'd seen anything, he would have told me already."

"You speak to him often?" she asked. "Really speak to him?" She hesitated. "Like the girl on the gurney this morning. Tara Grissom."

"Often enough," he said. He winced a little. "Zachary loves to play games. He finds it hysterical to make me talk to him when there are people around. He loves it when they stare at me as if I'm insane. I keep trying to tell him it's not a good thing to make people think that a Ranger with a gun is a crazy man."

She smiled at that but quickly turned serious again. "If he didn't die there, why does he haunt the Alamo?" she asked.

"Guilt, I imagine," Logan replied. "He was chosen to ride out the day before. His friends and comrades all died, and he didn't."

"But he risked his own life, riding through enemy lines to get the message out," Kelsey said.

"I agree. And yet if we feel guilt, if we

believe it in our own minds, that's what's true to us," he said.

He heard his own words.

It was certainly true for him.

But I am guilty! he told himself. *I arrested Rory Norton. I brought him down, and I brought him in, and he sat on death row. And Alana died because of it.*

Rory Norton had viciously killed at least a dozen people. He'd shot anyone who had gone against him, and if he hadn't carried out the murder himself, he'd ordered it. He'd also been responsible for dozens of other deaths with the hardcore drugs he'd supplied.

If Logan hadn't been so determined to bring him down, if he'd let another Ranger or another law enforcement agent take him in . . .

"We can carry guilt all the way to the grave," Kelsey said. "That's so sad." She stood suddenly. "We have to go and speak with him."

Logan groaned. "In broad daylight — two of us talking to a ghost? Kelsey, there are going to be tourists all over right now!"

He realized he'd just called her by her given name for the first time. She hadn't even noticed.

"Yes, but we need to find out what your

friend knows."

"He's not actually what you'd call a friend," Logan said.

"Why not?"

"He's a ghost."

"But he *was* living, and he must like you — I think he was trying to talk to you yesterday when you were so rude!"

"I wasn't rude. He wanted to make me look foolish in front of you, and I didn't appreciate it."

"Logan, he was trying to speak to you," she insisted.

"He would've told me if he'd known anything," Logan said again.

"*You* didn't learn about this last disappearance until yesterday."

"That's true, but if Zachary had seen a woman in distress, he would have mentioned it."

"Maybe he didn't realize a woman was in distress."

Logan thought about the morgue, and how the corpse had opened its eyes. "Tara said she was attacked in the darkness," he murmured. "She didn't say she was at the Alamo."

"I've been in the plaza at night, and even with the lights that focus on the chapel, it can be very dark. And the areas surrounding it are dark, too. But we do know that Chelsea's last conversation with her friend took place at the Alamo. The conversation that was interrupted by what she called 'a man in costume' — and by that voice we heard on the tape. Logan! What's the matter with you? We actually have someone who could steer us in the right direction, and you're hesitating."

He stood. "Fine. Let's go to the Alamo."

They sat on the same bench and watched as tourists came and went. It wasn't hot; the sun was bright and the day was beautiful. But Logan was anxious, worrying about the dozen tangible things they could be doing instead.

Mothers pushed infants in strollers, dads walked by holding the hands of toddlers. The citizens of San Antonio, along with the many tourists visiting the Alamo, passed by.

They waited an hour, and there was no sign of Zachary Chase.

"I don't understand. Why doesn't he come?" Kelsey asked.

"He's a ghost. He appears when he chooses to," Logan said. He hid a smile, looking at her. She was wearing a business suit again, this one a navy pinstripe with an attractive flare to the jacket and a tailored pale blue blouse beneath it. She wore little heels, maybe an inch high. They must look like an odd couple, with her so formally, even severely, dressed and him in jeans and a buckskin jacket. He was never without his service weapon, though. It was hidden by his jacket.

"Isn't there a way for you to contact him?" she asked, her eyes brilliant as she turned to him.

"What? Call him on his cell phone?"

She grimaced and wagged a finger at him. "We might've lost a valuable opportunity yesterday. You have to learn not to be so hostile."

"I'm not hostile."

"You just said that with tremendous hostility," she said.

He started to laugh; despite their circumstances, she could somehow make him feel lighter.

But then his laughter faded.

A black bird suddenly landed in front of his feet. It looked at him, tilting its head.

He thought he heard a flutter of wings, and turned to see that birds had begun to light down around them. He wondered if he was wearing aftershave with bird pheromones and felt an odd sensation of dread.

"The birds again," Kelsey said in a low voice.

Startled, he looked at her.

"There was a crow at the kitchen window yesterday morning," she told him. "And then here and, after that, in my dream."

"The Comanche believe differently from the Apache," he explained. "They believe all creatures bring power, and we can look to them for the particular energy and power they provide."

"I have to admit, I feel as though I'm in an Alfred Hitchcock movie," she said, frowning.

"I thought that, too. At first. Half these guys are crows. Like Jackson Crow," he muttered.

"You think Jackson Crow is controlling the birds?" she asked skeptically.

"No. I'm thinking along the Comanche line," he told her. "They're here for a reason. They're here to give us power."

The birds settled around them, but did nothing that was in any way frightening. He remembered the hawk that had taken down its prey in front of him. That had been just yesterday morning. The hawk had almost dared him to try to take its kill.

He hadn't done so, but he'd held his ground. Which was when he'd seen the mass of crows and myriad other birds.

"We can walk around the Alamo," he suggested to Kelsey.

She nodded. "All right. Since Zachary doesn't carry a cell phone."

She stood and he joined her. He took a step forward, then paused. One of the birds was swooping toward them. Instinctively, he reached out to draw Kelsey against his chest. He thought the bird might be attacking.

But it dropped something at their feet and flew on.

Kelsey straightened, pulling down her jacket and brushing back her hair.

"The little bastard was dive-bombing us!" she said.

"No . . . no, it wasn't."

Logan bent down to see what the bird had dropped. It looked like a small twig, tipped in red paint.

Kelsey gasped as his hand closed around it, and he realized what he was seeing wasn't paint.

It was nail polish. On the well-manicured nail of a finger.

A human finger.

CHAPTER 5

"This is what I think it is, isn't it?" Kelsey asked.

Logan nodded. Kelsey was prepared; she reached into her purse and produced an evidence bag. "We have to bring it right in," she said.

"I'm going to call Crow."

"But shouldn't we —"

"No, I'd rather we took it to someone else I know. Someone not associated with this case."

"But . . . Gaylord has to be competent. Otherwise, I'm sure Jackson Crow would've brought in a different medical examiner," Kelsey said. But that didn't seem to sway his opinion.

"Fine. Your call," she said, shrugging. He got through to Crow, and when he'd finished, he told her, "We're going into the office. Crow's calling someone. Someone I like better than Gaylord."

As she walked briskly toward his car — his strides were long when he was in a hurry — Kelsey asked him, "Who?"

He glanced her way. "There's a new, younger woman at the M.E.'s office. I've worked with her on a few cases. She's not as matter-of-fact as Gaylord. Don't get me wrong, Gaylord is competent, he's just been at it too long. To him, a body is a body. Kat Sokolov has a greater . . . I don't know, *investment* in her cases."

Kelsey grinned.

"What?" he asked.

"Strange. When I first met you, I took *you* for matter-of-fact."

He smiled slightly, and Kelsey realized she was pleased when she made him smile. And even though she prided herself on her abilities, she'd liked it when he'd protected her from the bird.

Stop thinking that way! she warned herself.

When they returned to the station, Jackson Crow was there with Jake Mallory and a pretty, petite blond woman with large blue eyes. She hugged Logan, then turned to Kelsey with an open smile.

"Logan already knows Katya, Kelsey, so I'll introduce you two," Jackson said. "Katya, Marshal Kelsey O'Brien. Kelsey, Dr. Katya Sokolov."

124

"Doctor, it's a pleasure," Kelsey said. "I —"

"It's Kat, please!" the other woman interrupted. "I'm not formal with my clients."

"And I'm just Kelsey."

"Here it is." Logan produced the finger in the evidence bag.

Kat lifted the bag first and studied the finger through the plastic. "Some decomp, but not too bad — not like the others," she said. "The finger wasn't severed. It was ripped off."

"Could the birds have done this?" Logan asked. "A crow dropped it in front of me."

"Sure. Birds have very powerful beaks. That probably means the body's nearby, which should make it easier to find the rest of her," Kat said. She brought the finger to the small lab area of their assigned space. "I'll have to send off samples, you know," she said, turning to Jackson.

He nodded.

Kat placed the finger under the microscope; when Jake hit some buttons on the computer, it appeared before them, larger than life on the screen. "Forefinger," Kat said. "And it belonged to a young woman. White, I'd say. The polish is a gel — the kind that stays on for two to three weeks." She looked around, and Kelsey wasn't sure if she was seeking Jackson's approval or Logan's. "We'll be able to get a good DNA comparison, and that'll tell you if this belongs to your missing girl. I'll send out samples today."

"There's a chance that . . . that there is no body, right?" Kelsey asked. "The finger might have been severed before death?"

Kat shook her head. "The way it's been dislodged, with no blood coagulation, makes me suspect it came from someone who no longer had a beating heart. But, to be fair, I can't be a hundred percent certain."

Logan took Kelsey's arm. "Let's go," he said.

"Where are we going now?" she asked.

"To look for crows."

They drove for what felt like hours, in every direction around the Alamo. But although they stopped more than a dozen times, digging through garbage pits, trash piles and any other place a body could conceivably be hidden, they found nothing.

Logan was frustrated. "We have to find Vanessa Johnston quickly," he said.

She laid a hand on his arm. "We will find her, but even if there's a flock of birds up there the size of a 747, I doubt we'd see them anymore. It's too dark. Time to quit for the night. Besides, we can't continue the search if we don't get some rest."

He sighed. "All right. Where's your car?"

"At the Longhorn. Or rather, the parking garage across the street. Jackson picked me up this morning."

"Then I'll take you back."

When they reached the inn, Kelsey said, "Why don't you come in with me? You're curious about the saloon. You can talk to Sandy, and she can tell you more about what was going on with Sierra Monte and the bloody disappearance in Room 207 a year ago. It's highly possible that Sierra died by the same hand that's killed these other girls."

He looked at her, shaking his head. "The Sierra Monte case is still open. It did occur to me, of course, except that none of the remains match her DNA. Honestly, we're not inept in Texas."

"I didn't mean to imply that."

"Bodies with no names. And now a name with no body," he murmured.

"Please, just park. Come in. The food here is good," Kelsey encouraged him.

He found parking, and they walked into the Longhorn together.

Inside, the saloon was lively. That night, Sandy had a trio — piano player, fiddler and guitarist — playing on stage, and the music was at a pleasant level. Poker games that involved peanuts were going on at a few of the tables, and people seemed to be enjoying themselves.

"Rodeo in town," Logan said. He set a hand on Kelsey's shoulder and whispered, "Over there, at three o'clock. The real deal. See how his jeans are worn and his hat's been folded a million times? And his boots are scuffed to pieces. There . . ." He turned her slightly. "Ten o'clock. A city slicker down to play cowboy. Shiny new boots. Designer cowboy shirt. Face clean and pure as a newborn babe's — no nicks, scrapes or scars from a tumble or an argument with a bull or a bronco. Or even a calf."

"Ouch," Kelsey said. "Judgmental, aren't we?"

"Nope. I hope they all come to San Antonio and have a good time — and keep the city prospering."

"Hey!" Sandy said happily, swinging past them, her fingers twined around a half-dozen beer steins. "Welcome, sit, I'll be right with you!"

"I can help," Kelsey called after her.

"Don't be silly! You'd be like a bull in a china shop. We've got it covered," Sandy called back.

Kelsey gave an offhand shrug as they went to scrub their hands. "She's remembering the time at camp when I spilled a whole tray of juice glasses — which happened to be full," she told Logan.

On their way back from the restroom, she noticed that Ricky, one of the bartenders, had come from behind the long saloon bar and was waving to her, gesturing to a small table near the stage. "C'mon," Kelsey said, and Logan followed her.

They sat, with Ricky promising he'd bring them a couple of beers. Logan looked around, studying all the renovations. "You're right. Your friend has done a great job. It's as if you stepped back into the nineteenth century. Very different from when I was last here, which has to be more than three years ago."

"The rooms are beautiful, too," Kelsey assured him.

Ricky brought their beers. He was twenty-four, eternally cheerful and he loved working in the saloon. "The special is barbecue beef. And it really *is* special."

"Barbecue beef for me," Kelsey said. "Would you like a menu?" she asked Logan.

"Refuse a special that's *special?*" he asked. "Make it two, please, Ricky."

He'd caught Ricky's name, although she'd

said it only once when he delivered the beers. Kelsey liked that he was cordial to those who waited on him. She glanced away, wondering again what was the matter with her. She was listing his good points as if she was planning to bring him home to her mom, and she had to remind herself that their relationship was professional — they were *working* together — and that he could be a real hard-ass.

She was startled when someone suddenly swooped down on her, giving her a mammoth hug, then stepping back quickly in acknowledgment of Logan. "Sorry, sir! But this young lady is my heroine. Forgive me if I got too friendly."

Kelsey turned to Logan, "This is Mr. Corey Simmons, Logan. Corey, Ranger Logan Raintree. Corey is here for the rodeo."

"Nice to meet you," Logan said, rising to accept Corey's outstretched hand.

"Pleasure is mine. Hey, now, we're not in any trouble for rabble-rousing, are we, Ranger?" Corey asked, his grin wide.

"I'm just here for the barbecue," Logan told him, taking his seat again.

Corey dragged over an unused chair, and set it, facing backward, in front of the table. He straddled it, resting his elbows on the chair back.

"Guess I'm being a little nosy, but I happen to know that the lady is a U.S. Marshal," Corey said. "And glad of it, I am. She's a brave soul, and I had to beg her not to let the world know that I'm willing to ride any bull — but afraid of my own shadow."

She'd wondered if Logan was going to be irritated by the cowboy joining them; he wasn't. He gave Corey a broad smile. "Any one of us can be spooked, Simmons," Logan said. "So, you're taking part in next week's rodeo?"

Corey nodded. "I'm going to stay on the bull longest, I swear it! And I ride a fine barrel race, too."

"Good luck to you," Logan said. "Tell me about your experience in Room 207."

Corey Simmons had the grace to blush. "Well, of course, now I'm thinking I let my imagination run away with me, you know? What with that awful story about the room. . . . Well, there's the older story, too, but it's the new one that scares the bejesus outta me!"

"But you didn't really *see* anything?" Logan asked him.

"It was like I opened my eyes and saw a sea of blood everywhere! Dripping down the walls, on the floor . . . well, I'm just glad to be outta there. I would've left the inn if it wasn't for the Marshal here!"

Logan looked at her with some amusement. Kelsey shrugged.

"We all get carried away now and then," she murmured.

They were close to the bar. As she spoke, she saw that a man sitting on one of the wooden stools at the end had turned toward them. He didn't look like a cowboy. He was tall and thin and wearing jeans, but with a tailored shirt and loafers. His hair was cut stylishly short, and there was nothing weathered about him. He saw her looking at him, and slid off his bar stool, coming toward them.

"Oh, Lord help us," Logan groaned.

"Who is it?" she whispered.

She didn't have to wait to find out. Corey grinned broadly. "It's the newspaper man!" he said, apparently pleased that they'd drawn his attention.

But when the man approached and said, "Why, Mr. Simmons, did I hear that correctly? You were scared out of your room by a vision of *blood* on the walls?" Corey wasn't so pleased anymore.

"No, you didn't hear anything correctly, Murphy," he said. "Listening in on other people's conversations is rude, and if you write about a conversation you *think* you heard, I'll denounce you as a liar!"

Kelsey noticed that Logan didn't stand. "You're interrupting a private conversation, Ted," he told the man. "You're not welcome here," he added.

No one seemed to want the man around. It didn't stop him.

"So, word is out that you spent the day at the morgue, Ranger Raintree. What's going on? Is there a serial killer loose in the city, and you're not alerting the public?"

Kelsey watched Logan's fingers clench his beer stein. It was made of heavy glass, but she was afraid it would shatter. He managed to look up at the man. "Actually, I'm not with the Rangers right now, Murphy, and if there's something to be said, you'll hear it from a law enforcement spokesperson. I'm here for dinner with a friend, and I'd appreciate it if you let us enjoy that dinner in peace."

Murphy was persistent. "Friend?" Murphy's eyes snapped to Kelsey. "What kind of slacker do you think I am, Raintree? *Friend?* This is Marshal Kelsey O'Brien, in from Florida. So, what is it? Drug running? Murder? Or *murders,* plural?"

Logan stood at last, towering over Murphy. "If you don't leave, we will. Kelsey, I'm sorry, but . . ."

She stood, too.

"I'll take care of this creep, if you want," Corey Simmons said, grinning. "You can't touch him. That would be Ranger or Marshal brutality. But I'm just an old cowboy, and I can take him out. It'd be worth the night in jail."

By then, patrons near them had heard the confrontation, and with Logan and Corey Simmons both looming over Murphy, the tension and testosterone seemed to be rippling through the bar.

Sandy came rushing over. "Ted Murphy! What are you doing? Get out! See that sign over the bar? It says the owner has discretion over who should and shouldn't be served. You're creating a public disturbance, and you're going to ruin my business, and if you do, I promise I'll sue you — and your paper — up the wazoo. Do you understand me?"

Ted Murphy had already taken a few steps back. No doubt he'd known he wasn't going to taunt Logan Raintree into pounding him and creating negative press for the Texas Rangers. Corey Simmons didn't seem to care about the consequences.

"I think I've gotten what I came for,"

Murphy said. "Good evening, ladies and gentlemen." He turned away, took the time to drop cash on the bar and walked out.

"That sniveling little bastard!" Logan said.

"He's gone now. Please, sit, enjoy the saloon," Sandy pleaded, glancing from him to Kelsey.

Kelsey nodded and glanced at Logan.

"Sure. I'm looking forward to a *special* special barbecue," he said with a smile. Kelsey sat, he sat and so did Corey Simmons.

"Ease up," Kelsey warned Logan softly. "You're going to break that glass."

He stared at his hand, at his white knuckles against the bronze of his skin.

Then he grinned, but it was a deadly grin. "God knows what the man is going to plaster all over that damn tabloid."

"Then it's a rag. Who cares?" Kelsey asked.

"Well, it's a local paper, a daily, but it sure ain't a very respectable one."

"My point exactly," Kelsey said.

"Hey, it's me he's going to skewer," Corey said. "Big 'fraidy-cat tough-boy cowboy. But you know what? He'll get his. I promise you," Corey said. "Drink up, friends, drink up!" He lifted his stein. Kelsey politely lifted hers in return. Obviously, Corey could see

135

that Logan's mood hadn't lightened. He stood, winking at Kelsey. "I'll just leave you two alone now. If you need me, you know where to find me!"

When he'd left, Logan looked at Kelsey. "Murphy truly is a rat," he told her. "He'll put all kinds of half-truths in the paper, and get the public going, screaming that the police and the Rangers are putting the city in danger."

"It may not be that bad," Kelsey said. She tried to smile. "Hey, I come from Key West. If news isn't bizarre, it's worthless."

He finally cracked a real smile. Then it faded. "Sorry. I don't loathe many people, but I loathe that man. When my wife . . ."

His voice trailed off. She was surprised to feel her heart sink.

He had a wife. Well, that wasn't a great surprise. The man was walking sexuality, rugged and masculine to a fault.

After a moment, he continued speaking. "When my wife was murdered, and I found her just minutes too late . . ."

He shook his head and then looked at her again. "It was one of those instances. The kind we've talked about. I found her because I heard her." He brought his fingers to his forehead. "In here," he said. "I heard her crying out, and then, after I found her, I re-

136

alized I'd heard her because she was dead. I'd put a killer on death row, and his brother wasn't happy. When the trial was over, he kidnapped my wife — and didn't give a damn if the world knew who'd done it. He said he'd heard I had 'Injun powers,' and that if I wanted her back, he'd give me clues, but I'd have to use those powers. I don't think he even meant to kill her — he buried her alive, but he didn't set up the oxygen supply right, and she suffocated. I got to her, but too late. We put her killer on death row, too, but . . ." He paused. "Reporters all over were writing about the case. I never said how I found her, never spoke to anyone about it. I was sent on leave. When Murphy got wind of what happened, he wrote an article about Indian dream states, one that actually suggested Texas Rangers with Native American blood used peyote, and that my, uh, supposed drug habit might have been the reason Alana was so easily taken. There was a protest, of course — the Department of Public Safety was going to sue. I didn't know about it, and I didn't give a damn about it at the time. But the article couched the insinuations so carefully that everything was merely a suggestion. An implication. And in the end there was no lawsuit. Murphy isn't stupid.

He's a vicious bastard, but he isn't stupid. If he puts anything out there now, it'll be filled with innuendo, but he'll manage to make us all look like bumbling idiots."

Kelsey wasn't sure what to say; she felt his pain and bitterness as if it were a tidal wave, washing across the table and sweeping her in. She wanted to touch him, tell him she was sorry, but he didn't seem the kind of man who wanted pity. Before she could decide what, if anything, to do, Ricky came bearing their dinner plates, oblivious to the recent conflict.

"Here we go, an extraspecial dinner special!" With a flourish he served them. "Right back with the barbecue sauces — hot, spicy and mild for the faint of heart."

Logan straightened, a forced smile coming to his lips, something of a mask slipping over his features, hiding his thoughts and emotions. "Thanks." He glanced at Kelsey. "Texas barbecue is famous, you know. And when it's special — well, there's nothing better."

She felt that Logan had long since learned to cope with both his fury and his agony, concealing them behind stoicism. She felt numb and awkward herself; she'd learned so much about investigating people, but it hadn't occurred to her to find out more about Logan Raintree. Then again, they were on the same side. But she didn't know how to react. She couldn't move so quickly from an agitated state to a relaxed one, and she must have stared at him, stricken, when she should have been doing or saying something — anything — else.

"God, I am so, so sorry. I didn't know," she said at last, her voice shaking.

"And you shouldn't have known. We can't work together with you tiptoeing around my feelings. I'm sorry — it's just that Murphy is the one person who can hit exactly the right buttons to send my temper over the edge."

She grinned. "But you didn't belt him one."

"Don't go applauding me on that. I'm afraid that if I ever touched him, I wouldn't be able to stop. I'd kill him."

She could tell he wanted to change the subject. But she couldn't help herself. "How long ago did this happen?" she asked him.

His jaw tensed for a moment. "Don't worry — I'm not going over the edge now. Alana died three years ago. I took my time dealing with it. I'm doing okay."

"I wasn't worried," she said honestly.

He studied her again and seemed to believe her. "Good," he said. "I don't think the food can be all that special if you don't eat it."

"I'm eating, I'm eating."

"The barbecue is excellent," he told her. "And messy." He grimaced and licked barbecue sauce from his fingers.

The food *was* delicious; Logan could handle the fiery hot sauce, while she had to opt for mild. They both concentrated on eating during the next few minutes, and only a few pleasantries and requests were exchanged — Logan's, "Pass the salt, please," and Kelsey's "Another beer?"

"Sounds fine," Logan agreed. Ricky brought them a second round. By the time they'd finished the food and lingered over their beers, Logan seemed to have his anger under control.

"Why did your friend Sandy buy this place?" he asked.

"She's coveted the Longhorn for years," Kelsey said. "She loves Texas history and grew up here, listening to stories about the Alamo and the Longhorn. She took business and hospitality courses, and managed to pull together the financing when the previous owner was ready to sell it and retire. Sandy worked really hard to get this place. Her folks died close together when we were about nineteen. She got her education, plus money for the down payment, from what they left her." Kelsey sighed. "She was devastated when Sierra Monte was killed while she was in the middle of purchasing it. Or, I suppose I should say, *disappeared,* leaving behind so much blood that she couldn't possibly have survived. They had to bring in a biohazard cleanup crew, and there were a number of police and legal situations she had to deal with — in the midst of such tragic circumstances. So, with all of that going on, the saloon has really been a labor of love for her."

He nodded. "Did Sandy know Sierra Monte?"

"No, not really. She was in and out of here at the time, and they might have passed each other and exchanged a few words, but they weren't friends or even acquaintances." She hesitated a minute. "Do you want to see Room 207?"

"Yes, I'd like to see it very much," he said.

They both rose. Logan started toward the bar to pay their bill, but Kelsey flagged Ricky down. "Don't worry about it. I have a house account," she told him with a grin. He stiffened slightly.

"I pay my way," he insisted.

"So do I," she said promptly. "You're up next time." They were going to be partners.

Paying their own way didn't mean they couldn't take turns — not that she'd ever been one to worry about that kind of accounting. She was happy to treat.

She hurried up the stairs, aware of being watched. When the saloon was in full swing, those not staying at the inn often watched guests mounting the stairs with envy.

Logan was right behind her.

As she reached the balcony, she paused.

She was used to being observed, casually or sometimes, with male appreciation. Actually, the drunker the clientele, the more appreciation she received.

But tonight, she felt someone watching her *intently.* She walked to the carved white wood rail that overlooked the saloon. Some people were eating, and some were still playing poker with their peanut shells. Quite a few were entranced by the music, while others were just interested in their drinks and the conversations they were enjoying at the long bar.

She surveyed the room below.

Ricky was out on the floor. He set down a beer, looked up at her, grinned and waved. She realized he'd seen Logan, as well; maybe he assumed they were both getting lucky.

She flushed and waved back.

Sandy was on the floor, too, and she waved. So did the cowboy, Corey Simmons.

She glanced at the slatted, swinging doors to the sidewalk. They were fitted into glass now, to protect the flow of air-conditioning demanded by modern patrons. And, in the glass, she could see a face. The eyes in that face, she knew, were directed at her.

The face belonged to the reporter. Ted Murphy.

Let him watch, she thought.

She decided not to say anything to Logan. The man was standing outside the saloon, doing nothing illegal. Better not to risk another confrontation. Or another reminder of the past.

"What is it?" Logan asked.

"Nothing," she said. "I was just thinking that the saloon probably looks just like it did a hundred-and-fifty-plus years ago. Sandy studied old drawings and photographs to get it right, and she had the furniture repaired or replaced with similar period pieces." Conscious that she was babbling, she dug in her bag for her room key.

"The historic societies in this area owe Sandy a big thank-you," Logan said, pushing open the door after she'd unlocked it.

Entering the room, he stood still for a moment and slowly looked around. "I wasn't here at the time the murder — or bloodletting — of Sierra Monte occurred," he said. "And homicide detectives from the police department handled the investigation. None of the bodies that were found are Sierra Monte — we know that from the DNA testing — but it seems more and more likely that she was a victim of the same killer."

Kelsey nodded thoughtfully. "Yes, she was obviously a stabbing victim like some of the others — like Jenny Doe and Josie Doe. They have that in common. But Jenny and Josie . . . where were they killed?"

He angled his head. "Every murder has to have a crime scene. We simply haven't found them yet. And there's another question. Was Sierra Monte killed in this room by sheer coincidence, or is there a reason that two different women living in different centuries were killed here?"

"What could the past have to do with Sierra Monte's death?" she asked. "The first murder was really sad — well, all murder is. But the whole *story* is sad. From the bits of legend I've picked up, Rose Langley started life as a sheltered plantation girl. She fell in love with a drifter, who pimped her out as they made their way across the states. And then she was kidnapped by another guy, who eventually murdered her." She broke off, frowning. "He wanted something from her," she told him.

"He?"

"Her killer."

"What?"

"I don't know. I can't tell from what I've . . . seen," Kelsey said.

"Can you describe what you saw? Where they were? What was happening?"

Kelsey tried to recall both the waking vision and her dream. The details hadn't altered from one to the other.

"When the vision starts, they're both in the room — Rose Langley and Matt Meyer. Rose was really stunning, even after all she'd been through. Slim and shapely, with a pile of dark curls that she'd pinned up, but they came loose and tumbled around her face. She and Matt must have been in the room for a while, fighting. Her dress lay on the floor — over there — and the bed was by the window that looks out onto the street. Rose was still wearing her corset and garters, her stockings . . . and Matt Meyer was dressed more like a businessman than a Davy Crockett or Daniel Boone type. He must have been considered tall for his day. He was at least your height, but heavier set. Maybe his drinking habit was taking its toll."

She flushed, a little embarrassed that she

was giving him her opinion when he'd just asked her to describe what she'd seen. But he was listening.

"Then Matt walks across the room to Rose. She's standing here," Kelsey said, striding to the center of the room near him. "He grabs her by the shoulders. And yells at her. 'You won't hold out on me! I want it, and I want it now.' That's what he says to her."

"And then?"

"Rose says, 'I don't have it.' The man's grip on her tightens and his face twists into a really cruel expression, and he tells her, 'You're a liar! I know what happened in Galveston that night, and I know your pretty-boy lover won it. I want it!' "

Kelsey swallowed. She'd watched it all before, but she hadn't stood where Rose Langley had. She felt such sorrow for the woman.

She turned away from Logan. "I'm trying to remember exactly what they said. And never once did either of them mention what 'it' was." She thought back and said, "Rose told him 'No! It's mine!' "

"Then he killed her?" Logan asked.

"Within the next minute or so. He taunted her first. He said, 'You think you'll get back to that no-good weakling? Well, give up that dream. He moved on the moment you were gone.' "

"And then . . ."

Kelsey closed her eyes, trying to recall what they'd said. She was surprised that the words came so easily to her lips, almost as if she were an actress, playing the part of Rose Langley.

" 'I hate you,' " Rose said. " 'I hate you, Matt. I *loathe* you. You forced me here, and you've used me enough. Even if I had it, I'd never let you have it!' "

She opened her eyes and looked at Logan.

"Matt Meyer responded with, 'You're an old whore, Rose. I want it, and I'll get it.' " Kelsey shuddered. "Then Rose said, 'I will *never* give it to you.' "

She wrapped her arms around herself, imagining the feel of the man's hands around her neck. Rose had clutched his arms, trying to break his hold. She'd tried to scratch and claw him, but she hadn't been strong enough.

He'd wrenched the woman to him, his fingers curled around her neck. He'd squeezed his hands tightly together; he shook her hard. She grabbed desperately at his arms, trying to free herself.

"She begged him then. 'Please, Matt?' " Kelsey said. "But his fingers were around

147

her throat, and he told her, 'I'll kill you, and I'll rip this place to shreds — and find it.' She was able to whisper 'please' one more time. And then she was dead," Kelsey finished. "He picked her up and threw her on the bed as if she meant nothing to him. I hope he never found *it*."

Logan shook his head. "He never did."

"How do you know?"

"Well, Marshal O'Brien, it's obvious you're not a Texan, and not from San Antonio. After hearing your description of the murder, I'm positive that *it* can only be one thing. And I'm sure a lot of people might have felt it was worth fighting for, killing for — dying for."

"Well, what was *it?*" she demanded.

"The Galveston diamond."

CHAPTER 6

Logan lay in his room, staring at the ceiling fan as it whirred. He'd spent all his time since he'd returned home going through the various files on the victims. The stories he'd heard about the Galveston diamond kept playing through his mind, but so far, all he had was the fact that if Kelsey's vision was true, Rose Langley had left Galveston with the diamond, and she might have died trying to keep it. Once the ring had disappeared after a poker game in Galveston, it had never been seen again.

Chelsea Martin had been a part-time gemologist. But he couldn't find anything relating to gems or gemology regarding Tara Grissom, and, of course, the as-yet-unidentified corpses had given them nothing about their past likes, loves or hobbies.

He started trying to find everything he could on Sierra Monte. There were plenty of newspaper articles, but he wasn't looking for background on the investigation. He wanted to know more about the woman herself. He was glad to discover that he could trace the articles and police interviews to some of her friends and find old references on their social networking pages. She'd written one friend about an "amazing" citrine she'd found on eBay, and another page had an old reference to a ring she'd bought in New York's diamond district. "A blue diamond! It's magnificent — and I could afford it!" Sierra had written.

Clearly, she'd had an interest in gems and jewelry. Just like Chelsea.

He tried all the social connections he thought the young women had most likely used. He turned his attention back to Chelsea and Tara and looked through the links, and discovered that both women had — like a high percentage of the country — kept up Facebook pages. The pictures of their past lives made him sad, and the many messages of condolence, addressed to their families and friends, were heartbreaking. He wasn't sure what he'd discovered; he hoped something would click in his mind at some point.

Finally, he'd tried to sleep.

And, of course, what he'd learned about the young women continued to dance through his head, but then he found himself thinking of his own life and events gone by.

He thought dully of the time it had taken him to get past the agony of losing Alana. He'd often wondered if it would have hurt any less if she'd died of natural causes. But ultimately, there was no way out of being human. He had met Alana soon after he'd become a Ranger, and she had loved his work and the history of the Rangers — that of the stoic, heroic frontier protectors, *and* that of the men who'd pictured themselves above the law. Her own father had passed away, but he'd also been a Ranger. The idea of Logan's changing his line of work to something safer had never come up.

But then, neither had suspected that *she* might become a victim of violence.

Alana had known he loved her. She'd known that he would have given his life in exchange for hers, without question. She had loved him in return. If they'd ever been able to discuss the situation, she would have smoothed back his hair and said, "Hey, Ranger. That's the way the beans fell, and that's that."

Since he'd come back, almost a year ago now, he'd worked on the tangible cases. A bank robbery. A gang war — with homicides. There was one case in which a clever killer had murdered his friend with gloves on, using the friend's own gun — but he'd forgotten about the way circumstantial evidence could pile up, and he'd wound up confessing, afraid of the death sentence, carried out with frequency in the state of Texas.

And then Logan had been told to meet with Jackson Crow.

Whir, whir, whir, the ceiling fan went.

Hearing Alana call to him when she was already dead hadn't been his first experience with the unacknowledged senses. He'd had opportunities as a child to embrace both Apache and Comanche ways — entirely different from each other. To the Comanche, it was natural to see signs and learn lessons from the creatures around them. They weren't gods; they were energy and strength and power. The Apache saw a different world, in which there'd be an afterlife, and you might meet an enemy there, just as you could on earth. There were ghost riders, because there was a soul, and the soul lived on. Dreams were seen as omens, or as visions that might help a warrior make a decision. The unusual was far more accepted among most Indian nations. Not to mention the fact that the American west offered certain natural flora that occasionally enhanced a dream-walker's quest.

"All natural," an Apache friend had told him once. "So is hemlock," Logan had said. Yes, the world was filled with the natural — and what some saw as the supernatural. Like all things, there was both good and bad in what was natural — and supernatural.

Logan's first supernatural occurrence had fallen on the beneficial side. A young Apache girl had been kidnapped, and it was suspected that her own father had done it. He was known as a cantankerous alcoholic, who'd taken a strap against his sons often enough. There was little love for the man among his people, and it was easy to point the finger in his direction. But while sitting with his grandfather, watching the smoke of a fire, Logan believed he'd *seen* the girl. She was crying and afraid, and he thought he saw her at an abandoned emu farm outside the Apache reservation. Although he'd been seventeen at the time, and a "tinted white boy," as some of his relatives called him, he'd been able to convince his father — who had brought in the Texas Rangers. The man who still owned the land had allowed them to investigate. They'd found the girl — with the corpse of another. They caught the pedophile who'd kidnapped the girls and assaulted them and accidentally killed the first.

Logan had lied, of course. He'd said he'd heard the information about the girl and, riding with his cousins across family land on the outskirts of the city, he'd noticed the buildings on the abandoned farm and put two and two together. That was the day he'd known he was going to be a Texas Ranger.

He'd learned to focus and had honed his abilities. At times, he'd spoken to his grandfather in the years since he'd died, and to other "souls," those he'd known and those he hadn't. He did understand one thing: If a soul had moved on, he would not be able to speak with that person again. He had heard Alana when she'd called out to him, because she hadn't intended to let her killer get away with her murder. But she was gone now. He'd sat at her grave site often and long; he'd wandered the house with the little picket fence that they'd owned together — now sold — calling out her name. He'd gone to the restaurants they'd frequented, spent hours in the park where he'd proposed, ridden the Texas plains where they'd often taken his cousin's horses, and no matter how hard he tried, how hard he focused, he couldn't find her. Not even in his dreams. But when they'd recovered her body, buried in the coffin, the oxygen supply not properly set, he thought he saw her eyes open. He thought she touched his cheek. He had heard her whisper, "Goodbye, my love. Do good."

They were the words she'd often said to him when he went off to work.

He had been convinced she was alive. He'd tried to drag her out of the coffin and into his arms. Insanity had struck him, and he'd beaten back his friends, heedless of injury to them. All he'd seen was that Alana needed help. It had been Tyler Montague, another Ranger, who'd finally taken him by the shoulders and wrestled him down, and it had been the tears in Tyler's eyes that made him see the truth. Alana was dead, and he was destroying the evidence they would need to see her killer convicted.

He'd taken a two-year leave. When he'd come back, he'd refused to deal with anything that smacked of the supernatural.

And yet here he was. Like it or not, he was sucked in. Last night had been the clincher. He wasn't sure why. But Kelsey O'Brien's vision in Room 207 had started the process, and he believed that the murder of Rose Langley had something to do with what was going on now.

The Galveston diamond. It had never been found. He wondered what it was worth in today's market. Millions.

But . . . what could the deaths of so many women have to do with a diamond that had disappeared more than a hundred and fifty years ago? Especially when they suspected that most of them had been living on the fringes of society, surviving as prostitutes or by doing whatever odd jobs they could get. People who were on their own, who hadn't even been reported as missing.

Or so he assumed. They knew about Tara Grissom and Chelsea Martin. And maybe they could uncover something about the others.

He thought back to the files with the bios and information they had thus far. Chelsea had been a teacher. And *part-time gemologist.*

After an unsatisfactory night's sleep, Logan rose, showered and dressed, then headed out, anxious to get to Jackson Crow's temporary headquarters.

He paused as he stepped out his door.

The birds were back. There were sitting on the eaves of his house; they were arrayed around him on poles and wires, and some even sat on his car.

They watched him, and he watched them in return.

They seemed to be exuding no ill will.

"Ah, my friends, are you offering energy and strength? Or are you warning me that what lies ahead should be avoided?"

The birds did not reply.

He opened the door to his car, revved the engine and the birds took flight.

Kelsey had brooded through the night. No other dreams or visions had come to her, but she'd spent hours thinking about Logan Raintree. She realized that what she'd learned disturbed her, and she woke feeling out of sorts.

Arriving in the kitchen early, she hoped for a little time alone, but that was unlikely. The inn was now full, and Sandy had hired help to prepare breakfast. Kelsey was glad to see that coffee had been brewed, but disappointed that there was nowhere she could be alone to enjoy it. She stood in a corner of the kitchen, trying to keep out of the way.

"Everything all right?" Sandy asked.

"Great," Kelsey assured her.

"You look upset," Sandy said. Then she grinned. "I wouldn't be. I love your Texas Ranger."

"He's not *my* Texas Ranger," Kelsey muttered. "We're just working together."

"Okay. Well, then, I wouldn't mind working with your Texas Ranger."

"Sandy, have you ever met Logan before? Was there information about him in the paper when his wife died?"

Sandy frowned, and her eyes widened. "Oh! Oh, he's *that* Texas Ranger! I didn't make the connection. . . . I definitely remember the case!" She shivered. "Oh, it was horrible. The poor woman died. The killer was playing a time game. Except that he had some kind of oxygen system supposedly rigged up when he buried her alive, but he didn't do it right. The Ranger — her husband — found her, but she'd been dead for a while, according to the papers. Oh, that's so sad! But Logan Raintree seems so . . . well, *normal.* Considering what he's been through."

"He is normal," Kelsey told her.

As normal as I am, she thought.

But her distress about the tragedy in his life — and her anger that she hadn't been told — continued to bother her.

"I've got to get going." Kelsey drained her coffee cup and put it down.

"Okay," Sandy said. "Oh, and, by the way, thank you again."

"For?"

"Oh, for dealing with Corey Simmons. He's a happy camper now, and I was sure he'd leave the inn and tell terrible stories about it!"

"Not a problem."

"And you're still okay with the room?" Sandy asked anxiously.

"I'm absolutely fine."

"I just remember when we were growing up . . ."

"What?" Kelsey arched a brow. She'd never shared any of her *impressions* or *visions* with Sandy, even though they were close friends. She'd learned early that it was too easy for people to misunderstand — or to make fun of her.

"When we were kids, at camp, you'd tell great stories about history. And those ghost stories you told by the campfire . . . You were so good, I always felt as if you knew something the rest of us didn't — almost as if you had imaginary friends whispering in your ear."

"I was an imaginative kid," Kelsey said. "Listen, I've got to get to work. See you this evening — and thank you. It's great to have a place to stay."

She didn't want to get involved in a discussion about the Longhorn. She wanted to accost Jackson Crow and find out why he hadn't told her anything about Logan Raintree.

Crow was alone when she walked into the dedicated room at the police station.

"You had no right to put me in the situation you did," she said angrily, marching toward him at his desk. "None."

"And what situation was that?" he asked her.

"Setting me up with a man — a potential team member — without any explanation about his past."

He leaned back casually, watching her.

"And why does his past matter right now? We're looking for a murderer, not planning a therapy session."

"Oh, I see. You're giving me a 'this is business' speech? Well, I'm sorry, that's not acceptable under the circumstances. You obviously want us using abilities we don't usually share. And just as obviously, that's going to bring us closer than most business associates, team members, whatever we're going to be!"

"Do you think Logan Raintree is emotionally crippled? Or that he's going to go off on some kind of rampage? Shoot up the streets?"

"No, of course not."

"Well, then?"

"I should have known. That's all."

"Logan's past is his concern. He chose to

160

tell you about it."

"Yes, but . . . what happened to him wasn't something like, oh, his house was robbed. His wife was *murdered.*"

"Yes."

"And you knew it."

"I make a point of knowing everything about anyone I'm asking to join this team," Jackson told her.

Frustrated, she scowled at him.

"It's important that you get to know each other on your own terms, not that I outline your lives."

"But —"

"A team only works when every member learns to trust every other member," Jackson said.

She would have spoken again, still irritated, but the door opened and Logan Raintree came into the room. He greeted them with a solemn, "Good morning."

They both responded. Kelsey felt guilty; she wondered if he could tell she'd been talking about him.

He probably could. But he didn't press it. "We need to get back on the streets. We have to find Vanessa Johnston. I read and reread the files last night. We can't compare lives and histories on all the victims, since we don't know who some of them are, but I

161

spent last night looking for a common thread between the two women we do have. So far, all we've got is that both were young, attractive, fascinated with the Alamo and headed there. But," he said, glancing from Jackson to Kelsey and offering them a crooked, almost sheepish smile, "I believe I've found a connection between one of them, Chelsea Martin, and Sierra Monte. And it's something that's been staring us in the face."

"The Galveston diamond?" Kelsey asked.

He nodded. "Sierra Monte was presumably killed at the Longhorn," he said. "The diamond was brought to Galveston by pirates. It was apparently stolen, then disappeared from history after it was won in a poker game in Galveston. Historians agree on that much. The legend that says Rose took it with her is based on conjecture but the diamond's never been found in Galveston. People with metal detectors have searched the beach for it often enough. I can imagine that someone might've thought Sierra Monte was looking for it at the inn, but Chelsea Martin never got there. She made it to the Alamo — her last known location. But in her spare time, she studied gems." Logan paused. "I went to her Facebook page," he said. "She truly loved stones and wanted to work with jewelry. But I'm willing to bet she knew about the Galveston diamond. Sierra Monte was a diamond girl, too."

"Did you find out anything similar about Tara Grissom?" Jackson asked him.

"Everything I read reinforced what we've already learned — she loved history, especially state history revolving around the Alamo, the massacre at Goliad and the road to independence for Texas. She must have been aware of Rose Langley and the Galveston diamond. Although a lot of it's legend, the story's been around in Texas as long as I can remember."

"But these other women . . . We're assuming they were runaways or prostitutes because we haven't been able to match them to any missing-persons cases," Kelsey said. "How could they be involved with the Galveston diamond? Do you really think it's possible that they all died because of a diamond that's been missing for a century and a half?"

"I think it's the only connection I've found between any of the victims," Logan said.

Kelsey sat on the edge of Jackson's desk and picked up one of the sheets he'd been studying, a synopsis of the medical examiner's reports.

"The Longhorn isn't far from the Alamo," she pointed out. "And if you've studied the Alamo, you probably know about the Longhorn. Most of us learned about Davy Crockett, Lieutenant Colonel Travis and Daniel Boone as school kids, no matter where we grew up, but the sad tale of Rose Langley isn't as well-known. All the local kids would've heard it, of course, and so would anyone with a fixation on the period. But the Longhorn's been torn apart over the decades. If there was anything hidden there, it would've been found by now. And where else would you look? But if the women never even made it to the Longhorn . . . Anyway, just because someone liked gems and knew Texas history, why would you murder her?"

"We need to know more," Logan said quietly. "More about all the women."

Jackson looked across the desk at Kelsey. "We're going to try to do that." Jackson was thoughtful. "And yes, we have to find Vanessa Johnston. Every officer in every agency in the city is searching for her. I'd like to take an hour and go back to the morgue."

"We're testing at the morgue — with Kat as the M.E.?" Logan asked. "We're bringing Kat in?"

"Yes, and I'm going to bring in our fourth and fifth team members, too. Jane Everett is meeting us at the morgue."

"She does facial reconstructions," Logan informed Kelsey. "And she's very good. She can work with all kinds of material, but she's worked with computer images, too."

"Jane's done assignments for several anthropological societies," Jackson added, "and also for the Rangers and the police."

"Why wasn't she brought in before?" Kelsey asked.

"Everything costs," Logan reminded her, looking at Jackson.

"We're also getting a computer whiz," Jackson said. "Film and sound effects, computers — every team needs someone who's good at those things."

"Do I know him or her?" Logan asked.

"You both do," Jackson said.

Kelsey was startled. "Oh?"

"Sean Cameron."

Kelsey almost fell off the desk. "Sean Cameron? My *cousin,* Sean Cameron?"

"Is there family rivalry, Marshal?"

"No, nothing of the kind. Sean . . . Sean is great. But he . . . works on movies. Documentaries — like the one he's doing now, about the Alamo."

"He's done computer work for us before,"

Logan said. "Crime-scene re-creations."

"But Sean isn't a cop." Kelsey frowned, looking at Jackson.

"No," Logan agreed. "Neither is Jane."

"Is it fair to bring them into . . . whatever this is?" Kelsey asked.

"It's up to them. If the team works out, they'll wind up with training, and you'll both have to take a few courses, too, for the proper certifications in weapons and such."

Kelsey wondered about the documentary. Would Sean still be working on it? He was no slouch. Besides being multitalented, he was what you'd consider a "man's man." Football, kickboxing and mixed martial arts were hobbies for him, and he'd turned down a chance to be college all-pro because he loved film and computers more.

"He's got what we need," Logan said, looking at her curiously.

"Does he know about this?" she murmured.

"We've communicated," Jackson told her.

"And he's a —" Logan began.

"Texan," Kelsey finished for him. Logan raised his eyebrows and smiled at her. He was smiling far more easily. She wished she wasn't so glad of that.

"When are they meeting us at the morgue?" he asked.

"In twenty minutes. At nine," Jackson said.

"What's the first order of business?"

"We'll start with Kat," Jackson said. "Most of the bodies are so decomposed that the best medical examiner in the world would have difficulty telling us much more than Gaylord did. But she has the ability to go a step further, especially now, as a member of this team."

Logan wasn't surprised by that, Kelsey realized. Of course, he knew Kat Sokolov because he'd worked with her before.

"She . . . speaks with corpses?" she ventured.

Logan turned to her. If he guessed she'd been talking about him earlier and felt angry about it, he didn't indicate that in any way. "I think Jackson means that she not only has a special ability, but she's got the money behind her now to do the kind of testing they wouldn't normally have done for unidentified corpses with apparent causes of death. Doing the appropriate tests, Kat can learn a great deal more. She'll be able to give us information that could lead us in the right direction."

Jackson spoke up. "Kat is excellent, and she'll be dedicated to this case."

He looked at them both. "We've already got our first report from her. We didn't need an exceptionally talented M.E. to find out about the DNA in that finger, but as we all suspected, it was Vanessa Johnston's."

"The killer seems to be speeding up," Logan said.

They were all quiet for a minute. Yes, they'd suspected that the finger had been the missing woman's. Now they knew it. Yes, any adept technician could have gotten them that information. But Kelsey had the feeling that things were just beginning, that Jackson Crow knew exactly what he was doing, and Kat Sokolov was going to be an important addition to their, as yet, uncertain unit. But although Kelsey hadn't made a formal decision, and neither had Logan, she *felt* as if they belonged. As if they were part of the Krewe of Hunters.

"We should've been able to help her," she murmured. Tears stung her eyes; she hadn't known Vanessa Johnston or the others, and she'd mastered some hard lessons in law enforcement, but the human element was always there. So was the hopeless, impotent feeling that came with learning another victim was past saving.

"We just figured this out," Jackson reminded her. "Now it's up to us."

"She's probably beyond help, but not beyond justice," Logan said. "Let's head out. The longer it takes us to discover the truth, the more opportunity there'll be for this killer to find his next victim."

Kat wore a white lab jacket and her hands were gloved as she worked over the body of Tara Grissom, taking blood and tissue samples.

Logan watched her, again studying what remained of Tara's face. He felt anger roiling inside him — a good anger, not a destructive one. It was the kind of anger that made him want to track down the killer. A completely controlled emotion. They needed to be methodical while they worked with all possible haste. He glanced over at Jackson Crow and thought about the power the man had and what they were being offered.

Certain tests were automatically done on corpses brought in for autopsy. In cases where cause of death seemed clear, some tests usually *wouldn't* be done. They were just too expensive, especially when X-rays or physical trauma pointed to the means of death — such as broken hyoid bones or the evidence of stab wounds.

However, in this case, they desperately needed more clues. That meant more time and money.

Jackson had the federal funds necessary to pitch in when the local budget was used up. And, Logan knew, if he joined Crow's unit, he'd have that same backing.

He saw that Jackson was staring at him, and he wondered if the other man suspected what was going on in his mind.

"I doubt I'll be able to find needle marks if the women were injected with any substance," Kat said apologetically. "In some of these instances we're down to almost no soft tissue. We could find metal poisoning in the hair or bones, but . . . we do have a few victims who may be able to tell us something."

"GC-MS?" Logan asked.

She nodded, looking at Jackson. "Yes."

To detect many of the possible substances that might've been used to subdue the women before they disappeared, GC-MS, or gas chromatography-mass spectroscopy, would be needed. The state of decay meant that no other approach was likely to yield results.

It seemed logical that the women had been influenced in some way to leave the Alamo — or wherever their location — without putting up any kind of fight or making a scene. They might've been persuaded to come and see something or invited to do something. What that *something* was Logan and the others had no clue — except for the phone call recorded between Chelsea Martin and her friend Nancy. The call was abruptly cut off. Someone had interrupted Chelsea, and she hadn't been seen or heard from again . . . until her corpse was discovered. Another possibility, as Kat had mentioned, was some form of sedative.

"I'm going to do more testing, a lot more testing," Kat told them. "As of now, I don't have much to give you, but I'll look for drugs, and I'll study the stomach contents — those tests were done, but not really followed up. I'll do whatever I can." She offered them a weak smile. "It's going to be nice to have first call on all the lab techs out there, and free rein for any test I need."

Logan glanced across the corpse at Kelsey, who was gazing down at Tara's face. He liked the quiet way she'd stood listening, and the empathy in her eyes. He looked at the corpse himself and wondered whether he'd lost his "talent" after Alana's death.

Had it diminished because he'd refused to make use of it? After all, what good was a "talent" that had failed him when he'd needed it most?

But he still had it. He knew he did. Something was eluding him, though. He could reach out, and he could see, but he couldn't see *enough.* He'd reached the young woman, but he'd felt blinded.

He walked over to Kelsey, who started, her attention drawn from the corpse. He took her hand; she scowled at him, taut and resistant, when he urged her toward the corpse.

"You need to see," he told her.

"Just like you do," she shot back.

He bent his head slightly, a bitter smile curving his lips. "But we're a team, right? And your eyes might be better on this one. You have to *feel* the hurt, don't you?"

She didn't allow him to force her hand onto the putrefying corpse, but she didn't make a show of fighting him in front of Kat and Jackson, either. She did let him guide her, though, and he felt some emotion rip through her as she touched Tara Grissom's arm. Her eyes flashed to his in green fury but she didn't get a chance to speak; the door opened and they were joined by a tall, slim brunette wearing a lab coat and carrying a camera.

"Jane," Jackson said warmly. "Thank you for coming."

Logan released Kelsey's arm.

But he met her eyes again and shrugged grimly. She'd gotten something, made some kind of connection. And while he was glad to welcome Jane Everett to the investigation, he was also anxious to get back on the streets with Kelsey.

She had what he'd lost.

Maybe it was simply the ability to give, and to love. To touch, in a way he no longer could.

CHAPTER 7

Kelsey tried to greet Jane Everett cordially, with professional courtesy, but she felt as if she were burning inside. Watching as Kat worked with the corpse had become painful. She kept wondering if Vanessa Johnston had been alive when she'd reached Texas, and though she knew the loss of a finger didn't guarantee death, she also knew they wouldn't find her alive. And as she'd listened to Katya Sokolov, she'd felt an almost overwhelming sadness for the young woman on the table.

Touching her had made it worse; it was as though she'd felt her own life ebbing through her fingers as the corpse's one good eye stared at her. Deep in her mind, she'd heard a silent cry for help.

Where were you? Kelsey asked. *What were you doing? How were you so quickly and easily taken? And why?*

"Kelsey O'Brien, Jane Everett," Jackson

said, introducing them.

They shook gloved hands, and Kelsey tried to smile as Jackson continued. "Logan, Kat, Jane, you three know one another and you've worked together, so I'm actually the odd man out here, along with Kelsey, of course."

Jane Everett had warm amber eyes and she seemed pleased to meet Kelsey. They didn't exchange small talk over the corpse; Jane went right to the heart of her expertise. "This isn't going to be easy," she said. "I can do better images when we're working with skulls," she told Kat.

"Tara's face we know." Kat spoke gently and respectfully of the dead. "On some of the others, most of the tissue is already lost, so we can take a look and then decide on an approach."

"Jane," Logan said. "I think it'll help us immensely if we can determine the identities of the other women."

"Kat and I will start on the images immediately," Jane assured him. "Then you can distribute the pictures." She smiled. "I haven't seen you in while. It's good to work with you again."

Jane liked him, Kelsey thought. At the moment, she didn't like him very much herself.

But Jane had barely entered the room

when the door opened again, and her cousin arrived. Sean came in, giving her a broad smile, and it was nice because . . . so far, she really had been an outsider. She wasn't Texan. Sean was, but he was blood, as well, and they even bore a family resemblance. She wanted to rush over and throw her arms around him, but the gravity in the morgue forbade it. And the sense that still seemed to vibrate in her fingers, the sense that Tara Grissom was *with* her, made any other kind of feeling — or interaction — difficult just now.

Jackson stripped off his gloves and shook hands with Sean, and the others greeted him as an old and esteemed acquaintance. He looked at Kelsey then, sheepish, his eyes trying to meet hers but slipping to the corpse that lay between them.

"Hey, Kels."

"Hey, Sean."

He was tall and lean, with hair that was similar to her own but much darker, and the same green eyes that were dominant in their family. While she stood awkwardly behind the corpse, Sean kept avoiding it and trying to speak to the others, saying he was glad to be working with them again.

"I'm not sure I'm much good in the morgue," Sean said, addressing Jackson.

"And I'm still involved with the documentary. But I'll do my best on searches and video re-creations as soon as I have something to work with."

"Kat?" Jane began. "How soon —"

"This afternoon," Kat said instantly. "I'll get an assistant in here, and we'll start with the photographs. I'll see what I can do about getting down to the skulls. If we can come up with a real idea of more of the victims' faces, Sean can start tonight." Kat turned to Jackson, Logan and Kelsey. "I'll do whatever I can in the tests, and get back to you."

"Kelsey's named our victims," Logan said. "I think we all believe that 'Jodie Doe' might have been the victim of a different killer — she was drowned. This doesn't mean we don't need justice for her, too. I'm just mentioning it."

"All right, I'll look for differences, as well," Kat promised. "I'll also do anything I can to find out if a common drug, synthetic or natural, was used on any of the women."

"Everyone at the office tonight at eight o'clock," Jackson said.

They were dismissed. Kelsey pulled off her gloves and went back to the hallway. Knowing Sean was behind her, she turned around and greeted him with a hug at last.

"I was hoping to see you soon," she told him, "but this is a surprise."

"It was a surprise for me, too," he said. "Well, not totally. Crow contacted me, but a lot of my time is committed to the documentary that's being shot. The good thing is, we've come back to the city to do some interior shots at Branch Studios. I'm here now, so you're welcome to stay with me. I figured you wanted to spend some time with Sandy, but if we're working together . . ."

"I'd love to come and stay with you, but right now I think it's more important to be at the Longhorn."

He nodded. "We're negotiating to shoot there, too." He grinned wryly. "The rodeo's in town, which is good on the one hand, since they can hire some of those guys as extras. But it's bad in a way, too, because Sandy may not want shooting done on the premises when she has such a great clientele — thanks, of course, to the rodeo. She won't want us closing off any areas. Then there's sound, of course. But I'm not producing. I'm just the special-effects guy." He glanced at his watch. They'd moved down the hall, but Jackson, Logan and Jane Everett had exited the autopsy room, as well. He looked quickly in their direction. "So, this is why you're here?" he asked her. "What do you think?"

My cousin! My blood, she thought. *Sean was here. She felt now that she really had someone she knew, and trusted entirely.*

"I'm not sure yet," she told him. "Jackson Crow seems to know what he's doing. It's a little scary. But very tempting."

"Yeah, it's intriguing. Who knew the world had so many strange people in it?"

"We're not strange," Kelsey said.

"Right. We're perfectly normal *gifted* people," he said dryly. "Let's face it, Kels, we're strange. But working where strange is normal might be really nice for a change."

She studied Sean's face. He was a few years her senior; they'd both seen and done some things that could definitely be considered strange. And they'd both learned that you didn't talk about any of these things to others.

She nodded. "We'll see, won't we?"

"We will," he agreed.

"Sean, you know the history and legends here, don't you?"

"Born and raised in San Antonio," he reminded her. "Any questions you have, I can answer later, okay?"

The rest of the group was coming toward them, and he backed away from her slightly.

"Going to my day job." He raised his voice. "I'll see you all tonight. And if anyone has anything for me . . ."

He waved and headed off.

"Let's go, shall we?" Logan said to her.

She didn't ask where they were going. Kelsey knew he was anxious to search for Vanessa Johnston.

She still felt a simmering anger against him over forcing her to touch Tara's corpse — forcing her hand in more ways than one — but she nodded.

They left the morgue together.

Kelsey could still smell the mixture of chemicals that seemed to permeate the autopsy room, even as they walked into the sunlight.

It wasn't a smell you ever forgot.

They returned to the Alamo, and sat on the bench not far from the entrance to the old chapel.

"This seems highly useful." He could hear the sarcasm in her voice. They'd been on the bench for nearly half an hour and nothing had happened.

"This is where the crow dropped the finger," Logan said patiently.

She was cool and aloof; she'd been angry since they'd left the morgue.

He turned to her. "Look, we're here because we can sit on this bench and possibly . . . hopefully, make some discoveries."

Her green eyes blazed. "Yes, we know we can do things differently. But, Raintree, we're supposed to use our gifts as we see fit to use them. I don't force you to do anything, and you don't force me."

He shook his head. "I tried. I touched Tara, and because of that, I know she was taken in darkness. You're better than I am. You might have discovered more."

"I'm not better! You . . . made contact."

"So did you," he said, turning away. "And, hey, if you don't want to use what you have, you should just go home."

"*I* should go home?" she responded furiously. "If you can't move beyond the past, there's no sense in working on this. And if you're supposed to be some kind of team captain, well, there's been a mistake."

He wanted to answer her sharply, but he tensed and found himself inhaling.

She was right. She was so right. He had to learn to find the truth again.

He exhaled. "Team. That means we all use what we have," he said. He turned back to her. "*Did* you get anything more?"

She shook her head. "Tara Grissom can't help us because she was taken in the dark,

181

and she doesn't know who killed her."

"She can still help us," Logan said.

"How?"

"We have to find out more about her. Learn about her friends and acquaintances. Who knew she was coming here? Did she meet with anyone once she arrived? We need to discover the little personal things. I thought —"

"You thought you could force me when I wasn't ready," Kelsey said.

He smiled crookedly. "Are we ever really ready?"

"Are *you* ready yet?"

Was he?

Looking past Kelsey, he saw Zachary Chase hovering a few feet away.

"Zachary," he whispered.

Kelsey whirled around. Logan supposed that, if any visitors were watching, they'd think the two of them were staring at an imaginary friend.

Kelsey didn't stand. She didn't act as if she was about to shake hands with the air. She smiled, though, and said in a soft voice, "Mr. Chase! I've been hoping to meet you."

Thus encouraged, the ghost of Zachary Chase came forward.

Kelsey made way for him to sit on the bench between them.

Zachary was in buckskin, the outfit he'd probably worn most of his life. His face was weathered and taut, but he was still capable of a shy grin as he looked at Kelsey. And, with him between them, they could converse as if Kelsey was talking to Logan, which would certainly create the appearance of a normal conversation.

"How do you do, miss," Zachary said appreciatively as he greeted Kelsey. "It's a pleasure to meet you."

"You, too, Zachary." Kelsey nodded at him.

"This is Kelsey O'Brien," Logan said. "She's a U.S. Marshal. We're both desperate for help, Zachary. Someone is stealing or seducing away women from this area, or so we believe — and killing them."

Zachary frowned. "I had worried," he said.

"Zachary, you didn't say anything to me," Logan chastised him.

"You haven't been around much," Zachary said. "When you were, it was as if you hadn't noticed me. And I didn't know the women were dying."

"Can you tell us what you've seen?" Logan asked.

Zachary sighed, glancing toward the chapel, and Logan had to wonder just what the man was seeing. He knew the Alamo as they couldn't, as the best scholar couldn't, as the most historically accurate filmmaker could never quite portray it.

"There was one rather plump, pretty girl. And she saw me. She saw me, the way you see me. I watched the man following her. I was trying to tell her. To warn her. Then he approached her, and touched her, and I couldn't hear what he said. She gave a startled look, and she seemed to fall toward him. I thought perhaps he'd given her bad news. They left together," Zachary said.

"You mean . . . she sank against him? But she was still conscious? Moving on her own?"

"From what I saw, yes." He pointed toward the street. "It was busy that day. I thought that if she was afraid or in trouble, she would cry out. But she didn't. She went with him. It was as if she knew him, and yet, when he was following her, I didn't think she did."

"Can you describe him? What did he look like? Who was he?" Kelsey asked anxiously.

"He was Davy Crockett."

Logan saw the surprise register on Kelsey's face.

"Pardon me?" she said.

"Zachary, I've never seen the ghost of Davy Crockett at the Alamo," Logan began.

"You've told me before that you sit here and think about him, but you've never seen him, either. I don't believe the ghost of Davy Crockett, if he *was* here, would be out to hurt people."

Zachary shook his grizzled head. "Not the *real* Davy Crockett," he said impatiently. "This man seemed to be one of the actors they bring in when they're doing reenactments. Lord knows, I've watched enough of those through the years!"

"So, someone dressed up as Davy Crockett?" Kelsey asked.

"Someone trying to dress up like Davy," Zachary said. "But he was ridiculous, this man. Oh, his clothing wasn't bad. Had on buckskin and fringe, rather like my own trousers and jacket. Had on a cotton shirt in a plaid pattern. What looked so bad was his face. Fakest whiskers I've ever seen, and bad wig. Worse hat."

"Think, Zachary," Kelsey urged. "Had you ever seen the man before?"

Zachary shrugged. "Don't rightly know. I mean, there's so many of those actors who come and go, and around here, on Halloween, there are Davy Crocketts everywhere. When I did see him, I was barely aware of him at first. I thought a school group was coming. Then I noticed that he was following the young woman, and I tried to warn her. I think she even saw me, and she was laughing. She supposed I was playing with her. I tried to get her to follow me into the chapel. There were people there. Living, breathing people. I just felt he was . . . odd. Then he went up to her and I couldn't get close enough to hear what he was saying. She sagged against him, like I told you, and they went away. I didn't think much more about it. I've seen a lot here over the years. Many people pass through this place. Sometimes they're smiling, sometimes they're serious. Sometimes they leave together, and sometimes they leave alone."

"Have you seen the man since?" Logan asked him.

"Don't think I have," Zachary said. "Hard to say, though. You get all kinds around here. The historical society is usually in on it, but you occasionally get folks who think they'd like to be heroes, too, and they dress up and come here. Every once in a while, you get the unemployed actor with a hat out for donations. But did I see this particular fellow again? I don't rightly know." He shook his head again and looked at Kelsey sorrowfully. "I didn't know women were being killed. And I'd planned to talk to Logan

186

the other day and find out if there was anything I needed to worry about, but he brushed me off. Rude, you know what I mean?" Zachary asked.

Kelsey actually smiled as she looked past him at Logan. "Incredibly rude," she agreed.

"Zachary, you know damned well that you enjoy making me look like a fool who talks to himself," Logan said. "We waited for you," he added. "The other day."

Zachary shrugged. "Sometimes I like to walk around where the walls once stood," he said. "Sometimes I like to walk on, heading in the direction I did the day I left to get help." He turned to Kelsey and said sadly, "Men might be willing to die. Don't mean they *want* to die."

Kelsey started to reach for him, but her hand ended up on Logan's thigh, and she yanked it back.

"Zachary, I'm so sorry about all your friends here," she said.

"It was a long time ago. I don't know why I stay. Can't help them now. I just keep thinking. . . . The provisional government was a mess. Who knows? More men might've come, and more might've died. And I didn't get to see everything, but I did speak to some of the women afterward. Santa Anna, he was a bastard, executing

187

people right and left. But he didn't kill the women or the kids."

Kelsey murmured sympathetically.

"I could never help them," Zachary said.

"But you can help *us*. You can help us now," Logan told him.

"What can I do?" Zachary asked. "You say women are being killed. I only saw what I did that one day, and even then . . . So what can I do now?"

"You can watch for us, Zachary. You can watch what goes on. I'll stop by every day. Tell me if you see this man again or anyone who might have been this man," Logan said.

"I can do that. Yes, I can do that." Zachary nodded vigorously. He stared at the chapel entrance again. Tourists were flocking around; docents and interpreters were on duty. The sun was shining, and the sky was blue, and it was a beautiful day in Texas.

Zachary spoke directly to Kelsey. "Davy Crockett died in the fighting, you know. That's what they told me. Travis, he was killed right away. Some say Davy was taken and executed, but I talked to Susanna Dickinson after the battle — she was the wife of my friend Almaron Dickinson — and she said there was a commotion, the women and children were hiding, but she heard that Davy went down fighting. Santa

Anna sent her and Joe — Travis's slave — on to Gonzalez to warn the folks they'd all be dead if they kept fighting. And can you imagine? Santa Anna offered to adopt her little girl! This was after her husband was killed. Good for Susanna — she didn't give an inch."

Logan let Zachary talk, although he'd heard his stories many times before.

They needed Zachary now. He could be a witness — the camera and the recording no one could find.

"I'm so sorry," Kelsey was telling Zachary.

He shook his head. "So long ago, now. So long ago." He suddenly turned to Logan. "What's going on with the birds?" he asked.

"What?" Frowning, Logan gave his attention to his surroundings.

The birds were back.

There were scores of them, and different varieties. Crows, of course. Black birds by the dozens, alighting here and there and everywhere around them. On cars, poles, wires, the eaves of the old chapel. And there were sparrows, pigeons, seagulls and more.

As he looked, an arrow of flapping wings passed overhead and soared toward the south.

He stood, saying, "Zachary, please keep watch for us. Tell me about anything you see, whether you think it's important or not."

Zachary was on his feet, as well, and Kelsey rose at his side, studying the birds. She frowned, then said to Zachary, "Thank you so much. I'm so glad to know you."

"My pleasure to serve you, beautiful lady." Zachary made a slight bow.

Logan regarded her for a moment himself. Kelsey was just that, a "beautiful lady." He believed she could be tough, and he was sure she knew how to use her weapon, and that she was effective in law enforcement. But there was a ladylike quality about her, in her movements, her manner of speech, the empathy in her emerald eyes.

And yes, she was beautiful.

"We have to go," he said.

Her level gaze reminded him that they'd searched before and found nothing.

But she nodded; they had to keep trying.

They returned to Logan's car. "The birds were flying south," he said.

"We already went south, but we could have missed something." She stared out the window intently while Logan drove as slowly as he could.

"Are we looking for an actor?" she asked.

"It could be an actor," he said. "Or someone who knows there are always actors and

190

would-be actors around. It's easy — strange as that sounds — to dress up in buckskin and look like you belong at the Alamo. I wish Zachary could've just said, yes, he saw the man — he was tall and light-haired or short and swarthy, blue-eyed, green-eyed, businesslike, a bum. . . . But all we know is someone's using history."

"Using history to find history," she murmured. She turned to face him, her focus now on their quest, the anger gone from her voice. "I wonder if Zachary knew Rose Langley. The saloon would've been frequented by men who were at the Alamo — not when the siege happened, of course, but when they first came. There was a community here. And some of them must have known Rose."

"We'll talk to him again," Logan said. "We'll talk to him every day until we learn the truth. Keep your eye on the street, okay?"

"We've been here before," she said.

"We didn't look hard enough."

"I'm keeping an eye out for trash piles, dumps, old construction heaps," Kelsey said. "Fresh gardens, old gardens . . ."

"I think this guy likes hiding his victims in plain sight, if that makes sense. He wants them to rot, and then be discovered."

"*If* he wants them discovered," she said.

"Oddly enough, I think he does."

"Stop!" Kelsey shouted.

"Where?"

"Anywhere around here."

He saw a space between a massive GMC truck and a Mini Cooper. He moved his car smoothly in and turned off the ignition.

"What do you see?"

"The birds."

He looked. They were across from a large wooden fence.

Black birds were perched on top of the fence.

On it were written the words *Danger. Keep Out. Fourscore Construction.*

He left the car and started toward it, aware that Kelsey was close behind.

There were chains where the wood ended and an aluminum gate had been erected. The fence itself had a jagged top — fine for birds, but not great for people.

Logan pulled out his Colt.

"What are you doing?" Kelsey snapped. "This is private property!"

"We're feds now, or acting as feds, right?"

"I *am* a fed. It's still private property."

"I hear a distress cry. Don't you?" he demanded, squinting at her.

As if on cue, one of the birds let out a raw scream.

"Well . . ." Kelsey shrugged. "We could just call someone from the company."

"That takes time," Logan objected.

The bird gave another loud screech.

"Hey, I hear a cry," Logan said next. "It might be nothing, but . . ."

He shot the chain that was keeping them out, then pushed the gate open and entered the construction site.

Kelsey said something under her breath and followed.

The site was large, but no one seemed to be working that day. An old building had apparently been torn down to make way for a new one. Old foundations stood, surrounded by cheap wire and warning signs. Plywood covered some of the gaping holes in the ground.

Logan gestured toward the south. "Start over there. I'll take the north corner."

"Yes, sir," she muttered, marching off in the direction he'd told her.

Logan went to the opposite corner. Here and there, sections of a wall had been built; he could see naked brick as he lifted the first plywood sheet. Below it he saw nothing but what would one day be a part of a basement.

He looked across at Kelsey. She'd lifted a sheet, too, and then let it fall. She was standing very still.

"Logan," she called softly.

"Yes?" he called back.

"The birds."

That was when he noticed them. They hovered over a section that would have been an entry, he imagined, or, perhaps a corner of the basement.

He heard sirens — someone had alerted the local police to gunfire.

They had to hurry.

He nodded, and they both skirted the other holes and went over to the area where the birds had been.

Facing each other, they raised the sheet of plywood.

Logan looked down expectantly but saw nothing except a hole in the ground littered with construction debris.

Kelsey hurried around to his side. "Slide me down there, Logan!"

She crouched close to the ground, heedless of her clothing — her tailored pants and jacket, her crisp white shirt. He caught her arms, guiding her, holding her tightly until she dangled just a few feet from the bottom.

Their eyes met, and in that moment, he

thought, *We* are *a team. We understand each other.*

She dropped the rest of the way and righted herself. He twisted around, sliding into the hole himself and then falling.

Old broken boards were everywhere. So were plywood shavings and sawdust, with the occasional coffee or soda cup and fast-food wrappers.

He began to raise boards and sift through trash, and then Kelsey cried out.

He turned.

There, protruding from the ground, was an arm, the hand dangling.

And the hand was missing a finger.

CHAPTER 8

"Fentanyl," Kat Sokolov said when they were back at the office.

Kelsey tried to recall what she knew about the drug. It was legally used as a painkiller and had improved the quality of life for many a cancer patient.

Not surprisingly, unscrupulous people were now selling it for use on the streets. Like all good things, it had been corrupted.

She waited for Kat to continue. Kelsey's mind seemed as exhausted and dazed as her body. It had been a long day. Logan had managed to keep the local cops at bay while contacting Jackson and getting Kat down to the construction site so the body could be recovered without losing any evidence that might exist. They'd spent hours in the April sun, working the scene along with local forensics and keeping the "team" in the lead. Jane Everett had come to photograph every minute of the procedure, and she,

Logan and Jackson Crow had kept watch to ensure that nothing that could provide a clue — a fiber, a fingerprint, a hair — was overlooked.

And once Vanessa Johnston had been removed from the ground, she'd been rushed in for autopsy while local investigators had set out to question every member of the construction team, from the contractor to the delivery boys. Kelsey had to admit that, like Logan, she didn't believe they'd get much help from that direction. The site had been closed down for several weeks due to lack of funds. Vanessa Johnston had only been missing for about a week. Still, there was the fact that the lock on the gate was new and there was no other point of entry, unless one scaled the wooden walls with their arrow-tipped tops. It was extremely unlikely that anyone could have crawled over the fence, especially carrying a corpse or a drugged or unwilling woman. That mystery was solved when Logan began walking the perimeter and discovered that two of the side-by-side slats were no longer embedded in the earth. They slid easily enough when pushed to create an entrance allowing passage for a man, even a man bearing a burden as large as a human body.

The neighborhood was canvassed, although no one had heard anything, and only one woman complained about noise at the site.

"Birds!" she'd told the officer. "Birds shrieking and cawing at all hours of the night. I called in to complain twice."

And she had; the construction site was on a list for the cops to check out.

The physical evidence at the site could take weeks to examine, even with all of Jackson Crow's power and contacts. There were hundreds of wooden boards, there was dirt, bricks, refuse, and many other surfaces to be tested.

Vanessa Johnston's body had not decayed to the same extent as the other bodies. Kat was optimistic that she'd be able to learn a great deal more about time and method of death than she could with the earlier victims.

Kelsey thought about Vanessa's family and friends, those who had feared for her and would now learn the worst. . . .

Everyone seemed as exhausted as she was. Jane had done what she could to establish images of the deceased; Kat, too, had worked without a break. Sean came later, having spent the day on the documentary. He'd plunged in without pausing for a meal.

Now they sat, the six of them, in the office, their chairs gathered in a circle, sharing the events of the day and discussing what they'd found out, with Sean listening.

"Fentanyl," Kat repeated. She looked at Logan and Kelsey. "I'm sure you've come across it. Fentanyl is a synthetic narcotic analgesic, and it's a hundred times more potent than morphine. For chronic pain, it's often delivered to patients through a patch. It's also combined with other drugs for surgery. Like I said, fentanyl's hit the streets, and God knows how many overdoses there've been because of it. It's sometimes mixed with Rohypnol — commonly known as a roofie — and I'm assuming that we've missed the combination because of the deterioration of the previous bodies and because we needed to use GC-MS testing. But that's how the killer is grabbing these women. I think he's mixing up a dose and getting close enough to prick them with some sort of needle or slap on a patch. I'm not positive of his method because I haven't been able to find a needle mark or evidence of a patch on any of the women, although I'll continue searching on Vanessa Johnston tomorrow."

"The drug is that potent?" Kelsey asked. "In my experience, roofies usually go into drinks, and I've worked cases where the women don't remember a thing that happened to them for hours afterward. In one rape, the woman didn't believe she'd ever been with the man, and he was only caught because the police found video."

"Yes, a roofie is a date-rape drug," Kat said. "Memory can be completely lost. But this is a mixture. The fentanyl is knocking the person out — right after the killer gets her to come with him willingly. Why? I have no idea. As far as I can tell, the women aren't being attacked sexually."

"I figured he had to have a method for getting so many women to disappear with him. If he was causing any kind of scene, someone would've noticed something by now and reported it," Logan said.

"I'll start on a grid, although I don't suppose we know where Vanessa was last seen?" Sean asked.

"Let's begin by putting all the women somewhere near the Alamo," Logan suggested. "And then indicate where the bodies were found. Let's include Sierra Monte in the investigation, so we'll need the Longhorn in the grid, as well. We know she was taken from there."

Kelsey glanced over at Logan. He seemed increasingly convinced that Sierra Monte's death was connected with the others. He also wondered if — and how — the Galveston diamond might be involved.

"I'll have preliminary sketches of the other women for you tomorrow, and we've decided it'll be necessary to remove the remaining flesh and soft tissue on several of the skulls. In a few of the other cases, that's what we're down to, anyway," Jane said. "I can provide images that will be almost real," she added. "There are even formulas you can use to come up with the most likely hair and eye color."

"That will help," Jackson said. "We need to identify the other women ASAP."

"Of course," Kat agreed. "And we have the best people in crime-scene forensics working on the site. Logan has seen to that. He knows the local technicians and scientists and labs. The place itself is a mess, but there's got to be *some* bit of evidence."

Logan cleared his throat. "This killer understands how to corrupt evidence. Somewhere along the line, however, he's going to leave something behind, something that doesn't become tainted. A skin cell, strand of hair, whatever. But even when we've got that, we'll need someone with whom to compare our samples. I think we should start looking at anyone who might be into costuming. We should investigate actors, interpreters, would-be actors and even historians," he said. "We need suspects."

"Why actors?" Sean asked.

"We found a witness who says he saw Chelsea Martin with someone dressed like Davy Crockett," Kelsey said.

"Can we all speak with him?" Kat asked.

Kelsey glanced quickly at Logan, still a little uncomfortable about blurting out such strange information, even in this group.

"Maybe." Logan shrugged. "His name is Zachary Chase and he hangs out at the Alamo."

"Zachary Chase?" Sean frowned. "That's the name of one of the couriers who rode out of the Alamo just before the final battle."

"Yes."

"A descendant?" Sean asked.

"No. Zachary himself," Logan said with a rueful smile. "He's a ghost. But he's still at the Alamo."

"Oh." Sean exhaled. "Well, I'm working on a documentary about the Alamo. I can give you all kinds of information — and dozens of actors."

Logan's house was fascinating. It had the feel of a hunting lodge; it was built of stone and wood, and a large stone fireplace was the focal point of the sprawling living room, with an extraordinarily fine headdress on the wall over the mantel — an Apache war bonnet from the 1870s, Logan told her.

He was casual about the house. He'd only owned it a year, and he'd bought it when he'd sold his last house because the back-yard was almost an acre, unusual in central San Antonio.

Besides having a number of authentic Apache and Comanche relics, he had a nice collection of art and seemed to be a fan of Mort Kunstler's Civil War pieces. "Most of them are prints," he explained. "The origi-nals are pretty pricy, but I have a friend on Apache land who is a fan, too, and frames them so expertly they look like they could be originals."

He'd just brought out two bottles of Lone Star beer and set them on coasters on the coffee table that stood in front of the soft leather sofa. He took a seat next to her, and for a moment she wondered why he'd asked her to come — and then wondered why she'd said yes.

She smiled and he looked back at her and laughed.

"We're an odd pair," he said.

"True, and yet a pair," she murmured, gazing at the fire. She found it pleasant to sit there and watch the flames. The day had been warm while the sun was out, but the evening was cool, with a definite chill in the air.

He leaned back, propping his feet on the coffee table. "Tomorrow, the documentary." He looked over at her again. "Thanks to Sean — and the fact that you're his cousin — we'll have nice, natural access."

"I'll find out tonight if they've negotiated space with the Longhorn," she said.

He was studying her and smiling. "You look like Sean. I don't know why I didn't see it before."

Kelsey laughed. "Great. I look like a line-backer."

He lowered his head for a minute, the same smile on his lips. "You know you don't. You always make sure you look professional — and not like a runway model."

She felt a flush touch her cheeks. "Sean and I have similar features, I suppose. Grandpa Cameron. He had the red hair and green eyes."

"Sean and I have been acquainted for a while," Logan said. "He's come in to work on digital re-creations several times, and they've been really helpful in court."

"I never realized he did that," Kelsey said.

"I guess it's because we're far away, and rarely see each other, even though we're close."

She sank back against the sofa. Sitting there felt good, as if the warmth of the fire was slipping into her bones, easing away the tension that had built up during the day. By the time they left the police station, she'd figured the kitchen at the Longhorn might have closed, and she'd thrown out a comment about heading back to dig through the fridge. Then Logan had said he had chili he only needed to heat up, and she'd found herself agreeing, even though Sean had assured her that he could find someplace to take them for a meal.

So now the chili was heating. She'd entered Logan's domain and she was glad of it. She was weary, and it felt all right to be weary with him, her defenses down. She'd been furious with him earlier, but the more they worked together the more she understood that he could be relentless in pursuit, especially when he was frustrated. Yet he knew the law — and how to work around it when necessary.

After she'd agreed to come home with him, she'd panicked, afraid she'd be going to a shrine — the house he had shared with Alana.

But he had sold that house and changed his residence, and despite the guilt and bitterness he carried like a brick around his neck, he was trying to move into a new life.

"I would've thought you'd have a dog," she told him, taking a long swallow of her beer. She glanced at him and grinned. "Like a pit bull or maybe a wolf."

"I had a wolf mix once. Loved her. She was a great watchdog, and yet incredibly affectionate. She died a few years ago. I've also had a little mutt about so high." He raised his hand a foot from the floor. "Lately . . . well, one day I'll get another dog. I like dogs. I just want to know I'm going to be a good dog owner again."

"I'd love to have a dog," Kelsey said. "But I feel the same. My training was hard, proving myself was hard — I didn't want to get a dog and ignore it. I'd like some big old mutt. Just a big lovable hound that wants to be loved and petted when I come home, and that I could take to a park or . . . well, we don't even know if this whole team will work, or if it does, where we'll be."

"And I took you for the Yorkie-poo type," Logan said.

"Oh, really!" she said, laughing, because he was obviously teasing her.

"I don't have your experience," she said a

few minutes later. "In law enforcement or in life. But I'm good at what I do."

"I'm sure you're good at everything you do," he told her. He'd spoken the words casually, but his voice had a rasp that they both heard, and it seemed to turn the words into a double entendre that she knew he hadn't intended. He stood with a wry grin of apology. "Chili should be hot by now, and I'm starving."

"Me, too."

She rose to join him. In the kitchen, while he took the chili from the stove, he instructed her to grab the instant rice from the microwave, which she did. Then she chopped tomatoes while he washed and broke up a head of lettuce. They sat at the kitchen table and said very little for a while, except when Kelsey took the time between mouthfuls to compliment him on his chili.

"Ah, well, Rangers come from a long tradition of survival in the wild," he reminded her. "Stephen Austin brought the first three hundred legal American colonists into Spanish Texas after his father died, soon after receiving an *empresarial* grant to colonize. They were known as the Old Three Hundred, and they were on dangerous frontier ground, so he created an informal group for protection — the Rangers. Poor

Austin had barely gotten started when Mexico gained its independence from Spain and the land grant was rescinded. There was trouble ahead for sure. So, the original Rangers were out there . . . ranging. Watching for outlaws, Indian attacks and bad men, protecting Austin and the colonists. They had to learn to forage." He grinned. "Any self-respecting Ranger has to know how to cook."

"And I wouldn't want you to be anything less than self-respecting," Kelsey said with mock seriousness.

"What about you?"

"I can cook," she assured him. "At least, I'm great with a microwave."

He laughed softly, but set his fork down, having finished his meal. "How did you know which plywood cover to pick up today?" he asked unexpectedly.

She grimaced. "I wish I could say I'd heard something, that Vanessa Johnston was reaching out of the ground for me." She raised one hand in a dismissive gesture. "Okay, I wish I could say that, but only to you. I noticed the birds. Is that crazy, or what?"

He shook his head. "Strange, when I was meeting Jackson Crow — and you — I had an incident with a bird. There were birds

everywhere. Although I'm not a supersti-
tious man and I've learned a lot of different
beliefs, I thought it might be an omen at
first, or a warning. Now . . . maybe it's just
because they're drawn to carrion, but the
birds seem to be helping us out. I don't
know. . . . Crazy or not, it was a bird that
dropped Vanessa's finger in front of us, telling us she was out there to be found."

Kelsey didn't speak for a minute.

"What are you thinking?" he asked her
quietly.

She was surprised by the tone of his voice.
She looked across at him and studied his
face. It was such an attractive face —
strong, with good bones, piercing eyes, the
bronze texture of his skin. She liked everything about his appearance. But attractive
men were numerous; with Logan, she realized, there was more. Even when he irritated or angered her, there was something
about him that compelled her.

Dangerous, she told herself.

But she knew he was attracted to her, too,
even if it was just physical. In their few days
together, they'd formed a strange kind of
bond.

*Yes, there are times when we can both com-
municate with the dead. We've touched a*

corpse, and felt the voice of her soul calling out.

And we share a ghost at the Alamo now, a man who died more than a hundred years ago.

Logan was looking at her. She hadn't answered his question.

"When we heard about Vanessa, I thought maybe we were brought together to save a life. Justice for the dead is so important, but I suppose I wanted to believe we were coming together to protect and save the living."

He nodded. "We still may," he said. "We haven't caught this killer yet. He may have other victims in his sights — he probably does — and we're on it now."

"We don't even have any suspects," she murmured.

"Trust me, we will."

He sounded confident. Kelsey watched him, knowing he wouldn't stop — whether their team was formed or not, whether he became a fed or stayed with the Rangers or worked freelance — until he found the man who had committed these crimes.

"I believe you," she whispered.

She would never know whether it was the simple words they exchanged, or something about that evening or the way they looked at each other. She would never even know if she'd moved to kiss him first or if he'd moved to kiss her. It hadn't been a romantic night. There were no roses or candles, no movie with dinner or a walk on the beach. . . .

But maybe it wasn't romance. Maybe it was more basic than that — the straightforward urgency of need.

Somehow they were suddenly locked in an embrace, a sweet touch that seemed to burn through limbs, that answered longing. He knew how to kiss, not with force but with confidence, and the feel of his mouth covering hers was an unbearable aphrodisiac. She parted her lips to his, hungry to explore everything about him, and before she realized how it had happened, they were both standing, tearing at each other's clothes. Their guns and holsters were the first to go. It wasn't until then — when she recognized what she was actually *going to do* — that she became conscious of the dirt and grime of the day. Some semblance of shyness tried to invade the hunger that surged through her with such insistence, almost as if she'd been without water for days, and she had to drink or die.

"I'm filthy," she whispered.

"I do have a shower," he said.

He hopped along, tugging at his boots as they headed from the kitchen down the hall to the shower. Her own pumps were kicked aside and he groped for the water while she struggled out of her suit trousers. Hot steam filled the bathroom. She caught sight of them both in the misting mirror just before it completely fogged. She thought there was something oddly right about the way they looked together. He was dark and she was pale, and her hair was streaming down over his fingers and they were close, so close.

"Birth control?" he asked.

"Taken care of," she said.

He dragged her into the shower, pulling the curtain around them, and the spray of the water seemed to enhance the feel of his lips, his tongue within her mouth, the touch of his hands upon her.

For a moment, as they were locked in a kiss with the water showering over them, she felt a panic rise within her.

He was still in love with his wife.

She was a substitute for a dead woman.

She wanted to cry out. She wanted to look into his eyes, deny nothing, but insist that he call her by name, acknowledge the fact that he was with *her.* It was all she wanted. No declarations of love or even caring, just the acknowledgment that she was Kelsey O'Brien, she was flesh and blood and she was here with him *now.*

But she said nothing. She felt the searing fire of the water again, or the fire that was inside him, the liquid heat of his lips on hers, and she let the thought slip by because she wanted to be where she was. She felt his hands on her breasts and between her thighs and the hot, slick feel of his dark hair as he bent against her, mouth and tongue over one breast and then the other. She clung to him, her fingers sliding against his back and digging into his buttocks. She would've said just moments before that she hated showers, that she was tall, that the shower was slippery, that it was far from her fantasy of making love. But he was strong and powerful, and she wasn't afraid — and it didn't seem at all bizarre that they hardly played in the water before he lifted her easily and she slid down onto him as if they'd rehearsed it all as a dance. She felt the tile behind her, and his movements against her and inside her, and she was aware of only the running water, the force of her own movements and his. Finding his mouth again as they thrust and writhed, feeling the explosiveness inside her, that was sweeter than she'd imagined possible. . . .

She climaxed with a shattering sensation she'd never experienced before. She'd been with other men, of course — in particular one Key West cop she'd thought she loved until their relationship ended a few months ago. But the intensity of these emotions, these sensations, was new to her. She felt Logan shudder as he finished, and then he held her close, still inside her, and she felt again the surge of water. She didn't know what to say or do so she said something ridiculous, whispering in his ear.

"We might have gone for some soap, as well, you know."

He chuckled, easing her down, making sure she didn't slip.

"I have soap," he said, and reached for it.

It might have been awkward; they might have stared at each other, naked in a shower, and realized what they'd done.

She could have spoken then. . . .

But she still didn't. He took the soap, and spun her around, caressing her with it. And she stood, feeling the water, feeling his touch, and it was so good and sweet again that she didn't dare think, didn't dare breathe. Until the friction she felt began to grow into something else, and she turned toward him, seizing the soap, and touching him slowly in return. She savored the feel of his flesh beneath the suds, and teased his body as he had teased hers, watching the movement of her hands against him, savoring the rise of his erection to her erotic touch — and wondering how such incredible passion and intensity could have escaped her all her life.

He kissed her while hot water sluiced the soap from them both. Then he lifted her into his arms and fumbled to turn off the taps. He carried her, dripping from the shower, down the hall. They stumbled onto his bed in the dark, and he began to kiss her again, taking his time. She tore at his shoulders and hair, and pulled him to her, then crawled over him, lying against him as she made her way down the length of his body, squirming and arching as she returned every last kiss. He took her in his arms and brought her to him, and as they made love that time, they twisted and turned, each atop and each below, panting and gasping and whispering incomprehensible words of pleasure until, once again, it seemed that the ground beneath them trembled and the heavens above exploded.

Kelsey lay against him, gasping for breath, hearing the pounding of her heart and his. Slowly, slowly, she began to notice the damp sheets. As she felt her heart calm, she realized she was still entwined with him. They both lay there in a silence so long she thought he was asleep, and she tried to ease herself from the sprawl of their limbs.

"What is it?" he asked.

"I don't live here," she said. "I have to get back to the Longhorn."

"But you don't live there, either," he told her.

She was ridiculously happy that he wanted her to stay the night.

"If Sandy knows I never came back, she might worry, and she's got enough on her plate right now," Kelsey said.

"You could call her."

"I could, but it's more than that. I'm not sure why — maybe because of you — but I feel it's important that I stay in Room 207," Kelsey said. "I really have to go," she added. "Thank you for a really wonderful night."

"Aw, think nothing of it, Marshal O'Brien. Thank *you* for a wonderful night."

He'd used her name. Well, he'd called her Marshal O'Brien, and only when it was over, but that still pleased her.

"Have to collect all my clothing," she said, and rose.

He followed her after a moment, dressed in nothing except jeans, and she thought he looked as attractive as ever, but younger somehow. He helped her, finding one of her lost pumps, then headed to the bedroom door, searching for his car keys.

"I don't think you should leave, but if you feel you need to, c'mon, I'll get you there safe and sound."

"Thanks," she said lightly.

He was silent as they drove through the streets.

"Actually, you don't live that far from the Longhorn," she said apologetically. "You didn't have to come out. I like walking at night."

He shook his head. "I don't think it's a great idea for you to go running back across the Alamo in the dark."

"I'm a U.S. Marshal," she said, as if he needed reminding. "I can fire my weapon, and I got excellent marks at the range, you know."

She saw that he was serious, although his eyes were intent on the road as he drove. "I don't doubt that. But I don't like what's going on. Each of these women was obviously taken by surprise. That can happen to *anyone* — any man or woman. I don't like to think about you, or anyone, really, taking chances until we understand what we're up against."

She looked ahead. "Well, then, thanks for the ride."

He pulled up in front of the Longhorn. It wasn't rowdy inside, but there were still lights on and people lingering at the bar.

Kelsey got out of the car quickly. "I'll be careful," she promised. "I'll go right up the stairs."

"I'll swing by for you in the morning, to get to the studio," he said.

She felt the greatest urge just to get back in the car. He was still shirtless in his jeans, and for the first time she wanted to forget that she was supposed to be focused elsewhere, that she was working on a truly horrible case. She wanted to forget she was strong and independent and following the course she'd chosen.

He was so damp and sleek and tempting. . . .

She managed to smile, and realized she was laughing at herself.

"Thanks. I'll be ready."

She hurried into the Longhorn. She tried not to pay attention to the stragglers as she dashed up the stairs. When she reached the balcony, she paused.

She hadn't been thinking about people watching her, and yet she'd felt that same strange sensation along her spine, that intense stare following her all the way up.

She walked to the rail and looked over. She could see nothing but the tops of a dozen ten-gallon hats.

Turning away, she opened her door, prepared for bed and crawled in.

She started dreaming right away.

But she didn't dream of days gone past. She dreamed of a darkened room, and the man who waited for her there, and she dreamed that he spoke her name.

CHAPTER 9

For the first time, Logan felt the extreme emptiness of his house when he returned to it.

The fire had died down low. Silence surrounded him.

He'd wanted her to stay. He couldn't remember when he'd wanted to spend the whole night with a woman and wake up beside her.

"I really should get a dog, shouldn't I?" he said.

Of course, no one answered.

He walked into the kitchen and began picking up the remnants of their dinner. As he rinsed the dishes and put them in the dishwasher, he thought of the way Kelsey had looked when she was in his kitchen and the way she'd looked in the shower, and then in his bed.

He groaned as he walked back into his bedroom. The sheets were still damp. The faint, ethereal scent of her cologne or soap or maybe just the woman herself seemed to hover in the air, and it was going to make sleep difficult.

He wanted to feel guilty. He hadn't merely had sex. He'd had great sex.

More than that — he'd *cared.*

That was why he should feel guilty.

But he didn't feel the corrosive pain he usually did. He tried to analyze himself. He knew Alana had loved him. She'd really loved him, the way he'd loved her.

And she would honestly want him to be happy. That was a revelation, although it shouldn't have been.

Ah, but what was *happy?*

He told himself that right now, *happy* would be discovering that he was being effectual in stopping the murders that had occurred beneath his nose.

But as he lay there, he was oddly at peace.

"I will get you, you bastard," he said aloud.

And he would, or die trying.

But he found that he could close his eyes, and that sleep would come, and that he could allow it. Because he would start again in the morning.

Hours later he woke suddenly, and he did so with extreme dread.

Kelsey.

Her name pounded in his head. He bolted up.

Kelsey didn't know what time it was. She didn't know what she'd heard, but she was wide awake.

There was . . . something. A sound that had wakened her from a deep sleep.

She opened her eyes in the darkness but made no sudden move. She'd left her Glock on the bedside table where she could grab it in an instant.

When she did make her move, it was swift. She sat up and reached for the gun, staring into the darkness.

"I'm armed, and I'll shoot," she said, and she meant it.

But her only answer was the ticking of the old-fashioned alarm clock. She leaned over and switched on her light. Shadows seemed to slide back into the walls.

There was no one there. She rose, always careful about the placement of her back, and walked quietly to the bathroom. The shower curtain was closed; she wrenched it open with her left hand. No one there, either.

Perplexed, she headed back into the room. It wasn't so large that she couldn't see every corner of it. Nothing stirred. She listened to the hum of the air conditioner, and wondered if it had kicked on, awakening her.

She knelt down and peered under the bed. Not even a dust bunny.

At last, she walked to the door. It was locked.

Perplexed, she went back to the bed. As she did, the phone rang.

"O'Brien," she said, looking at the clock.

"Kelsey?" Logan. He sounded anxious.

"Logan. Hey. Do you know what time it is?"

He ignored her slight sarcasm. "Six. Are you all right? Has anything happened?"

"I'm fine."

"Where are you?" he asked.

"My room. 207."

"And you're alone."

"Entirely."

"You're *sure* you're alone?"

"Yes. I've just been around the room."

"Stay there. I'm on my way."

Ten minutes later, there was a knock and she heard Logan's voice again. She opened the door. He was dressed, but his hair was askew over his forehead.

"What's wrong?" she asked him.

He came into the room. As she had previously done, he made a visual sweep of it.

"Logan, what's wrong?" she persisted.

He paused, looking at her in confusion. "I don't know," he finally said. "Were you dreaming . . . or having a vision again? Did you see the past? Matt Meyer strangling Rose Langley or . . . something more contemporary?"

She shook her head. She wondered if she should tell him that she'd awakened, certain that someone had been there, that she hadn't been alone. But he seemed so worried about her that she answered carefully.

"I'm all right. I woke up just before you called, but I searched the room and . . . well, I was the only one here. But I wish I'd see more in this room," she told him.

He relaxed. She smiled. "You need a hairbrush. Use mine. It's on the dressing table."

Sheepishly, he smoothed back his hair, then walked over to borrow her brush.

"Thank you — for being worried about me," she said, as he shaped his hair into its customary neatness.

"Hey, what's a partner to do?" he asked. "I guess I'll let you sleep for another hour or get ready. Or whatever."

He didn't have a chance to leave. There was another pounding at Kelsey's door, followed by Sandy's anxious voice.

"Kelsey?"

She shrugged and hurried to the door. Sandy was staring at her with similar concern.

"Did anything happen? Are you okay? Oh, Lord! Maybe I should never have bought this place!" Sandy saw Logan, but she obviously wasn't surprised. "Ricky opened the door when he heard Ranger Raintree knocking. . . . I was so afraid something had happened in here."

"No, I'm fine. Logan just wants to make an earlier start than we'd originally intended," Kelsey said.

"Oh." Sandy let out a sigh of relief. "Ricky came in early this morning — he was going to help me with the garbage disposal, but I'd already fixed it." She grinned engagingly. "You learn a lot about simple electrical work and Band-Aid types of repairs when you own a place like this. Actually, I didn't learn that stuff when I was doing my hotel and hospitality degree, go figure, but my dad being an electrician sure helped a lot. Anyway, to make a long story short, coffee is brewed and Ricky's got food going, too!"

"That'd be great." Logan turned to Kelsey. "Whenever you're ready," he said.

"You two have time for breakfast, don't you?" Sandy asked.

"Of course we do. Thanks," Logan replied,

smiling. Sandy flushed. She liked Logan, apparently.

"I'll be down as fast as I can," Kelsey promised. "Logan, why don't you go ahead?"

When she entered the kitchen, he and Sandy were seated at the table. Ricky and several other employees were working around them, cooking and gathering up plates for the guests who were filtering down.

Sandy looked up, almost as if she felt guilty about something, when Kelsey walked into the room.

"Coffee," Ricky said, handing her a cup as he hurried by. "I'll bet you need it."

She thanked him briefly and sat down at the table, noticing that Sandy had the local paper.

"You're not going to like this," Sandy warned.

The headline read Body of Vanessa Johnston Found. Where Are Rangers of Yore?

The byline belonged to Ted Murphy.

She glanced at Logan, but he seemed much calmer regarding Murphy than he'd been a couple of days earlier.

"What a help the little prick is to law enforcement," Kelsey said, shaking her head as she read the article.

Murphy hadn't written anything that wasn't factual. But he also knew that the FBI was involved, that she'd been brought in from Florida and that a special "task force" — including law enforcement officers who'd had some "interesting" experiences — was on the scene. He'd researched the small amount of information available on Jackson Crow and his unit, the Krewe of Hunters, and suggested San Antonio should bring in a tea-leaf reader, a medium or maybe a voodoo priestess.

"Yep, he's a little prick," Logan agreed.

"It's so sad, and so scary!" Sandy said.

"We just have to do our best to keep details from the man," Logan said, dismissing the paper. "Ricky made cheese blintzes today," he told Kelsey. "They're excellent."

"Sounds good," she said.

She wasn't really even hungry. She couldn't believe that Logan was accepting the newspaper article so coolly. She hoped the article — which really couldn't be missed if you saw the paper — wasn't going to hamper their investigation.

"Yes, you have to have some blintzes," Sandy said, starting to rise, but Ricky was already there with a plate for Kelsey.

"Sit, eat, relax, both of you. We've got it

covered," he told Kelsey, then Sandy.

"Thank you!" Sandy breathed, with Kelsey echoing the words.

Sandy waved a hand in the air. "He's such a sweetheart. Like he says, he's got me covered. He's worried about me because we're trying so hard to accommodate everyone, and I'm going insane. I've agreed that the host of that documentary can come in here and do a few minutes at the bar. It'll be a mess because we have so many people staying here, and I'm telling everyone that they don't have upstairs access — except for the fire escapes — from one-thirty to three-thirty this afternoon. I'll set up a bar in here, but it's disruptive. I don't know how I let them talk me into this. Oh, wait —" she rolled her eyes "— yes, I do. They offered me big bucks. Of course, if I really piss off my guests, and they cream me on all the travel sites, it won't be worth very much."

"The people staying here seem to be nice," Kelsey said.

Sandy placed a hand on hers. "Here I am, going on about a trivial problem while you . . ." Her voice trailed off, as she gestured at the paper. "While you're dealing with a *real* problem. Do you think the Sierra Monte case might actually be related?"

Kelsey winced inwardly. Sandy was such a good person and she worked so hard, Kelsey hated to dismiss her by saying they weren't supposed to talk about their cases.

Logan saved her from answering. "Who knows at this point? And it's only recently that anyone has thought this might be a serial killer."

"Of course," Sandy murmured, looking from one to the other. She suddenly seemed to remember her own dilemma for the day. "Kelsey, I should've said this earlier. If you're going to need anything from your room —"

"Don't worry, Sandy, I won't interrupt the filming."

Sandy brightened. "If by any chance you guys have some spare time this afternoon, you're more than welcome to watch. I've been told I can be there — nice of them, huh? I tried to tell them I could arrange far better circumstances if they'd wait until after the rodeo. But, with their budget, they have to wrap things up. I did suggest they might've asked me earlier, but it seems their narrator or whatever you call him came in for a beer the other night and fell in love with the place. He told the documentary people they had to do a location shoot here, not film the Longhorn scene at the studio.

So . . . Well, it's just for today. And bless Ricky and my other help! Like I said, we'll keep a bar going in here, as well. Thank God they put in a big kitchen! And drinks will be on the house for our guests tonight."

"Looks like you've got everything worked out, Sandy," Kelsey said.

"And maybe we can get back here to watch the filming," Logan added. "Now eat up those blintzes, Kelsey. We need to go soon."

She did. Logan encouraged Sandy to talk, and she explained how she'd admired the Longhorn and how she'd wanted it since she was young. Nothing Kelsey hadn't already told him, but Sandy was clearly enjoying the conversation. "Who knew what would happen right before I was finally able to buy it?" She winced. "Ouch. That sounds terrible. Of course, I'm so sorry about that young woman. Sierra Monte."

"Is there anything you can tell me about her?" Logan asked.

"I wish I could," Sandy replied. "I just saw her a few times when I came by, measuring, getting ideas. We exchanged comments like 'how are you' and 'nice to see you' and 'beautiful day,' " Sandy said. "She always seemed very pleasant, and she loved the inn, too. She knew the story about

Room 207, but she said she liked staying there, and that it was the main reason she'd come to the Longhorn. She was especially interested in poor Rose Langley. I've always been entranced by that legend myself. My grandfather told me the story when I was a little girl — I mean that's what got me so excited about this place from the get-go. But now . . . my heart aches for Sierra. She became part of the legend."

"Yes, she did, didn't she?" Logan looked at Kelsey's half-eaten food and seemed to know that she was just pushing it around her plate.

"Ready?" he asked her.

"Yes, I am." She stood. "Thanks, Sandy. Ricky!" she called. "Thank you! Blintzes were great!"

He smiled in acknowledgment, busy preparing.

"We'll be back for the filming, if we can swing it," Logan said.

They headed out to Logan's car. "If the filming's going to take place in the saloon, maybe we should wait," she suggested. "We want to check out the actors, but it might be difficult to do that here — and we don't want Ted Murphy to catch us at it."

"He can't be everywhere. I'm willing to bet he'll be bugging whatever public information officers he can find today. He'll probably try to wheedle something else out of someone at the morgue, as well. I would like to see the filming, but I think we'll have a better chance of observing the actors if we go to the studio."

"As you wish, oh, faithful leader," Kelsey said lightly.

She'd been worried that she'd feel awkward about the previous night, or that he'd act uncomfortable or reserved, but it was almost as if it had never happened. Maybe it *hadn't* been anything — in his mind at least. She decided that she'd act low-key and easygoing, concentrating instead on the horror and mystery before them.

The studio was some distance from the inn. Kelsey sat back for the drive, glad that Logan knew where he was going.

They arrived and found that their names were on a list. The gatekeeper let them through, and when they'd parked a receptionist called Sean to come out and get them.

"This building rents out space to a lot of producers and productions," he said, welcoming them. "Today, we're doing the room in the Alamo where Jim Bowie was on his sickbed and where it's presumed he died."

They followed Sean down a hallway as he

told them, "Alan Knight, the executive producer, isn't on set, but you'll meet Bernie Firestone, the director. He's a down-to-earth guy and really great at documentaries. I like working with him. He tells me what he wants in the way of the special effects, I tell him if it'll work and we go from there."

They came to a door that warned no one was to enter if the red light was on — it wasn't. A green light blazed, and Sean opened the door and ushered them in.

It was much more casual — and much busier — than Kelsey had expected. The director, Bernie Firestone, was with the cameraman, checking angles as the first camera zoomed in on the scene being depicted. Kelsey could see how the sets were constructed, and she watched a makeup woman adjusting the mustache on one of Santa Anna's men, who would soon burst in on Jim Bowie.

Bernie Firestone seemed happy enough to meet them, and while the preparations continued, he stood back and explained. "There are so many versions of Bowie's death. He was dying and in rough shape — that we know. Some people say he cursed the Mexican officers who came in so violently and he did it in such eloquent Spanish that Santa Anna ordered his tongue cut out and that he be thrown, alive, on the funeral pyre. Others say he killed himself. I just don't believe Bowie would do that. We offer all the different stories in our narration, but in the scene, we're going with the most widely accepted. The officers burst in on him, he propped himself up against the wall and he shot at them until he was shot and bayoneted to death." He shrugged. "Of course, he died with his famous knife at his side — we *have* to believe that!"

Kelsey watched as quiet was called and all the support personnel moved away. Firestone calmly announced, "Action!" and filming began. The narration would be edited in. The actors played out the scene, ad-libbing for greater spontaneity, Bernie had told them.

Bowie — or the actor portraying him — leaned heavily against the wall. The bed was in a corner, at an angle. There were guns in his hands, his knife in his belt. The door flew open and Mexican officers filed in. Bowie started to fire. One of Santa Anna's men clutched his shoulder, and another cried out in pain, clasping his knee and falling to the ground. The men attacked Bowie with their bayonets, and he clutched his knife, raising it high over his head as they slammed their bayonets into him. It was painful to watch.

But when "Cut!" was cried by Firestone, the actor playing Bowie sat up. He was dripping in fake blood, but he seemed pleased. "Bernie, how was that?"

"Perfect, Brant. We'll break and set it up again for a backup shot," Bernie said. He looked over at Sean. "You'll be able to edit out Henry Garcia, won't you? I want the blasting guns as the men burst in. You can do that, right? But Henry tripped on the doorframe. I thought the whole set was going to fall in for a minute."

"If that's the take you want, Bernie, no problem. That's easy stuff," Sean assured him.

"Okay, guys, grab some coffee, and then get back here and we'll do a second take," Bernie called.

The actors left the set, milling around a table laden with coffee and pastries. Bowie came over, still covered in his stage blood.

Sean escorted Kelsey and Logan to the table to join the performers. There were seven of them, including James Bowie, who was really Brant Blackwood, a local actor. He was polite and apologetic as he met them in his spattered clothing. "Kelsey O'Brien, Sean's cousin. A pleasure. You look like him except that you're pretty. Oh, hell,

Sean's pretty, too, but he hates when you tell him that."

"Blackwood, you're an old goat," Sean said. Obviously, he liked the older man, and the feeling was mutual.

"Hey, I know you," Blackwood told Logan. "Oh, I'm sorry. I mean, you were on the news," he finished awkwardly. "Anyway, glad you're back in law enforcement."

"Thanks," Logan said, shaking his hand. "Nice to meet a star."

"Hell, I'm not the star in this," Blackwood muttered. "That's Jeff Chasson. He's the narrator. We get all mucked up and dirty. Chasson puts on a buckskin outfit, gets his hair done nice and walks in front of a few locations to explain what the scene's been about. I've been proud to play Bowie, though. He must've been a tough old dude."

"Well, you seem to be doing him justice," Logan said.

Sean went on to introduce them to Santa Anna's men — the clumsy Henry Garcia, Ned Bixby, Arnie Rodriguez, Liam Swenson, Donald Chou, Victor Lyle and Doug Bracken. They were very affable, and for a few minutes they talked about the documentary. All of them seemed to feel a part of it, and to get on well together. They were a mixture of nationalities, Kelsey learned, with Henry Garcia being the only one who thought he was "mostly pure Mexican."

"Do any of you ever dress up at the Alamo?" Logan asked.

"Sometimes, when they have reenactments," Henry said. "Like in March, when the anniversary rolls around. But it's a shrine, you know — a national shrine. They're careful about filming there, and they don't like bums getting dressed up to con tourists out of money."

"I haven't done one of those reenactments, but I'd like to," Victor Lyle said regretfully.

None of these men seemed to be a mass murderer. Least of all, the guy playing Bowie . . .

When the break was over, and everyone was recalled to the set, Logan whispered to Kelsey, "I'm going to keep the director busy. Grab up the paper cups. Oh, and mark them with each man's name."

She frowned at him. Collect them without being noticed? Maybe. *Mark them?*

But Logan was good. He and Sean managed to get the cameramen and Firestone paying attention to them, with their backs toward Kelsey. The actors were milling around the stage; the makeup and prop people were in the dressing rooms. She quickly dug a marker from her purse and wrote initials on the cups, praying she wasn't making any mistakes.

Firestone turned around once. She smiled and took a big bite of pastry, then had to swallow down the mouthful of guava and cheese.

She joined them a few minutes later, the paper coffee cups in plastic bags inside her large purse.

They stayed to watch as the scene was filmed one more time. Afterward, they heard Firestone complain about the position Jeff Chasson had put him in, with regard to the Longhorn Saloon.

"We were just going to film it here — in fact, the sets were ready to go. But Chasson is convinced he's not only the expert, he's the star. When I told him we were sticking to the schedule, he went over my head. To the important people," Firestone said. He grinned ruefully at Kelsey. "That would be the money people."

"Jeff Chasson," Kelsey murmured. "I'm not sure I've heard of him before."

Firestone irritably waved a hand in the air. "He's written a few books on the history of Texas, the South, the Civil War. And he's been interviewed in some of the big documentaries." He paused. "This is a labor of love for a lot of us. We're trying to tell the story that keeps our heroes heroes without romanticizing them. The producer wanted Jeff Chasson, and he wanted to be part of it. Don't kid yourself — a director can be fired by the producer. My power is limited."

"Sandy, who owns the Longhorn, is a good friend of mine," Kelsey told him. "We're going to be there and watch for a bit, if we may."

"Your friend did us a tremendous favor, despite Mr. Chasson's interference." Firestone smiled. "You're more than welcome."

"Sandy was happy about the income," Kelsey said. "Her upkeep is high."

They spoke a while longer, then Sean walked them out. "There are other people who can do what I do here," he muttered. "But when I suggested to Jackson that I quit, he asked if I'd stay on and work with you all at night. But he also said to talk to you, Logan."

Logan stepped back for a moment. Kelsey sensed that he was startled by Sean's words. "I think it'll be good if we can keep our connection to the film, and that's you, Sean. Stay with it, okay? I hope the hours don't wear on you too badly."

She loved Sean, and she knew he worked

hard. He'd worked at a special-effects studio in L.A., a job he'd loved, for many years. He'd come home because his high school flame had been dying. Although they hadn't made it as a couple, they'd never stopped being close. He'd always called Billie Jo Riley the true love of his life. He'd stuck with her until the end, and then, maybe a little broken, he'd stayed on in Texas. He wasn't married and he didn't have kids — and he still worked ridiculous hours.

Sean shook his head. "No, I'm in."

He gave Kelsey a hug. "Hey, remember, if you want out of the Longhorn, kid, just holler."

"Sean, you cannot call a U.S. Marshal *kid*, even if she's your cousin," Kelsey chastised, smiling. "But I need to stay at the saloon. It's another connection we have."

She and Logan left the studio and returned to the station and their dedicated room. Jackson was there alone. "Poorly collected evidence, but we have these if we need them," Logan said as Kelsey took the coffee cups from her handbag. "They were intended for the garbage, and would have been in the garbage."

"Technically, *would have been* is not the same as actually being there," Jackson pointed out.

"We can't use it in court, but if they help us find a killer, then we'll look for a way to make our case," Logan said.

Jackson nodded.

Logan checked his watch. "We're going over to the Longhorn," he said. "You never know what we might learn. So far, we don't have a shred of evidence — or, I should say, we have a mountain of it that means nothing."

They went back to the Longhorn, coming in through the kitchen. Ricky was there, along with a few of the guests who seemed happy enough to be sitting around, enjoying the free alcohol.

Corey Simmons was among them. He greeted them warmly. "Hey! This worked out just great for me. I met the director, and he said he liked my look. And he found out what I do for a living, that I'm the real rodeo deal. I'm going to be a performer! I mean, on film. They hired me to be one of the couriers when they do the scenes with the fellows slipping out across the Mexican lines."

"That's great," Kelsey said. "I'm happy for you, Corey."

He gave her an enthusiastic hug. "And to think! If it wasn't for you, I probably wouldn't have stayed on here!"

Ricky interrupted them. "You can go into the saloon now. Quietly, I've been told. They're running film. Jeff Chasson wants his practice filmed, in case it's better than any of the takes."

"We won't make a sound," Kelsey promised.

She led the way, Logan close behind her. They entered the saloon on tiptoe and walked around the seating area in a wide arc.

Bernie Firestone, standing near one of the cameramen, turned and waved to them, urging them in.

Sandy, who was seated at one of the saloon tables, waved as well, inviting them to join her.

They slid into seats at her table.

One of the other bartenders was dressed in the vest, cotton shirt and string tie that a bartender might have worn in the mid-1800s.

Jeff Chasson leaned against the bar like a rugged frontiersman on the day of the Alamo.

He was blond and clean-shaven, but he did look convincing as he stood there, a hat on the bar, beside a long rifle.

"It was here that the men came when they needed respite. Remember, the defense of

Texas fell into the hands of a mixture of people — old settlers and new settlers, those who came hoping for land and glory. They were a ragtag band, not a regular army. So, while many a rancher, Ranger and drifter passed through, their station in life didn't really matter. We're in the old Longhorn Saloon. Famous for the best whiskey in the area and the prettiest girls. Among them was the legendary Rose Langley. She sang, and she served, and she flirted — the most coveted of all the girls. But she'd come to San Antonio with one of the roughest men to ever draw a bead on Texas. He died in the fight for independence, or so it's assumed, but he was hardly one of our heroes. Before he disappeared, part of the massive death toll that brought Texas independence, Matt Meyer became enraged with the beautiful Rose, and strangled her right here at the inn, up in Room 207."

The narrator turned dramatically to indicate the staircase. "Up those stairs. Room 207. And the history and the legends live on," he added ominously.

Kelsey saw the horror on Sandy's face.

"Rose was strangled, but in the aftermath, in the years that followed, like the legend of the Alamo itself, the legend of the Longhorn was destined to continue. So will we ever know? Is the Alamo really hallowed ground, drenched with the blood of heroes? Is it haunted by the men who died there? And is the historic Longhorn just as haunted, with spirits — old and new — drifting along that staircase?"

Chasson let the sentence fade away.

Sandy was tense, waiting for what he'd say next.

Then he settled back at the bar. "Jeff Chasson at the Alamo, now and then."

The knowing smile left the man's face as he pushed away from the bar and started toward Bernie Firestone. "That's bullshit, pure bullshit. We need to add the part about the murder of Sierra Monte. The Alamo now and then —" he snorted. "We've talked about the massacre in Goliad and what happened in San Antonio. It's bullshit not to mention the murder last year! We can sell this thing ten times over if we talk about blood dripping through the woodwork. Not then but *now*."

CHAPTER 10

Sandy was distressed. She got to her feet, wanting to protest, clearly not knowing how. Kelsey leaped up, too, and Logan, afraid that Kelsey would try to defend Sandy first and use diplomacy second, decided to take the matter into his own hands.

He winked at Sandy, then walked over to the director and Chasson.

"Excuse me," Logan said. "I couldn't help overhearing," he began.

Chasson turned and stared at him in irritation. "Who the hell are you?" he demanded.

"I'm a friend of Sandy's, and I'm also a Texas Ranger, Mr. Chasson," Logan said politely. He went on before Chasson could ask what business he had interfering. "I should warn you that you're in the Longhorn due to the largesse of the owner. The events that occurred here in the 1830s are well-known, but for you to sensationalize the presumed death of an innocent girl is in extremely bad taste. If you simply present known facts, that's one thing. But you're doing a documentary on the Alamo, not on unsolved murders in Texas. You could be setting up this production for a major lawsuit — by the owner, by the victim's family — and you'd be named right along with the production company. Or Ms. Holly might determine that the production should be thrown out and you could be banned from ever stepping foot in the Longhorn Saloon again."

He smiled as he spoke. He'd lost his temper with Ted Murphy, and he wasn't going to do that again. He was really getting his life, *himself,* back; dealing with arrogant assholes like Chasson in a smooth and politic way was actually far more satisfactory than losing his temper.

Chasson scowled at him before turning back to Bernie Firestone. Firestone had been grinning, but he tried to appear stern when Chasson looked at him for help.

"I'm sorry, Jeff. You said you wanted to film here. And if we're filming here, Ms. Holly does have a say. You didn't tell me you planned to talk about Sierra Monte."

"But —" He stared over at Sandy. "But it's history!"

Kelsey walked up to them, Sandy beside her.

"It's Sandy's property now, Mr. Chasson," Kelsey said. "And she has the right to call the police and have you evicted if you're breaking an agreement."

"I didn't agree to anything," he said angrily.

"You can leave," Sandy offered, apparently delighted with the way things were going.

"We . . . we paid to film here!" he sputtered indignantly.

"However, I *was* given script approval," Sandy said.

Jeff Chasson might have been a jerk, but he knew when he was outnumbered. He smiled again, the practiced smile he gave the camera. "All right, forgive me. I wasn't aware of your script approval, Ms. Holly. But if that's the case . . . You see, the documentary traces the history of the Alamo, along with that of Texas. We follow the Alamo through to the present time. Ms. Holly, the Longhorn is a huge part of that. Now, we can leave, and I can say anything that's fact, and there's nothing you can do about it."

"That's true," Sandy murmured.

"Or you and I can work on a script together, ensuring that the truth is told, but that you're happy with what I say."

Sandy looked uncertain at that. Her eyes darted to Kelsey, who shrugged. "Sandy, it's totally up to you."

She still hesitated. Chasson placed a hand on her shoulder. "Please, Ms. Holly? It looks bad if we avoid the truth. Bernie, what's the schedule? This is all we had for today, isn't it? Could I have a few minutes with Ms. Holly?"

Bernie Firestone nodded. "Whatever Ms. Holly decides."

"Or did you want a larger check?" Chasson asked.

Sandy straightened regally. "I made a deal. I'm not reneging because of money."

"Fine. Sandy and I can hammer this out. It won't take us more than twenty minutes," Chasson said.

Guiding Sandy to another table, Jeff Chasson withdrew a pen from his jacket pocket and a cocktail napkin from a longhorn-shaped holder.

Bernie shook his head. "I knew better than to take on this project."

"Jeff Chasson calls the shots?" Logan asked.

"Not all of them," Bernie said wearily. "On some of the narration. Like I told you, he really wanted this project, and the executive producer really wanted him. To be honest, he looks good on camera, he's got credibility and he has a great voice. This is my first real snag. A lot of the film is action, reenactments of what happened, based on the historical record." He paused. The cameraman, no longer filming, had taken off his headset, set it over the tripod and waited with weary patience. "I'm not sure you met earlier. This is Earl Candy. An amazing cameraman."

Kelsey and Logan shook hands with him, introducing themselves.

"I wait around a lot," Candy told them with a good-natured shrug.

Kelsey laughed, and Bernie Firestone flashed her a smile. "Your cousin Sean is an important part of the process. There are dozens of maps spread across the screen as the narration goes on — he does those. And he's a whiz with film, working with shots that look like hell until he's added his smoke and black powder or blazing sun."

"What about the cast?" Logan asked in what might have sounded like a non sequitur but wasn't.

"You saw today. Most of them have been a dream. Very professional."

"And you've hired on a real cowboy," Logan noted.

Bernie nodded. "The guy's got the look, you know." He smiled at Kelsey again. "I'd love to have you in a few shots, all dressed up like a saloon girl. And, Raintree, you'd make a damned good Alamo defender."

Kelsey immediately demurred. "I don't think it's for me, but it sounds like Corey Simmons is pleased and excited."

"Yeah, I'll just have to work around the rodeo schedule. There's always something. And we're supposed to wrap this up by next week. That'll be a miracle."

Jeff Chasson rose and returned to stand before Bernie. "I've got everything settled with Sandy. We'll film the last part in Room 207. She's approved the script."

"What?" Earl Candy asked. Logan saw that his camera was big and heavy; there were also lights and screens, along with sound equipment.

Logan saw that Kelsey was frowning, silently echoing his own reaction.

"Kelsey, do you mind?" Sandy asked, hurrying over to her excitedly. "He's going to introduce me as the new owner up in your room. We'll be quick — we have to be. I need to reopen the bar area soon."

"You did a wrap-up on the practice tape," Bernie said.

"And you can edit it, and I damned well

know that," Jeff Chasson snapped. "Come on. Sandy and I have this all worked out, and it's going to make for a better piece. Our market is the history and learning channels. You have to offer them something new. Something out of the ordinary."

Chasson turned away, starting for the stairs with Sandy.

Bernie Firestone glared after them. "Yeah. How about history?" he muttered. But Chasson didn't hear him, and Sandy had apparently become his best friend.

"Want me to carry some of the camera equipment?" Logan asked. "I don't know much about it, but I can haul and take directions."

Bernie and Earl Candy looked at him with gratitude. "Wait, I'll get you more help!" Kelsey said cheerfully.

A moment later, Kelsey was back with Corey Simmons, who was happy to assist with the equipment. Kelsey grabbed a couple of the screens, and with all of them participating, they were able to take up the entire video and sound ensemble in one effort.

When they reached the room, Sandy was applying what had to be Kelsey's makeup and trying to move Kelsey's belongings out of the way. Logan watched Kelsey's eyes as she surveyed the scene; she held her temper and stepped forward. "Sandy, I can shift my belongings into the bathroom and closet for now. Finish your makeup and let me clear everything away."

Chasson had already studied the room, and he started giving directions. "Bernie, get the room, and then me, with the curtains just so, like that, looking out on the street. We'll have Cameron play with the film and get some mist going. And shadows. That'll be great."

Logan held still. It was up to Sandy. If she wanted to go along with the arrogant weasel, that was her choice.

"I'll set it all up," Earl Candy said. "Don't mind me," he added a little bitterly.

"Let me just, uh, get out of the way," Corey Simmons said. He'd put down the heavy camera he'd carried, looking torn. He'd run screaming from this room, Logan remembered.

"I'll be back in the kitchen for now, in case y'all need me!" Corey said next. Maybe he was expecting the director or Jeff Chasson to ask him to stay. Neither did. Logan wasn't sure if Corey was relieved or disappointed.

"Thanks, Corey," Logan said. The others hadn't really seemed to notice him, once his function had been fulfilled.

"I'm here, if you need me," he repeated. Then he left, heading back down the long stairway.

"Is this the way it usually works?" Logan asked Earl Candy in a low voice.

"Well, there isn't always a *usual* in documentaries, but no," Candy said. "Hell, I make a good income and I'm paid by the hour. Guess this'll let me get the wife an iPad."

Chasson did have an eye for the dramatic. He started to tell Bernie what to film, but Bernie took over. "I know what you want, Chasson. And I'll make it work, but listen to me now. They call me the director for a reason."

"We'll get out of the way, too," Logan said.

Kelsey frowned, and he almost smiled. She wasn't leaving what was currently her room with these people in it.

"We'll wait here, in the hallway," he said.

Kelsey nodded slightly and joined him.

What Chasson had planned wasn't derogatory, or disrespectful. He spoke softly, with a reverent hush to his voice as he said, "We've come to Room 207. When some guests phone to book it, they call it the murder room. This was where Rose Langley entertained men from the Alamo, and where she met her death. And where, nearly two centuries later, another young woman encountered a terrible fate, although the truth of that fate is still not known. With me is Sandy Holly, current owner of the Longhorn Saloon and Inn. Sandy, can you tell us more of the story?"

Sandy looked very pretty — shy and sweet — as she stepped closer. Chasson laid an arm across her shoulders. "Ms. Holly, you bought the Longhorn right after the incident with Sierra Monte, didn't you?"

"I was in the process of buying the saloon, yes, and it was so tragic! We don't know what happened, other than that a tremendous amount of blood was found in the room. But after the police were finished, a clean-up biohazard crew came in and, as you can see, the room is beautiful now."

"But, Sandy, twice in the same room . . . Do you think the spirits of Rose Langley and Sierra Monte are still here?"

"No. I think that if there *are* spirits, they're the souls of those who have gone on, and both women know I revere the history in this place, and that they're as welcome as any other guest of the Longhorn Saloon," Sandy said earnestly.

"Thank you, Sandy," Chasson intoned, "and I'm Jeff Chasson for the history of the

Alamo and Texas, old and new."

"All right — was that brilliant, or what?" Jeff asked, coming forward when they were done.

Logan realized that Sandy was smiling from ear to ear.

She came forward, as well, hurrying out to the hallway to throw her arms around Kelsey. "That was great, just great! I think it will bring tons of people to the inn!"

"I hope so, Sandy," Kelsey told her. She looked at Logan, and he grinned in return. He could tell that they were both wondering what Sandy had been so worried about.

"Drinks on the house!" Sandy announced. "If you're available, of course."

Earl Candy nodded. "Works for me."

"Me, too. I could use a drink," Bernie said. "Earl, give Cameron a call first. Have him get a gofer to pick up the film and ask him to take a look. I want it back with his effects in it as soon as possible, just to make sure we've got something really decent."

"Thanks for letting us hang around, Sandy," Logan said. "Let's get Corey Simmons back up here, and we'll carry the film equipment down so Kelsey can have her room back."

"Kelsey, wow. You'd be a great interview!" Chasson said, homing in on her.

"No, no, I wouldn't be. I'd ruin your documentary."

"But you're staying in this room. Have you been scared? Do you sleep with the lights on?"

"It's a room, just a room. An ordinary room." Kelsey spoke evenly and smiled as she looked at him.

"Well . . . anyway. Thanks," Chasson said, turning to Sandy. "I'll take that drink, Ms. Holly. In fact, I'll have two. I'm done for the day!"

They started down the stairs. "I'll get Corey. He does know how to tote and haul," Logan told Kelsey. He left her in the hallway, watching the crew take apart the camera and sound system again.

He came back with Corey and they helped carry down the equipment. By then, the young gofer who'd been summoned had arrived; he collected the film, and Kelsey's room was cleared out at last.

Logan waited with her as she went through her room. She didn't seem to mind spirits or ghosts at all, but openly resented having Jeff Chasson in her temporary domain. Chasson did have a smarmy charm; Sandy had fallen for it in no time flat. Despite himself, Logan could suddenly envision the hours he and Kelsey had spent together, and it was an almost painful and too-physical memory. He urged himself to abandon the thought. "Let's run by the Alamo," he said thickly, "and then get to the station."

She nodded. "Sorry. I just feel . . ."

"Invaded?" he asked.

She laughed. "Yes."

"You have your key."

"Oh, yes. But then, Sandy has a key, too."

"True," he acknowledged. "That's why you should just come and stay with me." The words were out of his mouth before he knew what he was saying, but as he spoke, he realized he meant them.

Kelsey shook her head. "Sean needs to stay with this documentary. By the same token, I need to stay in Room 207."

He nodded. "We should get moving," he told her. The days were too short for everything they had to do. The killer might already have another woman. But at the moment, he needed to move for another reason. He had concentrated too fully on Kelsey.

"The Alamo — and our bench?" she asked.

"Yeah." He hurried down the stairs. Jeff Chasson, Bernie and Earl Candy were already at the bar, drinking. They were joined by Corey Simmons and several other guests. Chasson was talking to Corey, which didn't seem to bode well, but there was nothing they could do about it.

They left the Longhorn and headed out.

Kelsey hadn't liked Jeff Chasson in her room, and she couldn't shake that feeling. Even though he'd kept his words and tone careful, there'd been something nearly salacious as he talked about the murders. And she was worried about Sandy, falling for such a slimy manipulator, but Sandy seemed to be smitten.

They walked to the Alamo from the inn.

"Now the rat bastard is talking to Corey Simmons, who wants to be in the documentary. If Chasson finds out that he was in that room, there'll be hell to pay," she said to Logan.

"Don't worry, Corey won't say anything."

"You're sure?"

He grinned. "I'm pretty sure. Corey Simmons is happy as a clam to be in that film. He's been hired to portray a rugged frontiersman willing to brave the lines of Santa Anna's army to bring help to his comrades. He's not going to risk that — or his rodeo career — by admitting he was scared silly in a 'haunted' room and had to be saved by a woman."

"A U.S. Marshal," she corrected him.

He didn't reply but grinned again.

"Never mind." she groaned. He was right about Corey's frontier mentality.

They reached the Alamo and claimed "their" bench, the place Zachary Chase would expect to find them. He didn't come right away, of course, and they studied the flow of people around the historic shrine, speaking softly about the case as they waited.

"The actors at the studio seemed wonderful," Kelsey said. "Of course, we've only met a fraction of the people involved. When Sean was out on location, there were hundreds of extras at a time."

"Yes, but some of those people live out there."

"There still have to be other people working here, in San Antonio, if they're doing more scenes at the studio. I mean, they just about have to include the famous scene in which Travis tells the men they can fight or leave. He draws a line in the sand, and James Bowie has himself carried over the line, even though he can't stand. And there have to be scenes between Santa Anna and the women and children he spared, and Joe, Travis's slave."

He nodded and leaned his head back, catching the last rays of the dying sun.

"And we're taking the word of a *ghost* that we're looking for a man in costume," he said."

"You doubt Zachary?" Kelsey asked, a little horrified.

"Not in the least. But could you begin to explain that to anyone else?"

"No," she said. "So, we met some nice actors today. Except for Jeff Chasson, and he's an idiot."

"I can't disagree. But being an idiot doesn't make a man a murderer, nor does the fact that he's charming — or can pretend to be — make him innocent."

"Of course not. But . . . did you see his eyes light up when he talked about Sierra Monte? It gave me chills," Kelsey said.

"He's creepy, but that still doesn't make him a murderer," Logan responded. Then he straightened. "Here comes Zachary."

And indeed, their friendly spirit was coming toward them, excusing himself as he moved past others who had no idea he was even there. Sometimes people would pause and look around, as if they felt a strange stirring or the whisper of a chill. Maybe they were really feeling the past and the sacred sorrow of the ground on which they walked.

Zachary made his way to the bench and bowed awkwardly, greeting Kelsey, then took the seat between her and Logan.

"I have kept my eyes open, and I have been vigilant, through the day and through the night," he assured them. "I'm sorry to say I have nothing to tell you."

"Nothing is good," Logan said. "We're afraid that another young woman is going to be kidnapped and killed. We don't know why this man is taking them, but I was thinking it might have to do with Rose Langley and the Galveston diamond."

Zachary Chase frowned. "The Galveston diamond? It disappeared in Galveston, or so I thought. I always heard it had existed, but that in the scuffle — when Matt Meyer took Rose Langley — it was lost in the sand."

"I believe Rose brought it here," Kelsey said.

"That's interesting, that she might have held on to it." Zachary spoke very quietly.

"You knew Rose, didn't you?" Logan asked him.

Zachary nodded, and there was something wistful in his eyes. "I wish . . . I wish I had been braver. That I had been a better man."

"In what way?" Kelsey asked gently. "You must have been a very brave man, to have

261

done all that you did."

He shook his head, gazing down at his hands. Then he raised his eyes, a rueful expression on his face. "You have to remember, we didn't expect Santa Anna when he came. We thought it would take him much longer to march here. And when it all began — well, we still thought the provisional government would send reinforcements. I wasn't brave just being at the Alamo. And when we were manning the mission . . . I went to the Longhorn often. I was in love with Rose," he admitted.

"You were in love with her?" Logan repeated, and Kelsey realized that this was something he hadn't known or guessed.

"She was beautiful, and no matter what was done to her, she was so sweet and refined. I wanted to take her away with me. Run in the night. Go somewhere, anywhere."

"But Santa Anna's army was coming," Kelsey said.

"I could've made my move. I could have slipped away with her and we could have ridden east, ridden as hard as the wind, and escaped. But Rose was afraid for me. He'd nearly killed her man, Taylor, back in Galveston, and she'd seen him shoot another in cold blood over a poker game. I said we should go, anyway — just get the hell out of Texas. But Rose would tell me no, she wouldn't risk my life, and God help me, there was cowardice in me, because I didn't insist."

"How curious," Kelsey murmured. "Because, as I said, I believe she did have the diamond. And that, at the cost of her life, she refused to give it to Matt Meyer."

"What makes you so certain?" Zachary asked.

Kelsey decided not to tell him she'd *seen* the woman he'd loved, seen her murdered — over and over again, in her dreams and visions.

Logan didn't say anything; he waited for her to speak.

Kelsey took a deep breath. "I believe she had it, Zachary, because people have searched for it for years and years — to no avail. Of course, time passes, seas and sand change, hurricanes almost wiped out Galveston, and still . . . I think she had it. I suspect she was waiting for her own courage not to fail her, and then she would have ridden away with you."

Zachary smiled and looked at her. "Do you really think so?" he asked.

"I do."

"If I could only reach her . . . touch her,"

he said, his ghostly voice wistful. Then he seemed to give himself a shake. "But . . . even if Rose had the diamond, what does that have to do with someone kidnapping women from the Alamo?"

"We haven't figured that out yet," Logan said.

"Are you sure? Are you sure it's the same man, and that it could be connected to Rose and the diamond?"

"No, we're not, but we need someplace to start." Logan got to his feet. The darkness was descending upon them. "Thank you, Zachary," he said. "Kelsey?"

She rose, too, and so did Zachary. He began to walk by, then quickly turned.

"Thank you," he told Kelsey. "I will do my best not to disappoint you."

She watched as he moved toward the chapel and disappeared into the dusk and shadows of nightfall.

"He may be in love again," Logan said dryly.

"Jealous?" she teased.

"I'm pretty sure I'm a bit ahead of the poor guy, being flesh and blood," Logan said. He added briskly, "It's time to get to the station. I'm tired — and hungry."

"Yes, we really should remember that thing called lunch," Kelsey said.

They retrieved Logan's car and drove to the station. When they entered their office, Jane and Kat were already there, leafing through a sketch pad with Jackson. "May we?" Logan asked Jane, and the other three were quiet as Logan and Kelsey looked through the pages together.

"These are just sketches," Jane said. "I have computer renditions that may be better. I don't know yet. I'll compare the women and the sketches, and you decide which you want to go with. The sketches give an opaque quality to the faces — it makes them a little dreamier. The computer images are sharper."

"The sketches . . . have so much life," Kelsey said. Jane was a talented artist. The faces on the page seemed to have an individuality. Each woman was drawn with medium-length hair, and yet the personalities all seemed different.

"We can put them out tomorrow," Jane said. "Copies are already at the paper. They just need an approval."

Kelsey realized that the others, including Jackson, were looking at Logan. He met Jane's eyes. "Have them printed, please."

She nodded and just then, the door burst open. Sean entered, pulling a computer from his shoulder bag even as he shoved his way in.

"You have to see this," he said urgently.

"What? Did you come up with something in a grid?" Logan asked.

Sean was shaking his head. "No, no. I hear you and Kelsey were *there* for this! I thought Chasson had fiddled with the image somehow. I thought . . . I don't know what I thought. But I haven't given it back to anyone yet. I haven't shown it to anyone. I just called Earl Candy and asked him if they'd been playing around with Halloween props or anything of the sort, and he swore they hadn't. All he'd seen through his lens was Sandy and Jeff."

"What's in the film?" Logan demanded.

CHAPTER 11

Logan glanced covertly at Sean, curious about his excitement regarding the film.

There was nothing unusual in it. At first.

He saw what he'd seen earlier that day, in a smaller version on the computer.

Jeff Chasson stood by the window, posing for the camera. He spoke with a husky tremor in his rich voice. "We've come to Room 207. When some guests phone to book it, they call it the murder room. It was where Rose Langley entertained men from the Alamo, and where she met her death. And where, nearly two centuries later, another young woman encountered a terrible fate, although the truth of that fate is still not known."

Logan thought Earl Candy was a damned good cameraman. He'd caught the room at just the right angle, getting in the period dressing table and drapes; he'd used a lens that created a mysterious, ethereal quality.

Chasson spoke again, gesturing Sandy toward him. "With me is Sandy Holly, current owner of the Longhorn Saloon and Inn. Sandy, can you tell us more of the story?"

And then Sandy stood next to him, looking sweetly innocent as she faced the camera, Chasson's arm around her shoulders. "Ms. Holly, you bought the Longhorn right after the incident with Sierra Monte, didn't you?"

Sandy nodded. She was a natural, speaking to Jeff, but cheating toward the camera. "I was in the process of buying the saloon, yes, and it was so tragic! We don't know what happened, other than that a tremendous amount of blood was found in the room. But after the police were finished, a cleanup biohazard crew came in and, as you can see, the room is beautiful now."

Logan cleared his throat. "Sean, I'm not sure what we're supposed to be seeing."

"Wait," Sean said.

"But, Sandy, twice in the same room . . . Do you think the spirits of Rose Langley and Sierra Monte are still here?" Jeff Chasson asked.

"No. I think that if there are spirits, they're the souls of those who have gone on, and both women know I revere the history in this place, and that they're as welcome as any other guest of the Longhorn Saloon," Sandy said, passion in her voice.

And then Logan saw it, but he had to blink to be certain. A shadow seemed to step out of the wall. A shadow in the shape of a woman. As the computer continued to play the scene, they heard something that sounded like a sob.

As Jeff Chasson wrapped up, then stood there, giving the camera his final half smile, the sob turned to a wail, and then it, and the shadow, disappeared.

There was silence as they all stared at the blank computer screen.

"Play it again," Logan said.

Sean did.

And it came back, exactly the same.

"No one's had the opportunity to alter this film?" Jackson asked.

"I don't see how they could have," Sean said. "I got a call from Bernie, and he seemed really annoyed with Jeff, except that he thought they'd gotten some good stuff. He wanted to see it, and he wanted me to play with shadow and light, to make the room look spooky and haunted. But this is what I saw *before* I did a thing." He shook his head. "I don't think there was time for anyone to look at it, much less alter it in any way."

Kelsey turned to her cousin. "You did say you haven't given them this footage, didn't you?" she asked.

Sean stared at her, exasperated. "Of course not! I kept this and copied it, and cleaned up the sound, then exaggerated the shadow so they'd assume I put it in. I brought the original here." He glanced from Logan to Jackson, and then at Logan again. "I knew you wouldn't want any of them seeing this, especially knowing Chasson as I do. He would've turned this into a media circus. I figured we didn't want them following anything related to our dead women right now."

"Kelsey, that's the room you sleep in?" Jane asked.

Kelsey nodded. Logan felt as if his stomach twisted and every muscle in his body tensed.

"I don't think you can go back there," he told her softly.

But she looked at him with bright eyes. "Logan, everything I've seen so far has been like a repetition. It's just a residual haunting. Now I know there's someone in the room who can be reached. What I couldn't tell from the image was whether the woman was Rose Langley or Sierra Monte."

"You shouldn't be in there alone," Sean said, sounding like a big brother. He was her cousin, Logan reminded himself. But at the moment, that didn't matter.

"She won't be there alone. I'm going to stay with her," Logan said firmly.

"That's kind of cute — they're fighting over you," Kat said, trying to be light.

"I don't think Sean's fighting to be with me," Kelsey retorted.

Logan ignored them both. "Kat, anything else from your end?"

"More of the same. I was able to get more test results from Tara Grissom. And we're looking at the same mix in her system. She was definitely drugged when she was taken — the same as Vanessa Johnston," Kat said.

"How's he getting to them? Wouldn't you find needle marks?" Kelsey asked.

"Well, I'm not sure yet, but . . . I probably mentioned that when it's used medicinally, the drug is often delivered through a patch. The killer might be using the same method, with his own little drug cocktail. That would explain why we can't find any pinpricks, and it would explain how they became so docile. I'm still looking, but soft tissue decomposes quickly," Kat said. "You should also know that you didn't fail anyone," she added, looking around at the team. "There's a high probability that Vanessa Johnston was killed the night she disappeared. She was covered by plywood, dirt and other grime, but . . . well, the development of larvae and flies can help a lot in determining time of death."

Logan watched Kat, glad she was on the team. Or with the unit. Yes, they were going to be a *unit*. She was a tiny blue-eyed blonde with more energy than a hummingbird; she was thorough and open-minded, never dismissing the suggestions of law enforcement officers, and always going the extra mile.

Logan turned to Sean Cameron. "Have you done a grid on the bodies that can help us any?"

"Yes." Sean gestured to the desk where Jake Mallory had set up his computer and the connections to the large screen. "I need about two minutes," he said. "May I?"

"It's your show," Jackson replied.

Sean nodded and started his own setup. A minute later, a map of the area with an overlay noting the names of the victims appeared. "I'll explain, although it's pretty self-evident," Sean said. "Here we have the Alamo, the Longhorn and the locations where the bodies were discovered. There are only a few blocks between the Alamo and the inn. We're going to include everything here, in case there is a connection. Rose Langley was found in Room 207, soon after she was murdered. I don't think anyone *proved* it was Matt Meyer, but apparently everyone knew it. Due to the amount of blood in Room 207 last year, forensic scientists and medical examiners agree that Sierra Monte didn't walk out of there alive. If we were to draw a line around the locations where the rest of the bodies were found, including those of our other known victims — Chelsea Martin and Tara Grissom — we have a circle, and the center of that circle would fall right between the Alamo and the Longhorn."

"Do you think the locations mean anything?" Jane asked.

"Well, it means that a killer is staying within his familiar area," Logan said. "Every time he's dumped a body, he's known exactly where it could be left in plain sight and still remain hidden. So he knows the area. He also knows something about drugs, decomposition and how to manipulate people. Some of these things anyone can study online. And I'm afraid we're a huge city, so there are plenty of drugs on the street. Plus, it's really not that hard to go to lectures or read books on criminal science these days, although it would be interesting to find a suspect with knowledge of criminal science in his background." He looked around at the others. "We believe this person is never seen accosting the women, because he doesn't accost them. We also believe he's taking them from the area of the Alamo. If he's not creating an obvious problem, there's no reason for tourists or anyone to notice him. Also, if he's walking around the Alamo in costume, people just assume he's part of the program. When Jane's images go out tomorrow — online and in the paper — we may get more help from the public."

He walked over to the board Kelsey had covered with the women's J. Doe names and locations of death. "This is conjecture, but . . . A gem worth probably millions in today's market disappeared from Galveston right before the Alamo. If it did come to San Antonio, it came with Rose Langley, who was killed in Room 207. We've learned that Sierra Monte was exceptionally fond of gems and intrigued by jewelry, and so was Chelsea Martin. We've also learned that Tara Grissom was fascinated by the history here, so she likely had knowledge of the Longhorn Saloon, Rose Langley and the Galveston diamond."

"How would the killer have known who

these women were, and why would he have suspected they'd even heard of the diamond?" Kelsey asked.

"That's a good question." Logan looked at Sean. "I've done computer searches and I've checked our identified victims' email and social network accounts. What we need to find out is whether they were communicating with someone here, in San Antonio, who might've been giving them information — and maybe getting ideas or other information from them. That's just a theory."

"What if some of them were killed so it would *look* like there's a serial murderer?" Kelsey asked.

Logan turned the question over to Jackson. He was old FBI; he'd worked as a behavioral specialist.

"It's possible," he said thoughtfully. "Our scientific investigations have giant holes because most of the bodies were found in such severe states of decomposition, but as far as we can tell, these murders haven't had the markings of a sexual psychopath. The victims were murdered in different ways. They're similar only in sex and age. And again, as far as we know, their relationship is to the Alamo or the Longhorn Saloon."

"The killer almost has to be local, as we've discussed, partly because of the time elapsed. Of course, a killer could come and go, but the time and location grids suggest he's local," Kelsey said.

Logan nodded. "I'm going to say local for those reasons, too. We'll accept the fact that Rose Langley was killed by Matt Meyer. And we'll work on the theory that the Galveston diamond did come to San Antonio. Rose was the only one who knew where the diamond was, but it seems likely that it was hidden somewhere at the inn." He looked at Sean. "Can you research the known victims, try to find out if they believed they were psychics? I didn't see anything about that when I researched them, so I figure we'll have to ask friends and family directly."

Kelsey raised her eyebrows. "Kat," she asked. "Could the killer have kept them alive long enough to question them, or try to get them to a séance, or anything like that?"

"Yes, of course, it's possible. But still, how did the killer know which women to snatch?"

"I might have an answer to that," Sean said. "He saw their pictures, which made them easy to identify. They're all over the internet. It's a reasonable place to start."

"We believe he's dressed up, so we're looking for someone who does costume events, has access to costumes or might own a costume." Kelsey glanced at Logan, and then at Jackson Crow. "I honestly think we have that on good authority."

"We use everything we get," Jackson assured her.

"There's something else to keep in mind. We need to discover who might have had an unhealthy interest in the Longhorn, perhaps because of the murders," Logan said. "I'm almost convinced that one victim — our drowning victim — was killed by someone else, and if we determine her identity, we have a chance of finding her killer. But as to the killings that could continue, our answers may very well revolve around the Longhorn Saloon."

"We really have to do better with this meal thing," Kelsey said, popping a piece of cheese in her mouth as she cut pieces from a block of sharp cheddar to add to the salads. "I'm *starved*."

Logan hardly heard what she'd said. He was deep in thought, trying to create a list of everyone he'd seen at the Longhorn in the past few days. Which, of course, meant very little, since the rodeo was in town.

But there was Ted Murphy, for one.

All right, he hated the man, but you couldn't go blaming someone for serial murders simply because you found that someone to be an unbearable prick.

"Want to share your thoughts?" Kelsey asked, putting the salad on the table and taking a bottle of red wine from a nearby shelf.

"Sure," he answered. "Sorry. I was thinking about people at the Longhorn."

"Sandy, Ricky and a host of bartenders and hired help for starters."

He nodded. "We'll get the Rangers and the local police to follow through on employee dossiers," he said. "I was thinking more about the people we've come across there. Like Ted Murphy."

"He certainly seems excited by the prospect of blood and guts." She made a sardonic face.

"Jeff Chasson."

"He's sort of a celebrity. Popular historian and performer. And he's also huge on the blood and guts, or so it seems," Kelsey said.

"Corey Simmons — but he's here for the rodeo, and I'm not sure if he's ever been to San Antonio or the Longhorn before." Logan reached into the broiler for the steaks he'd thrown in. He set their food on plates and turned off the oven. "I'll have profiles run on these people. And if we're going to look at Jeff Chasson, there's the rest of the film crew. The director, Bernie Firestone, and the cameraman, Earl Candy."

They began their meal. At one point, Kelsey put her fork down and sighed. "Logan, this is like looking for a needle in a haystack. Even trying to narrow down some kind of profile seems next to impossible. San Antonio is the seventh-largest city in the United States. Most Americans know the story of the Alamo, if not all the details. Anyone can rent a costume."

"He's going to make a mistake or he already has made a mistake, Kelsey. We have to find it," Logan said.

"We can only hope. . . ."

He wasn't sure when or how, but they'd tacitly agreed that she'd come home with him. They'd slid into this naturally. When the meeting had broken up, he'd spoken first, suggesting steak. Now they were here, back in his house, as they'd been the night before. Of course, they were still talking business, trying to come up with new possibilities; it was hard to erase a mindful of theories and facts and conjecture.

But just as natural as his suggestion of

steak and her agreement was the way they rose from the dinner table and melted into each other's arms. Kelsey headed down the hall, and he practically raced after her, then paused to run back and make sure the broiler was off. When he returned, it was to find a trail of clothing leading to the shower.

Maybe touching the softness of her flesh and breathing in her scent was like a drug. Maybe making love gave them both the mindlessness they needed, if only for a few hours.

There was something about her. It began with her eyes, the emerald green that seemed so pure and untainted, even with the world around them so ugly and cruel and torn. She was lithe and beautifully golden with a fading tan; against that, her hair was like fire, a fire of temptation and seduction. She was vital in her passion, eyes flashing, whispers ever more erotic, and she moved with the fluidity of water. She could tease and excite and arouse with a sweep of that lustrous burning hair. Making love with her was like a sea of sensation. All-encompassing.

Shower and then bed. Making love in a stream of water, then making love in the softness of mattress and pillows. Afterward, he lay spent in a way he barely remembered, his mind telling him that sex was just physical heat and desire shared by a man and a woman, and yet somewhere in his soul another voice was telling him there was a difference and he should know it well. The difference between sex and making *love* . . .

As he lay with her, the sudden coolness of the air-conditioning was sweet against the heat of his damp flesh, and he didn't want to move. Didn't want to be reminded that his world was a place where the ugliness of day could intrude on the beauty of the night, where there was no escaping who he was or what he did.

She nudged him. "I need to get back to the Longhorn," she said.

"No," he protested.

She rose up on an elbow and smiled. "Logan, you know I have to go back. You're the one who's so convinced it all has to do with the Longhorn."

She looked down at him, the fall of her hair curling around her naked breast, her eyes that extraordinary green, even in the darkness.

He reached out for her and drew her to him, his lips just an inch from hers when he whispered, "Not yet."

She eased against him as their lips met in a slow kiss that became deep and passionate. Time stood still and yet passed by swiftly. And when she lay beside him again, they didn't speak, and she didn't move. As he held her he began to drift off. . . .

He saw nothing but darkness before him, and then he felt as if he'd zoomed in somewhere with a camera, going in close. He wasn't immediately sure where he was. Then he saw that he'd zoomed into Room 207 at the Longhorn, and that he was standing just inside. It was as though a movie began to unfold. There was someone speaking in a raspy voice and he recoiled. He needed to watch, but he didn't want to, because he was human, and it was agony and anguish to watch another person's pain and do nothing to stop it.

A shadow was coming from the wall. But Sandy wasn't there, and neither was Jeff Chasson. Just the shadow. He thought he'd see Rose Langley step forth in a corset and garters and chemise, and that he'd witness Matt Meyer placing his fingers around her neck, killing her.

Because she wouldn't give him the Galveston diamond.

But it wasn't Rose, and the woman wasn't clad in anything old-fashioned, although he couldn't have sworn exactly what era, if any, such a simple white gown belonged to. He didn't need to pinpoint the age of the clothing, however; he recognized the woman's face. He'd seen it in his files, on the news, perhaps even on a TV screen, but he hadn't been affected by it back then as he was now. Crime had gone on when he'd left the world for his grandfather's land and enclosed himself in his circle of mourning. Horrible things had happened but they hadn't really touched him, hadn't seemed *personal.*

He'd since learned that the world was shared, that he'd gotten into law enforcement with a true desire to find justice, to save the vulnerable and innocent from the brutal and vicious.

He knew the face. *Sierra Monte's.*

The shadow coming from the wall seemed to be looking straight at him. Her smile was sad, and her whisper was broken and pleading as she whispered, "Help me. Help them. Help *her.*"

She didn't fade away, but rather disappeared in an explosion of flapping wings. She'd been a shadow, and then she'd been form, and her form had burst into dozens of black crows that flapped their wings and flew away. He started, and realized he'd been sleeping and that now he was awake.

Kelsey was gone.

He leaped out of bed and ran naked down

the hallway, to the kitchen. Her clothing no longer lay strewn about.

He raced back into the bedroom and looked at the clock. He thought he'd barely closed his eyes, but it was 3:00 a.m.

He was suddenly so anxious, so desperate to find Kelsey, that he nearly dashed out of the house nude. He remembered the shadow with Sierra Monte's face whispering to him.

Help me, help them, help her.

Kelsey was *her,* and Kelsey was in danger.

He managed to jump into his jeans and moccasins, grab a shirt and buckle on his gun belt. Then he tore from the house.

San Antonio was different by night, especially in what Kelsey considered the heart of it — Alamo plaza. The Alamo shone beautifully in the night lights, while across the street and grass and trees of the plaza, some neon still burned. Ripley's Believe It or Not offered the visitor a trip through the extreme and the exotic and the plain old weird, and ghost tours were, needless to say, available. Tomb Rider 3D promised to be an entertaining attraction, and for those who wanted a good scare, there was Ripley's Haunted Adventure, where guests could ride a haunted coffin cage into a world of "bone-chilling" special effects, animatronics and live-action thrill-chill actors.

But it was three in the morning, so there was no one about. Kelsey decided she loved the city this way.

She was surprised that she'd been able to slip out of bed without a protest. She'd noted before that Logan seemed to wake at the slightest movement or sound. Not tonight.

He wanted her to stay, she knew, but men went into protective mode, especially when they were sleeping with a woman. They both understood that she had to stay in Room 207, and that her talents and abilities were why she'd been chosen, why she was with him. Talents and abilities she had to use . . .

They all realized there was something in Room 207. Even if she hadn't already seen the past reenacted there, they'd watched the film.

Logan would have to forgive her for walking out — and he would, because it was the right thing for her to do. He wanted to come to Room 207 to be with her, but she knew innately that neither one of them wanted to *make love* in that room, tainted as it was by pain and brutality, so they'd gone to his house with wordless consent.

It didn't change the fact that she needed

to be in that room. She didn't mind if he came back with her; she'd actually like it if he did. It was just that . . .

He'd been sleeping so deeply. He'd been at rest and she thought that, for Logan, such a deep and encompassing sleep was rare.

A moon rode high that night, casting a gentle glow along with the streetlights. Turning from the modern attractions to the historical ones, Kelsey saw the old chapel of the Alamo gleaming. With the modern world at her back, it seemed even more hallowed.

Not until she'd crossed over toward the old chapel was she aware of being followed.

She paused for a moment, pretending to adjust a shoe. There was no sound. Straining to hear, she caught the rustle of leaves, the sighing of a breeze at night. She straightened, reminding herself that she was a U.S. Marshal. She was armed and deadly with her weapon, and she was smart enough to be a little afraid. It also occurred to her that she just might have a chance to lure someone who might be a killer.

As she began to move again, she heard a click. *Click, click, click.*

Up ahead lay the historic Menger Hotel and other buildings. She needed to move away from the open plaza and find a place to wait.

Once more she pretended to stop, just to gaze at the chapel in the moonlight, and reflect upon its sanctity and beauty. She listened and thought there might be someone between her and the side of the plaza.

Kelsey resumed walking, and when she'd cleared the open area, she crouched close to the buildings on her way down the street.

She slipped into a tiny alley and waited, drawing her Glock, releasing its safety.

She looked back and heard another sound. *Not close yet.*

Kelsey leaned against the wall, closing her eyes, and prayed for strength and intelligence in every move, then peered out carefully.

There was someone there. All she could see was a silhouette, moving slowly, stopping, moving slowly.

She felt her heart beating and wondered, *Could this be the man? A killer, stalking by night?*

She prepared to meet him. She looked out again.

He was coming closer and closer, and the shadow he cast seemed to dwarf the chapel of the Alamo and the street itself.

She braced herself to accost him. She

turned and faced the man with the mammoth black shadow.

Chapter 12

Before she could open her mouth, Kelsey heard Logan Raintree's voice in the night.

"Stop! In the name of the law, stop. I have a Colt aimed at your back and will shoot to kill or cripple. Hands above your head. Turn slowly!"

Kelsey stepped out from her hiding place. By the glow of the moon and the streetlights she could see that a man stood in the plaza. Logan's gun was aimed at him, and he was slowly turning, as ordered.

She walked out, her own weapon drawn. She saw that the man was big — tall and big, not fat, but heavily muscled.

Corey Simmons.

"Logan!" Corey said with relief. "What the hell?"

She could see that Logan wasn't smiling. As she walked back to the plaza to skirt around Corey and join Logan, she saw that Corey was starting to lower his hands.

"No! Keep them up!" Logan shouted.

Corey did. He now had a Colt and a Glock aimed at him.

His handsome face appeared puzzled.

"What's wrong? What's this about?" he demanded.

"You carrying a weapon?" Logan asked Corey, flashing an angry glance Kelsey's way.

She frowned in return, indicating her own grasp on the Glock.

"I got me a little peashooter here, and it's legal! Totally legal. Hell, Logan, you know that. This is Texas!" Corey said.

"Get his gun," Logan told Kelsey.

She went over to Corey. He was carrying a Smith & Wesson, stuffed into his waistband.

As she took it, she saw his eyes on her, wide and disbelieving. "What's this all about, Kelsey?" He sounded hurt and confused.

She backed away from him. "Why were you following me?" she asked.

"I just left a bar up the street, over there, on the other side of Ripley's."

"The bars are all closed now," Logan said.

"Yes, it's closed. That's why I left!" Corey returned indignantly. "Smell my breath!"

He exhaled a rich plume of alcohol that

spoke for itself.

"So, why were you following me?" she asked again.

"Hell, I didn't know I was following you. I didn't intend to follow anyone. But if I *was* following you — or anyone else — it would be to make sure you got where you were going safely! Some bad things have been happening here, which you know! Can I put my hands down now?"

"Not yet. Kelsey, see what else's he's carrying," Logan said.

"Sorry," Kelsey murmured, patting him down.

"Best thrill I've had all night," he told her. "Except I'd like to know what gives you the right to do this."

"Probable cause!" Logan said, walking forward.

Kelsey turned to Logan. "He's got his wallet, Logan. His wallet, his keys and nothing more."

"Please, could I put my hands down?" Corey asked.

Logan nodded as Kelsey stepped away from him. Corey let his hands fall, shaking his shoulders, then rubbing his arms. "What the hell is the matter with you two?" he grumbled. "It's me! Corey. The coward who couldn't stay in 207!"

"It sure looked as if you were following Kelsey," Logan said.

"Well, I wasn't. And you can check out Mike's bar tomorrow. He'll tell you I'd been drinking, and that when he closed the place, the two of us were still shooting the breeze, and then I left. On foot. No driving under the influence. Can I have my gun back?"

Logan's jaw locked; Corey saw his expression.

"Fine," Corey said. "You keep it. For now. Check out my story with Mike tomorrow. Then you can give it back to me."

He probably expected Logan to return the gun after that, but Logan didn't.

"Great. You're being a good, responsible citizen," Logan said.

"So, now what? We stand here in the street?" Corey asked. "Ah, come on! I want to get back, I want to get some sleep. And you know, don't you, that I can complain about this?"

It was the wrong thing for him to have said.

"You go ahead and complain." Logan's voice was quiet. Deadly.

"I'm sorry!" Corey said. "I'm just tired."

"Then let's move on," Logan said.

"Walk ahead," Kelsey suggested.

He did. They followed at a distance.

"Why did you leave without me?" Logan whispered fiercely.

"You were sleeping so soundly, I didn't want to wake you."

"But we *know* stuff goes on around here!"

"I was armed, Logan, and I heard him. I was ready for him. Please, have some faith in me."

"We're talking about someone who can drug people in a heartbeat and lure them away, Kelsey."

"I was okay, Logan, really."

He paused, looking at her. "If I start to wander off alone, stop *me,* will you?"

Up ahead, Corey sensed or heard the friction. He came to a halt. "Guys? Do I get to keep walking? What's going on here?"

"Yes!" they both snapped.

"Keep walking," Logan added.

They reached the Longhorn together. The saloon was quiet; the bar was shut down for the night.

Kelsey moved ahead to use her passkey to let them in the front door. Corey Simmons had one, too, as did the other guests.

She moved back so he could go ahead of her.

"Now, that just doesn't feel right," Corey said. "Me, stepping in front of a lady."

"Don't think of me as a lady, Corey. Think

of me as —"

"Yeah, yeah. A U.S. Marshal."

He went in, but waited for her and Logan. "Am I allowed to go to bed? Wake up and have coffee and breakfast in the morning?"

Logan studied him and nodded. "Of course."

"But now I'm on your radar. You suspect me of something. God Almighty, all I did was walk back to my hotel after drinking. I was being a responsible citizen, Raintree."

"Yes, you were."

"You harassed me for nothing," Corey said angrily.

"Perhaps," Logan agreed.

"I didn't do anything!"

"I'm sorry. It *appeared* that you were following a young woman at three in the morning, and there's been bad stuff happening, as you pointed out yourself," Logan said.

"Corey," Kelsey told him quietly, "if you're waiting for an apology, you're not going to get one. You're probably totally innocent, but if Logan hadn't accosted you when he did, you would've met up with my Glock. Go to sleep, all right? What were you doing out so late drinking, anyway? I can see having a few beers, but shouldn't you be getting ready for the rodeo? Don't you want to be in top form?"

That made him even more indignant. "I'm a cowboy! The real deal. We know how to drink and smoke and cuss — and still be in top form!" Corey shook his head as if they'd never understand. "Besides, I wouldn't hurt a fly. Hell, I even wrangle a calf gently!"

"I'm sure you do," Kelsey said.

Corey muttered under his breath. He stared hard at Logan, and then Kelsey. "Well, good night, I guess."

"Good night, Corey." Kelsey spoke in a low voice, but Logan didn't respond.

He started up the stairs. Logan and Kelsey watched him as he approached his room — her old room — at the far end of the upstairs gallery. He walked to the railing and looked down at them.

"Going to bed now," he called softly.

"Sweet dreams!" Kelsey called back.

Logan just watched him. He'd make sure their door was locked that night. And bolted.

Corey Simmons waved, and moved away from the balcony. They heard a door open and then shut.

"Is it Corey?" Kelsey whispered.

"We don't know, do we?"

"Well, he wasn't going to drug me, Logan. He didn't have a thing on him, I guarantee you, no needles or anything of the kind."

"Maybe not. It still seemed suspicious."

"And his story could be completely true," Kelsey said.

"Could be. I'll check at Mike's bar tomorrow."

"All right. So. Now what?" Kelsey asked him.

He shrugged. "Now we go to Room 207. And we see what it offers tonight."

Logan lay awake. He'd stripped down to his jeans, but he'd been tempted to keep his boots on. He was glad he'd gotten the few hours of dream sleep he had, because he had a feeling he wouldn't be getting any more that night.

He wondered why. The bed was comfortable and the night quiet, and he liked having Kelsey beside him. He respected her. He knew she'd been good when she'd worked for the U.S. Marshal's Office; if she hadn't been, she wouldn't be here. Jackson Crow still seemed a somewhat elusive character, but Logan was convinced that he did know his business and that he'd chosen his people carefully.

At night like this, with her by his side, he could forget for a few seconds at a time what they both did. Her breathing was soft, the feel of her hair against his bare skin as soft as a whisper, and the warmth of her body touched him. He felt an urge to protect her — and to experience ease and comfort, as well.

The old-fashioned clock on the bedside table ticked the seconds away. The drapes were drawn, but they were gossamer and lace, much as they would've been years ago, when the Longhorn was built.

The room was quiet. That night's shadows seemed to be natural ones, caused by the glow of artificial light from beyond the delicate curtains.

He drew her closer to his chest, and felt the movement of her breath as she slept. She seemed at peace.

He remembered waking earlier and discovering that she was gone. He thought about Corey Simmons and reminded himself ruefully that, yes, she was capable, and yes, she'd been prepared if someone had accosted her.

But the strange image in his dream kept coming back to him. Shadows, and then a face, and a face he knew, not from life, but from the pictures he'd seen of her.

Sierra Monte. Appearing as a face in the shadows and crying out.

Help me. Help them. Help her.

Even if he was learning to forgive himself, he could never forget the words that first warned him Alana was in trouble. The call from a bitter man, asking him, "Do you know where your wife is, Ranger Raintree? I think she's calling you. I'm going to give you a chance because you seem to follow the law, Raintree. Instead of shooting people, you arrest them, and I respect that. You arrest people and they wind up on death row with a little extra time. So I'm giving *you* time to find your wife. They say that you're some kind of soul sucker or psychic. Anyway, I hear her calling. *Help me, help me, help me.*"

He felt sweat bead on his cold skin, and he fought hard not to relive the past. This was the present. And there'd be another dead woman if they couldn't stop what was happening.

He'd been lost in his own thoughts for a long time when he suddenly realized that Kelsey had stiffened beside him. She pushed herself into a sitting position.

"Kelsey?"

Her eyes were open; she stared straight ahead.

"Kelsey?" he said again.

But she didn't seem to hear him. She seemed to still be asleep and yet she was staring across the room.

To Logan, nothing had changed. The room looked exactly the same. The drapes seemed to float as if a breeze was coming in, although the windows were closed. However, this was no paranormal phenomenon — the air-conditioning ducts sat directly beneath them. The dressing table was to the left of the windows as he looked at them, and the wall was to the right, a bare corner. The second tall period chest broke up the expanse of wall; a swivel mirror sat atop it. When he looked at the mirror, it returned nothing but darkness and shadow and the wall across from it.

Kelsey was staring into the corner of the room where there was only wall.

"Kelsey." Once more, he said her name, and again, she didn't respond.

He watched her for a moment, wondering if he should wake her.

He decided to wait.

She slid over him, as if he weren't there at all, as if she were rising from an empty bed. Unmoving, she stood beside him, still staring at the corner.

He hesitated, just watching her.

She took a hesitant step toward the wall, then paused. Her face was creased with pain and empathy. He began to fear for her, but he fought the temptation to grab her and shake her. Was she sleepwalking? If so, it might be dangerous to startle her into wakefulness. And if not . . .

She took another step. And then she slowly reached out, leaning forward as she extended her arm, fingers dangling in the air as though she was trying to touch someone.

It was then that the subtle change came.

There were shadows in the room, yes. But now those shadows began to flicker, to dance, following the movements of objects or people that could not possibly exist.

One of the shadows moved from the wall. . . .

It was there, the way it had been on the film. So far, it hadn't taken any form, but seemed to be a mass.

Like birds. Like birds forming some kind of image, their wings flapping as they hovered.

He waited. There'd be a face. And the face wouldn't be that of Rose Langley; it would be Sierra Monte's.

He blinked and the shadows seemed to darken, to cover the walls and the furniture and drip down them, like shadow blood.

Kelsey took another step, and another, still reaching out.

Suddenly, he was afraid for her. He didn't know what he was seeing, and he certainly didn't know what she saw. He didn't want to wake her, but neither could he leave her as she was.

He rose from the bed and stood behind her, wanting to touch her, to draw her back.

She stepped forward, and he followed.

They moved toward the shadow, and again he waited, expecting the face to appear. . . .

But it didn't. Kelsey reached the shadow, and she was almost within it. He slid an arm around her shoulders, determined not to let her know that darkness alone.

No face appeared before him, but in his mind, he heard the plea again.

Help me. Help them. Help her.

He stepped back, drawing Kelsey with him. There were no birds in the room, but he thought he heard a flutter of wings. As he'd dreamed earlier, the shadow seemed to burst into dozens of shadowy black birds, wings flapping as they disarticulated the shape they'd been, and disappeared.

The room seemed lighter.

Logan stayed next to Kelsey. She looked confused, and her arm dropped to her side.

The room *was* lighter, he realized. Morning was coming, dispelling the last of the darkness as the sun began to rise in the eastern sky.

A shaft of bright light found its way to them. Kelsey turned and blinked and looked at him.

"Logan? Why are you standing there like that?" And then she seemed to notice her own position. "Why am *I* standing here like this?"

"What did you see?" he asked.

"See where?"

"In the corner."

She turned again, still half-asleep and confused. She seemed to wait for him to speak first, and then said, "That corner?"

"Kelsey, you were sleepwalking. Or something," he told her. "You don't remember anything? Anything at all?"

"No. Logan, it's so strange. You know I've seen what I assume to be an incident of residual haunting in here. I've described it to you as precisely as I can remember. But just now —" She broke off. "I don't remember. I don't remember a thing."

He looked at her anxiously, but her eyes were so lost, he didn't want her worrying anymore.

"Maybe it'll come to you," he said casually. "Anyway, we can try for another hour or so of sleep."

She touched his cheek. "Logan, I'm so sorry I woke you."

"I'm awake half the time on my own." With a broad smile, he swept out an arm. "After you, Marshal."

"More sleep." She yawned. "That'll work for me."

She walked to the bed and crawled over to the far side. He got in beside her, lying on his back, and she curled against him.

Once again, he lay awake. The room was bathed with light.

He remembered being with Alana one time, remembered her asking, "Why do ghosts only seem to appear at night?"

"Maybe they like subterfuge," he'd told her. But then he'd recalled things he'd seen in the light of day, and he thought about Zachary Chase walking the Alamo and the plaza, in both the mornings and the afternoons. He'd said to Alana, "I suppose ghosts are like the rest of us. Some like the daytime hours, others the night. Some are brazen and some are shy. Some don't want to be seen. And some want you to hear them."

"That *would* be the same as people, wouldn't it?" Alana had mused. "Some know how to ask others for what they need, and some don't. And will simply go without."

Alana was gone. Truly gone. Whether to the heaven of her Christian fathers, or the great hunting plain of the western tribal people, she had passed on. She had said her goodbyes and embraced whatever new world she'd entered.

Murder victims often did stay behind. At least until their murderers were apprehended. And if they never were . . .

He hoped that victims like Chelsea Martin and Tara Grissom never had to see what they'd become. He vowed silently that he'd do whatever he needed to find them rest.

He felt Kelsey shift beside him again; she'd gone back to sleep. He smiled slightly.

So easy for her . . .

He closed his eyes.

Logan had already gone downstairs when Kelsey finished showering and dressing. She was about to strap on her gun, grab her bag and head down after him when she paused. She could remember waking, with the two of them standing in the corner together, and she could remember what he'd told her. She could even remember that she'd been exhausted. And yet despite all that, it had been incredibly easy to go back to sleep.

She thought of the day she'd come up here after Corey Simmons had run screaming down the stairs.

That was when she'd seen it. Matt Meyer killing Rose Langley.

If only everything could play out so clearly before her mind's eye!

She held very still and waited, but the spectral image didn't come again. And yet as she stood there, she felt there'd been a subtle change in the room. It hadn't just occurred; it had happened since her room was invaded by the film crew.

She considered the film Sean had brought them. Had something else come into the room, something that had lain dormant and was now awakened? She didn't know. She waited for a few minutes, but nothing moved or changed. She'd opened the drapes. There wasn't even a shadow in the room.

She started to walk out, then paused again.

"I want to help you," she said. But although she waited another full minute, nothing happened. Nothing at all.

She went downstairs to find Logan sitting at one of the saloon tables. Ricky had just poured him a cup of coffee and seemed to be expecting her. "Morning, Miss Marshal," he said.

Kelsey laughed. "Good morning, Ricky. That makes it sound as if my last name is Marshal, but, hey, you call me whatever you like. Although Kelsey will do just fine."

"Coffee, Kelsey?"

"Please," she said.

As Ricky went off to bring another cup, Logan spoke softly. "He told me it's quiet this morning because their cowboy guests left early for a preliminary meet out at the stockyards. Apparently, our friend Corey was quiet and a bit grouchy."

"That's not exactly a surprise," Kelsey said.

Logan shrugged. "Sorry. I can't seem to trust him. Oh, wait. I'm not *supposed* to trust him. I'm law enforcement."

She didn't get a chance to reply. Sandy came hurrying over to the table, a newspaper clutched in her hands.

She set it down in front of them and pulled up a chair, saying, "Here's today's front page."

Jane's sketches, created from what remained of the faces she'd seen, the skull bones she'd recorded and measured, and her own intuition, stretched across the paper beneath a headline that read Have You Seen These Women?

Kelsey looked at Sandy. "This is great.

We're trying to identify these women," she said. "I'm glad the paper's being good about helping law enforcement."

Sandy tapped one of the faces. "I knew this girl!"

"Really?" Logan asked sharply. "Sandy, who is she?"

"I can't tell you her name. She stopped by and asked if I needed any more help. I didn't, but I thought about her after she left. I began to think maybe she'd been a runaway, and that I might have done something for her. And now . . . now she's one of the dead women, right?"

"Yes," Logan said. "Sandy, can you remember *anything* about her? When did she come by?"

"Three months ago, maybe four. I feel dreadful! If I'd done something, she might still be alive."

"There's no reason to feel that way. Try to think back. She didn't give you a first name?" Kelsey asked.

"Susan, Sally, Sarah . . . it began with *S*."

Ricky had returned with a cup of coffee for Kelsey. "Sherry," he said.

"Sherry," Kelsey repeated, turning her attention from Sandy to him. "Ricky, did you talk to her?"

"Yes, we talked for a while. She seemed at

least twenty-one. She was a nice girl, fascinated by the Longhorn, and I swear she knew more about the place than I did. Her last name started with an *H*."

Logan gave an encouraging nod.

"Boy, we're batting a thousand here, aren't we?" Ricky sighed. "Higgins, Highland, Hilbert — something like that. We were slow at the time. So much so, there were some nights Sandy and I were the only ones working. And we survived because of the local crowd." Ricky frowned and looked at Sandy. "We were getting a lot of newspaper people in then, Ted Murphy among them. He's always been a jerk, but he's a jerk who built up a bar tab and paid it, so we were actually glad to see him. You might want to check with Ted Murphy. I think he sat at the bar with her."

Sandy sniffed. "Murphy wanted to set up cameras and stuff in Room 207 and see what he could get. Unlike him, I don't want to sensationalize the place. Of course, other than his bar tab, which he's always paid, he wants everything for free."

Logan was on his feet. Kelsey swallowed a few sips of her coffee, preparing to leave. But Logan wasn't ready to go. He pointed at the paper again. "Sandy, Ricky, please take a good long look at all the women on this page. Do you recognize any of the others?"

They both stared at the paper, and then at Logan. "I'm sorry," Sandy said.

"Thank you." He nodded. "Who else was local around that time? Did you ever see Jeff Chasson or anyone from the film crew?"

"I don't think so," Sandy said.

"Think harder."

She chuckled. "If I'd seen that Jeff Chasson before, I'd know it, trust me."

"What about the other men? The director, Bernie Firestone, or Earl Candy?" Kelsey persisted.

Sandy shook her head.

"A lot of the rodeo guys were around back then. There was some kind of local rodeo thing going on," Ricky said.

"Corey Simmons?" Kelsey asked.

"He wasn't staying here," Sandy replied. "This is the first time I know of that he's gotten a room here. I think he was at one of the chain hotels, but he used to come to the bar at night with the others."

Ricky studied the paper, and his eyes seemed sad.

"As far as the film guys go, I might've seen both of 'em in here, maybe on a Saturday night — or another night when we had entertainment. It was busy — half the world was around." He looked back down at the paper again, and then up at Logan. "This girl . . . I think I've seen her, too, although it's hard to tell from sketches, you know?"

"You saw her here?" Kelsey asked. "At the Longhorn?"

"No. I saw her at church. The Congregational church, about five blocks behind the Ripley's side of the plaza." He shrugged. "It's my church. I like it there."

"Was she a regular?" Logan asked.

"No . . . but I saw her a few times. I'm sorry. I can't remember better than that, and I may be wrong."

"That's great, Ricky," Logan told him. He turned to Kelsey. "Ready to go?"

"Ready," she said. Waving goodbye to Sandy and Ricky, they left by the front door.

Logan was moving quickly that morning. He jogged to his car, pausing at the passenger side, as if remembering he should open the door for her — and then deciding that he shouldn't because they were partners and not a couple going out on a date. He slid into the driver's seat, and Kelsey got in beside him.

"The phones will probably be ringing off the walls — or they would if they were on walls these days," Logan said.

She agreed. They drove to the station

where they were greeted by the desk sergeant before they could head over to the task force.

"Ten calls already. Some are crackpots, telling me they envision the girls on a lily pad or some such thing, but I've got everything down. I'm assuming you want even the crackpots."

Logan thanked him. Kelsey saw that it was just eight when they entered the room, and so far, they were the only ones there. Logan got on the phone, returning the calls they'd received, while Kelsey studied the information they had on the unidentified women she'd given *J* names.

She brought out the files she'd been working with and read them through.

"Jane Doe, strangled, discovered by a rock pile, semihidden, near a pond in a public park. Jenny Doe, found in a trash dump, stabbed to death. Judy Doe, strangled, again found in a public park. Jodie Doe, dragged out of the river, drowned. Julie Doe — most recent victim until Vanessa Johnston, dead about a month — strangled and left in a pond, discovered by divers. Josie Doe, found in a compost heap, stabbed to death."

She compared the names to Jane's sketches and notes, and started adding her own comments.

Josie Doe was actually Sherry H-something, according to Sandy and Ricky. And the girl Ricky had seen at the Congregational church had been their drowning victim, Jodie Doe.

Logan covered the phone's mouthpiece. "This caller believes that our Jane Doe is his niece, Linsey Applewood. She's from New Orleans, and no one's heard from her since she disappeared out of her uptown apartment."

Kelsey nodded and included that information. Logan asked the man questions, making notes as he did, then took another call. He was quiet, listening.

He hung up and looked over at her. "That was Reverend Milton from the Congregational church. Ricky was right. She was there. She and her husband didn't stay long, because he didn't think the church focused enough on family issues. That they were too permissive and not following the dictates of the Bible." He hesitated. "Reverend Milton paid a courtesy call on the family, and the husband said his wife had left him and moved back to New Mexico."

"I guess she didn't move back."

Logan looked at her a moment longer. "The husband's an actor," he said. "And we met him yesterday."

CHAPTER 13

The fact that they knew that one of their victims had been married and never reported missing because she'd supposedly left her husband and moved back home did not make that husband guilty of murder. It did, however, make him a "person of interest."

Jackson accompanied Logan when he went to pay a call on the actor, Ned Bixby, who'd been portraying one of Santa Anna's men in the documentary.

He knew that he wished the "person of interest" had been Jeff Chasson, and he knew, too, that was wrong.

He just didn't like the man.

And Ned Bixby had seemed humble and nice enough.

They'd phoned his home and gotten no answer, and when they'd phoned the studio, they learned that Ned had called in sick that day.

They tried walking around the man's house, and they spoke to his neighbors. He'd gone out that morning, and they hadn't seen him since. He hadn't looked sick.

They visited Reverend Milton, who was sad to hear that the young wife, Cynthia Bixby, was dead. "She was a sweet, quiet little thing. Her husband seemed to answer for her all the time. I had a lovely talk with her once when she came to church alone. She was excited to be living in San Antonio — both of her parents have passed on and she was an only child — and she loved the area. She was big on the history of San Antonio. She had a teaching degree, but her husband wanted her to stay home and raise a family."

"Did they seem to be having any marital problems?" Logan asked.

"No — I mean, other than the fact that she looked to him every time she was about to speak. They sat together. They even held hands. Then he called one day and said thank you, but they wouldn't be back. He was looking for a church where he could be closer to God, and where he would know that he was on the right track to do God's will. As I said, I went by after that, just a courtesy call, and I found Ned alone at home. He told me Cynthia had woken up one morning and told him she didn't want to be married to him anymore, she needed to break away and live a life that was more fulfilling."

"Was he angry, bitter, nonchalant? How did he appear?" Jackson asked.

"A little bitter, I think. He said she didn't seem to understand that no matter what society dictated, God felt that a wife should stay home, raise children and honor her husband. She wanted to get out and see the world. He said he believed she wanted to drink and cavort and perhaps sleep with other men." He shrugged, tapping his fingers on the desk. "I thought maybe she just wanted to make her own choice about what to order off a menu."

Eventually, they left the reverend, and had an all-points bulletin sent out so they could find their "person of interest" and talk to him.

"We'll have to leave it to the patrols and get back. Kelsey's going to have her hands full at the station, even with Jane and Kat helping her and Jake returning. We're not getting anywhere here," Jackson said.

"I have an idea, one last try before we go back." Logan mentally consulted his notes. "Come on, one more drive. That's it."

Logan drove to the edge of the city. Jackson didn't question him until they pulled onto a quiet road.

"Is this where the pond is?" Jackson asked.

Logan nodded. "I gather it's down there. Divers were cleaning it out when she was found."

Jackson followed him as he walked across the park. Logan saw the man perched glumly on the rocks by the pond and motioned to Jackson, who walked around the other way.

Ned didn't look the same as he had the day before, when he'd been a member of Santa Anna's army. Gone were the beard and mustache, and the hat. He was clean-shaven, his hair dusky blond. He was young, too, no more than mid-twenties.

"Ned," Logan said, approaching him.

The young man looked up. Panic streaked across his face and he stood, obviously planning to run in the opposite direction.

"Don't. Don't run," Jackson said. He had his gun at the ready. Jackson wasn't going to shoot; Logan knew that. But Ned Bixby didn't.

Bixby turned to him again, then back to Jackson. Defeated, he looked at Logan.

"I didn't do it," he said. He lifted his hands and let them fall. "I was angry with her, yes. But I didn't kill her. I couldn't kill her. I could never raise a hand against her. I loved her."

"We just need to ask you some questions," Logan told him.

"Sure. Oh, yeah, sure. I believe that in the eyes of the world, I'll be judged quickly. Guilty," he said wearily. "Isn't it always supposed to be the husband?"

"Two out of six?" Jane asked Kelsey.

"I'm sure we'll have more once we piece together everything we've got," Kelsey said.

Kat cleared her throat. "We have a definite ID on our first victim, Jane Doe. I've just compared the dental records, and the young woman is Linsey Applewood, out of New Orleans. She'd lived there since graduation from Tulane. She didn't have a roommate, and she didn't say a word to anyone, just packed up one morning and left. But she must've intended to come back. The apartment was full of her belongings and the landlord finally put them up for auction."

"What was her major at Tulane?" Kelsey asked.

"History."

Kelsey drummed her fingers and started shuffling through the pile of messages they'd received. She found the one from

Linsey Applewood's uncle. "Kat, do you have a number for the landlord?"

"Right here," Kat said. "Mr. Dillard. I'll dial it, just pick up the line."

"Thanks."

The landlord seemed to be a nice man who was truly disheartened to hear that Linsey was dead. Kelsey let him talk and consoled him the best she could. Then she said, "It sounds as if you knew her fairly well. I'm so sorry, Mr. Dillard. Perhaps you could tell me more about her. What did she like and dislike? What were her hobbies?"

Dillard told her that Linsey Applewood had loved animals and spent many an afternoon at the zoo. She enjoyed jazz music, and kept talking about buying a saxophone. She was cheerful and sweet. She dated, but hadn't been serious about anyone, and she liked to spend time with her girlfriends.

"Those girls, they just cracked me up!" Dillard said with a sad sigh. "They were so silly. They had these Ouija Fridays and they'd come over and drink wine and eat cheese and 'conjure the spirits.'"

"Really? Do you have any information on the other girls, Mr. Dillard?" Kelsey asked.

"Bijou went to Europe before Linsey left," Dillard said, "and I don't know her last name, or even if that was her real first name. I can get you a number for Dottie Hicks. She's still in town. In fact, she bought one of the tea-reading places down in the Quarter. Give me a minute — I'll be right back."

Kelsey waited. He returned with a number for Dottie, and when she'd ended the call, Kelsey dialed it. A young woman's voice answered. "Tender Tea Leaves."

Kelsey asked to speak with Dottie and found out she already was. Dottie hadn't heard about Linsey, but although she was dismayed, she wasn't surprised. "Oh! Oh, no! I was afraid of something like this, but I hoped . . . I mean, when she just disappeared . . . Oh, no, this is horrible."

"I'm so sorry," Kelsey said. "I spoke with Mr. Dillard. He said you and Linsey and another girl were fond of the Ouija board and that you had parties every Friday night."

"Let me close the door." Dottie was gone for a second and came back. "Honestly, we try to read people rather than leaves. But I don't want the customers hearing that. Linsey was . . . well, she wanted it all to be real. She wanted to see the future, and she believed we could contact ghosts. One night, the planchette went flying right off the board and the lights began to flicker. I swear, it's true."

"What ghost were you contacting?" Kelsey asked.

"I don't remember. A pirate, someone in Lafitte's crew, or . . . I don't remember. But Linsey started thinking she knew things. She was always trying to get me to go to Texas with her —"

"San Antonio?"

"Yes. She wanted to stay at an old inn there."

"The Longhorn?"

"I'm not sure. It might have been."

Kelsey was on the phone a while longer, making notes. When she hung up, Jane handed her the sketch of the girl Sandy had recognized. "Sheryl Higgins. Drifting waitress, pothead and self-proclaimed palm reader. Her last known residence was Houston. She was recognized by the truck driver who gave her a ride out here. He happened to be back in San Antonio and saw this morning's paper."

"So, Sandy and Ricky were right," Kelsey said. "Did you say palm reader?"

Jane gave her another piece of paper. "Truck driver's number. His name is Billie Joe Glover. He's expecting your call, and he'll come in if we wish."

"Thanks." Kelsey made her next call.

Billie Joe was shocked to hear about Sherry. She'd been cheerful, he said, even if she didn't seem to have a lick of common sense.

"She told me she could sling hash, and if you could sling hash and pop the top on a beer, you could work anywhere in the country. She sang while we were driving, and she had a right pretty voice. Real sweet girl. I'd look for her every now and then when I came back to San Antonio — but hell, I didn't know she was missing. She just wanted to travel and see the sights. And she wanted to live near the Alamo. It called to her, that's what she told me."

Jake Mallory arrived as Kelsey hung up after talking with Billie Joe, the trucker. Jake had flown back to the D.C. area, but returned when Jackson called him. He was ready to pitch in by manning the phones and interviewing anyone who claimed to have information.

Impulsively, Kelsey stood. "Jake, here's the chart, my notes, the old information and the new information. I'll be back soon."

She smiled at the others and headed out, not sure why she didn't want to say that she was going back to the Longhorn.

She simply felt the urge to return to Room 207.

They'd wondered if the murdered women

had some kind of belief in the paranormal. And so far, they were learning that their now-identified victims did. Linsey's planchette had flown when she'd been trying to contact a pirate who'd sailed with Lafitte. That was where the story of the Galveston diamond had begun — with pirates. Of course, trying to contact a pirate didn't necessarily connect to the diamond showing up in San Antonio, but it might. The legend wasn't discussed in history books, but it was certainly well-known.

Kelsey considered the facts they'd already accumulated.

The women had died at different times, and so far, they did have an interest in the occult and in the Alamo. They'd been drugged, and although the highest percentage of what they'd been given was a pain-killer, it had also included a "roofie," a drug that made them pliable, a date-rape drug. It was also a drug under the influence of which they might have said or done anything.

Logan was on the right track; she was sure of it. The killer was looking for the Galveston diamond. His killing wasn't as random as it seemed. He was luring women to a place where he could drug and seize them.

He wanted them to contact Rose Langley in the spirit world and have her tell them what she'd done with the Galveston diamond.

Kelsey asked the desk sergeant for a car. She drove back to the inn and entered through the main doors, since there was really no way to slip up to any of the rooms. Sandy had told her once that outlaws had shimmied down the drainage pipes and leaped to the trees from the windows, but she didn't think that would work so well today. Most of the trees were gone, and the drainage pipes were made of far cheaper and more fragile material.

When she came inside, the place was quiet. The lunch crowd had left, and it was too early for the cocktail group. Ricky was behind the bar wiping glasses, and Corey Simmons, looking worn and groggy, sat on a bar stool.

He swung around when she entered. "Well, if it isn't the beautiful Marshal. Welcome, ma'am, yes, welcome. Did you come back to have a drink with me? How'd you lose the long, tall Texas Ranger? Doesn't matter. Good riddance."

He was drunk, she quickly ascertained, and it looked like too much alcohol brought out a nasty streak.

"What are you doing back here, Corey?"

He scowled. "I lost. What do you think? I lost — and it's your fault!"

"Corey, if you lost, it was because you decided to stay out drinking all night," Kelsey told him calmly. "It's not my fault you didn't get to bed until after three!"

He wagged a finger at her. "It was past three-thirty when I hit the hay. See? It *was* your fault!"

"Oh, Corey. I don't think so. I'm sorry — are you out of the competition altogether?"

"No," he admitted. "I'm still in the bull riding."

"Well, that's good. Sober up and get some sleep, and you'll do fine."

"Yeah, fine. But why don't you come and have a drink with me first?"

"Because I have to get back to work. I just have to grab a few things from my room," Kelsey said.

"One drink?" he wheedled. "Just one —"

"Corey," Ricky broke in, walking over to him. "Kelsey is working on murder cases. Leave her alone, okay?"

Corey raised his beer mug. "Oh, yeah. She thinks I'm a murderer. But I'm not, and she knows it now, don't you, Kelsey? Word's out that they identy-fied one of those girls, and it was the husband that done it, and he's one of those actor types. He was probably a sicko right from the get-go. Her murder case is solved, even if Kelsey and that loco Ranger wanted to make *me* out to be the killer. One drink. Come on, please?"

"I think you should start worrying about the bull. I'm not having a drink, Corey, thank you," she said, her words polite but firm. She hurried on up the stairs and felt his eyes following her all the way. A chill raced down her spine. This time, however, she didn't have to wonder about the reason for it. Corey Simmons was angry with her.

She ignored him and closed the door to her room. She looked around, but everything seemed perfectly normal. Setting down her purse, she sat on the bed. Logan had found her in the corner of the room, staring at it. She'd been sleepwalking; she'd never done anything like that before.

But she wasn't afraid of ghosts. She needed to stop, and wait, let her mind go, and hope they'd come to her, not in her dreams but now, when she was awake. When she could understand.

From below, she heard the distant noise of the door opening and closing, and the occasional clicking of glass against glass. Someone had come in to play the old piano, and she could hear the soft and plaintive strains.

The drapes lifted in the false breeze of the air conditioner. Dust motes drifted on the air.

After a while, she lay down on the bed. She closed her eyes, then opened them; she was overtired and didn't want to fall asleep. But her eyes fell shut again. She forced them open, and this time, when she did, she saw the shadow in the corner.

A young woman. She wore a pretty nightgown, and her hair was tied back at her neck with a ribbon.

Sierra Monte.

"Help me," she said plaintively.

Kelsey rose to go to her. She moved slowly, afraid the apparition would vanish if she moved too fast.

As she came closer, she saw that a second shadow was joining the first.

Kelsey paused. Those who were decent in life, she told herself, would be decent in death. But what about those who *hadn't* been so decent?

Be careful!

She didn't know if she spoke the words out loud or in her mind. For a moment, she was seized with fear — fear that she'd come back to urge something evil out of hiding.

But Sierra turned slightly and smiled. The second shadow behind her began to take shape, and Kelsey saw that it was the woman she knew from the scene replayed before her twice — it was Rose Langley.

The women had come to her together.

"Tell me what I can do," Kelsey begged. "We're trying, I swear, we're trying. Can you help us? We need your help, don't you see?"

Rose set a gentle hand on Sierra's shoulder. "It's the stone," she said. "They always want the stone."

"Where *is* the stone?" Kelsey asked.

"I . . . don't know," Rose said. "But it was cursed. They said it was cursed. And so it was, and so it is today."

"Sierra, did you find the stone?" Kelsey asked next.

"They thought I could." She shook her head. "It was my fault. I pretended I knew so much, that I could reach out and touch the dead. And now, I *am* the dead." Her melodic, thin-as-air voice seemed to break.

"Who, Sierra, who?"

"I don't know! I remember sleeping, but I don't remember waking. . . . I don't even remember dying."

Like the others, she'd been drugged.

"I will help you, I swear. I'll do anything I

can," Kelsey promised.

"No . . . no . . . you mustn't! They know about you. They'll slip in when you're sleeping. They'll come, and you won't remember. If you can't find the stone, you'll fail them, and you won't remember what you said or how you died, and you'll wake up and you'll be with us."

There was a sudden, loud knock at her door. Kelsey jumped; her apparitions vanished not in a flurry of wings, but as if they'd never been.

"Kelsey? Kelsey! Are you all right?"

It was Sandy. Kelsey cursed her bad luck or her foolishness. She should've tracked down Sandy, told her she was there, explained that she was working.

She gritted her teeth, not wanting to look angry when she opened the door. She managed a smile.

Sandy stared at her for a minute. "I'm sorry, but Ricky just told me Corey was being a pest and you ran up here. You're not usually back in the middle of the day, and there's so much going on. . . . I was just worried."

"That's sweet of you, Sandy. But I'm fine. I had a few things to do that I needed a bit of privacy to accomplish, so I came back here and holed up."

Sandy still looked worried, and Kelsey gave her a hug. "I swear, I'm fine."

"Okay, then. I'll leave you to your own devices."

As Sandy backed away from the door, Kelsey called out, "Oh, Sandy, thank you!"

"For what?"

"You helped us tremendously. We identified at least one of the girls with information from you and Ricky."

"That's great," Sandy said, then sighed loudly. "Oh, Kelsey! Why couldn't you have been a runway model? Then I wouldn't have had to worry about you all the time."

Kelsey laughed. "For one thing, I'm not that thin. For another — well, then you'd *really* have to worry about me. I'm a klutz, and if they'd put me in high heels, I'd have broken my neck on the runway. So, kid, I'm fine, I swear it!"

Sandy nodded and started to go, but came rushing back, obviously flustered. "Kelsey, he's down there!"

"Who is?"

"Him, *him!* That hunk-a-hunk Jeff Chasson!"

"Well, go and play hostess."

"He came back here!" Sandy said in awe.

"You're the best-looking innkeep in town. Go on! Buy him a drink!"

Kelsey finally got Sandy to go downstairs. She looked around the room, but whatever momentum she'd found was gone.

"Why can't we figure out how to do dial-a-ghost?" she muttered to herself.

She sat on the bed again, gazing at the corner. A moment later, she stood and walked over to the wall, then went out to the hallway and studied the rooms and the doors. It didn't tell her anything. She came back in, staring at the wall again. The longer she did, the more convinced she became that she was right.

Now she had a plan.

And now, all she had to do was work out how to implement it.

Ned Bixby cried when they showed him the photo of his deceased wife. He laid his head on his arms and cried.

He was oblivious to the other women; he barely glanced at the photographs of the dead.

But he cried hard tears over his wife.

Despite that, Jackson and Logan took turns questioning him. He didn't want a lawyer. No matter what they said, he denied killing his wife.

Jackson spoke very softly to him. "Ned, you've got to help us out. We're looking at a series of killings here. All the bodies were found in similar condition — decomposed, as you can see. I want things to go easy for you, but this is murder. They'll search your house, Ned. They have probable cause because of what witnesses have said about your marriage, because you claimed that your wife had gone to New Mexico when it turned out she was dead. They'll connect *all* the killings to you, and this is Texas, Ned. There's a death penalty in this state."

"I didn't kill those women," he said.

"Just your wife?" Logan asked him.

"No, no!" he shouted.

"Tell us something to give the district attorney," Jackson said. "We don't quite understand what —"

"I didn't kill my wife or anyone!" Ned exploded before Jackson could finish.

"If you're guilty," Logan began. "We —"

Ned went very still. He wiped his eyes and cheeks, and stared at them. "I deserve to die," he said suddenly.

"Ned, we need to know what happened."

"It was me! I did it. I killed them. I killed them all," he burst out. "Now I'm done. Arrest me. And I want an attorney."

Ten minutes later, Ned Bixby was arraigned. Now, they had to wait until he had an attorney before they could talk to him again, although a search warrant was being issued for his house and car. Logan reminded the D.A. that the document had to be carefully worded; they didn't want to discover that Ned Bixby had a toolshed or other extra building that, if not included, couldn't be searched. They were looking specifically for a knife and for drugs and drug paraphernalia and, Logan added, for any reference to the Alamo, the Longhorn Saloon or the Galveston diamond.

The D.A. listened to Logan and then sighed. "Half the people in Texas and ninety percent of San Antonio have books that refer to the Alamo."

"We'll weed through it all," Jackson said. "Please. It's important."

At last, the two of them returned to the task force office. Jake, Jane and Kat were there, taking calls and making notes.

"Where's Kelsey?" Logan asked, concerned.

Jane raised her head from a file she'd been attaching notes to. "She left. Actually, a while ago now."

"She didn't say where she was going?"

"No, but she sounded like she wouldn't be long," Jake said. He frowned. "Sorry, this place is a madhouse. We've got a bunch of calls from palm readers who want to visit the corpses and touch their hands."

Nodding, Logan tried to appear calm as he slid his cell phone from his pocket.

What was it with the woman?

Still, she had a firearm and was trained to use it. She knew what she was doing.

He was almost certain that she wasn't going to answer her phone.

But she did.

"O'Brien."

"Kelsey, where the hell are you?"

"I'm at the Longhorn. Logan, can you come here?"

She was speaking in a hushed voice.

"You never came back to the station. Kelsey, we picked up Cynthia Bixby's husband. He confessed to all the murders."

"And you believe him?" she asked.

"No," he admitted.

"I know I should be there, but . . . can you come here?"

"Yes."

Logan closed his phone. "She's at the Longhorn and she asked me to meet her there," he told Jackson. "I'll call in."

As he started out, Kat called him back.

"Logan, she was talking to friends of our victims. You should know that Linsey Applewood was big into the occult. Kelsey also talked to the truck driver who drove Sheryl Higgins to San Antonio. Apparently, she made spare money as a palm reader."

"Thanks," Logan said.

"We're still weeding through tips," Jake assured him.

Logan thanked him, then headed out. He was tempted to run his siren, but he didn't allow himself to do it.

Help me, help them, help her.

He'd just talked to Kelsey on the phone, and she was fine.

The saloon had filled up when he arrived. Cowboys crowded the bar stools and the tables. He noted that Ted Murphy was there and that the film crew had returned. Absent was Corey Simmons.

He made his way to the bar, where Bernie Firestone hailed him. "You have one of my actors," he said glumly.

"His wife is among the dead, I'm afraid," Logan said.

"He didn't kill her, I'm sure of it. Ah, well, thank God I'm not the producer on this thing. I can take a day or two to drink away my frustration!" Bernie lifted his glass. "Join me?"

"Maybe in a bit."

Murphy was behaving himself, eyeing Logan but not talking and not trying to entice him into a drink, either.

Ricky, rushing about with a tray of filled glasses, finally noticed him.

"Hey, Logan. You look like you need a cool one."

"Thanks, but I'm looking for Kelsey."

"She's in her room."

He started to leave, then hesitated. "Where's Corey Simmons? Doesn't he usually hang out here around this time?"

"He was going to pass out," Ricky said. "I convinced him to go to bed."

Logan dashed up the stairs. As he reached the gallery, his heart quickened when he heard a sharp cry from the area of Kelsey's room.

Room 207.

And Corey Simmons was up here, too.

He ran the rest of the way to her room and tried the door. It was locked. He stepped back to slam his shoulder against it to break in. As he did, Kelsey opened the door. She was covered with white dust, but she stepped back quickly, letting him in.

He looked around the room. Plaster dust was everywhere; part of the wall had been torn out.

Logan turned back to Kelsey. She gave him a wistful smile of both triumph and sadness. "I've found Sierra Monte," she said quietly, and pointed to the gaping hole in the wall.

CHAPTER 14

Kelsey took Logan over to the wall she'd begun to dismantle and the corpse that had been lodged there.

Tearing the wall apart hadn't been easy.

Using only her pocketknife, she'd systematically cut through the drywall and old lathing. She'd done her best to keep the damage down, knowing that this was her friend's place of business, and yet she'd been absolutely convinced the woman's ghost clung to that area for a reason.

Logan closed the door and locked it.

"Did you just cry out?" he asked.

"Yes, I didn't mean to, but when I found the body . . ."

He leaned against the door, giving her a chance to explain.

"I know it looks crazy, but the logic is really simple. Think about it. The blood had been all over the room, nowhere else. Sierra Monte was definitely killed here, but the team working the case believed the body had been taken elsewhere because she wasn't here. The inn was being renovated at the time. Most of the rooms had just been redone, so no one would notice this particular section of wall. . . . And while Sandy would've repainted, there was no reason for her to dig into walls that had recently been repaired when she had so much else to work on. It's all logical," Kelsey insisted.

He was watching her, his expression skeptical.

She sighed. "Okay, screw logic. The shadow on the film was in this area, and today I saw them, Logan. I saw them both. Sierra and Rose. They were hovering in this corner."

Logan walked toward her, still silent. He came to stand directly in front of her, and then he reached down, planting an enormous kiss on her lips.

"You're brilliant!" he told her.

She smiled. "And now you're covered in plaster, too. I've got a disaster going here, but I didn't want to make too much noise and I didn't want to ask Sandy's permission. . . . We have to call in forensics, though. I'm not sure of my sanity in this — Sandy has so much to deal with right now — but this is a murdered woman, someone who was flesh and blood."

Logan pulled out his phone. "I'm calling Jackson. He'll do this from the FBI end, and he can bring in Kat and he'll let me call the shots on the crime scene, though God knows we never seem to get anything from the bodies. Still, there's always that one time a killer makes a mistake, and we could get a hair or a fiber or *something*. Maybe even DNA that matches DNA in the system."

As he spoke to Jackson Crow, he inspected the wall she'd dug out, using nothing but that small knife. She'd ripped through dry-wall and lathe, slowly and methodically. It had been worth it.

Within twenty minutes, Jackson Crow had arrived with Kat Sokolov. He inspected Kelsey's finding, as well, and stood silently for a few minutes, considering the situation. "We need crime-scene people here," he said flatly.

"I need her out of the wall," Kat told them.

"But Ted Murphy is down there, not to mention the fact that the place is jumping," Kelsey said.

"Murphy is going to be a sensationalist no matter what we do." Logan shrugged. "Nothing's going to change that. Kelsey, do you want to tell Sandy what you found? We don't have to clear the bar — there's no point. But we have to have our people in here. We can rope off the upstairs, and only overnight guests can have access to the gallery."

"What do we tell the customers down there?" Kelsey asked.

"Nothing," Logan said wearily, wiping plaster dust from his cheek. "We'll get a spokesperson on it. Other than that, they can guess all they want."

Kelsey walked over to the door.

"Kelsey." Logan stopped her.

He sent her a wry grin. "If you go downstairs looking like that, people are going to think *you're* the ghost of Room 207."

"Oh. Yes." Kelsey nodded, and headed into the bathroom. She tried washing her face and shaking out her hair. Kat came in behind her and began patting at her clothes.

Kelsey studied herself in the mirror. She and Kat seemed to have gotten off most of the paint chips and plaster dust, and she looked more or less presentable. She brushed her hair and put on some fresh makeup, then squared her shoulders.

"Ready."

It was with an almost unbearable pain in her heart that she went down and sought out Sandy. She was going to tell the friend who'd given her hospitality that she might be about to destroy not just her business but her dream. However, the Longhorn had survived before. It would do so again.

She saw Ted Murphy, ostensibly chatting with friends at one of the tables. He'd stay away from Logan, she was sure.

But he watched. He watched all the time.

She saw Bernie Firestone and Earl Candy at the bar, and they both hailed her with friendly waves. She waved back, but kept searching the crowd for Sandy.

She found her sitting, enthralled, with Jeff Chasson.

Kelsey wondered why she felt so protective of her. Sandy was very pretty, and there was no reason she couldn't attract the sexiest man in any crowd. But Kelsey didn't believe that anything about Jeff Chasson was real. Why he would want more information on the grisly doings at the Longhorn, she didn't know. But she felt he was a worm, trying to wriggle his way into something.

And now, of course, he was there when she needed to speak with Sandy alone. As she walked over to the table, Chasson looked up at her and stood, offering her a strange smile. She had the feeling that he was always on the lookout for whatever he might be able to use. Or another conquest, perhaps . . .

"Marshal O'Brien. Have a drink with us?"

"I'm so sorry," Kelsey replied. "But I've come to steal Sandy away from you for a few minutes. Sandy, please?"

Sandy frowned at her. "Kelsey, Jeff and I were sharing some experiences. Can't you just talk to us both?"

"I *really* need to speak with you alone," Kelsey said.

Sandy got to her feet, giving Kelsey a look of confused anger.

"Please," Kelsey murmured.

As she gripped Sandy's arm to lead her toward the stairs, Sandy pulled back. "What are you doing to me? He's the best possibility I've had of sex with anything decent in, like, forever!"

"Sandy, you have to give me a minute."

But Sandy wrenched her arm away. "What? What? I know your work's all-important, and that you're big-shot law stuff but, Kelsey, come on! We lower mortals need lives, too!"

That startled Kelsey and angered her. "Sandy, I found Sierra Monte!" she snapped.

"What?" Sandy's cry and the white look of pure horror on her face made Kelsey feel

instantly sorry and apologetic that she'd blurted out the words.

"She was in the wall," Kelsey said.

"You . . . *you* . . . found her? In the wall? My wall?" Sandy asked. "No, oh, no. No, no, no. Not all this again. Oh, my God. Oh, Lord."

Kelsey was afraid Sandy was going to faint. But when she tried to help her, Sandy shook her off and stood on her own. "Why?" she asked, and it sounded as if she was going to cry. "Why were you digging in my wall?"

"It was logical, Sandy, and she was there."

"I didn't know for sure she was dead . . . and if I didn't know, I didn't have to care. Oh, Kelsey!"

"Sandy, please! The girl was brutally murdered."

"I know, and I'm sorry, and . . . and now —"

"We're going to handle it as carefully as possible. All we have to do is block off the gallery, so our crime-scene people can make it through. We have to get her out of the wall, Sandy."

Sandy stared at her blankly.

"You don't have to clear out the bar, and you don't have to do anything tonight. I'll bring them in discreetly. Overnight guests will still be able to get to their rooms," Kelsey said quickly.

Sandy seemed to be letting it all sink in. "No. No. I'll take care of this. You go ahead and call the people you have to call."

Sandy escaped her and headed for the bar. She crawled up on one of the stools with the help of the surprised cowboy she'd rather rudely unseated.

"Everyone, please!" she shouted.

The piano player stopped playing. People were still talking, but Sandy raised her voice and shouted again. "Please! I have a very important announcement!"

At last, the room went silent.

Sandy pointed toward Kelsey. "My very good friend Marshal Kelsey O'Brien has done the Longhorn, and the city of San Antonio, a great service. God knows how she figured it out, but Kelsey has just solved a mystery that's plagued our city's finest — she's discovered the remains of Sierra Monte, the young lady who disappeared from Room 207 about a year ago. And she found her right in Room 207."

A shocked murmur rose and grew louder; everyone looked over at her.

"My God!" someone shouted. Ted Murphy, of course.

"But!" Sandy roared above the crowd,

quieting it again. "I've been informed that we don't need to close down. Forensics people are coming. We need to give them free passage and easy access to the stairs, so no one up in the gallery, okay? Unless you're a guest and you want to go to bed. I don't know anything more at this time, and I don't think even Marshal O'Brien does. I beg you, however, to stay, to drink, to play. Tragedy struck the Longhorn — that's something we already knew. But the saloon is still an incredible piece of history, as is our beloved Alamo. Thank you, my friends."

Sandy accepted the cowboy's help in stepping down from the bar stool. She stared across at Kelsey, and with a nod of thanks, Kelsey hurried back up the stairs.

The forensics people were going to be at it through the night, surveying the wall and determining how best to remove the corpse. Kat planned to stay and supervise, and after a while, it seemed that there was nothing left for Kelsey to do but leave.

Logan told her, "Pack up a few things. There's no sleeping here tonight."

"I know this puts Sandy in a bad position," she said, "but there was nothing I could do. I still feel as if I pushed her right over the edge. Ted Murphy is downstairs.

It'll take a crane to get him out of the place. It's like death has become a spectator sport."

Logan mulled that over. Sadly, throughout history, death sometimes *had* been a spectator sport.

"Kelsey, you did the right thing. You realized Sierra had to be in the wall. You dug her out. What else could you do?"

She shook her head. "This turns everything around. Now we have to find the previous owner, and we have to find everyone who worked here at the time."

Kat walked over to them and said, "The previous owner is dead. There was an article about him — written by none other than Ted Murphy — several months ago. The guy was elderly and he lived in Austin, where he died of some kind of flu. He didn't spend much time at the Longhorn to begin with, and he would've been questioned back then, so whatever he had to say will be in the police reports. But he wasn't here when the blood was discovered by one of the maids. He was in Austin. He'd been there for weeks before it happened."

"Sandy will know who was working here," Kelsey said. She turned to Logan. "I'm really tired," she murmured.

He didn't put an arm around her the way

he wanted to; they were in a professional situation. But he wanted to get away from this place as fast as he could. With Kelsey.

And he was going to be the head of this unit?

Maybe *unit* was the key word. People who worked together, who had one another's backs. Because, before he could ponder the situation, Kat spoke up.

"You two get out of here tonight," she said. "I have this covered. Go to your house and get some sleep."

"Thanks," he said gratefully.

"I'm the one whose job it is to deal with the mortal remains." She laid a reassuring hand on his arm. "You have to catch the living who commit the crimes."

He smiled at her and took Kelsey's hand, and he no longer cared who saw him. "Come on," he said. "We're leaving."

"I think I'm ready to exit by the fire escape."

"Aw, come on, tough girl. I know you can handle it."

And, of course, she did. They went downstairs, and when people crowded around them, Kelsey was the perfect professional.

"There's nothing to say," she explained. "Remember, we *assume* it's the body of Sierra Monte. We won't know any more

347

until the medical examiner has examined the remains, and that won't be for a while."

"Why wasn't that body found before?" Ted Murphy demanded.

"I guess no one looked in the wall," Kelsey said coldly. "And beyond that, Mr. Murphy, I have no idea. I'm just in from Florida. And, as we all know, this is Texas!"

Murphy was going to question her again. But, somehow, the man no longer ignited Logan's temper as he had earlier.

"There's nothing else to tell anyone tonight. Please have some respect!" he said loudly. "This was a living person who died tragically. Please give the people working for the state and the country time to get in there and do their jobs."

He walked through the crowd, drawing Kelsey along with him.

They were in the car before she turned to him and said, "What the hell is wrong with people? With all of us? Why isn't there more concern about the fact that someone *died?*"

He was quiet for a minute. "I don't think the issue is that people don't care. We're all horrified to hear about an earthquake or some other disaster that killed thousands. But we can't help taking it more personally when someone close to us dies. Besides, the news media told everyone a year ago that

Sierra Monte had to be dead. So, our mutual grief over a young woman who had her life cut short has already been felt. Now, it's more of a curiosity."

Kelsey sat back. "I think I care too much," she said.

"If you didn't, you wouldn't be who you are, and you wouldn't be so good at what you do."

She looked at him and smiled slowly. "Thank you. I just feel bad that I betrayed a friend."

"Kelsey, I'm sorry, but murder takes precedence, and Sandy will have to realize that. Besides, it didn't appear that we harmed her business any."

She seemed to agree with that.

When they reached his house, he suggested she might need food, but she said she wasn't interested. He poured her a glass of wine, and she drank it, and afterward, she walked into the bedroom. He left her alone until his own sense of exhaustion took hold. He went in as quietly as he could, doffed his clothes and slid into his side of the bed. A few minutes later, she moved against him; he was surprised.

When they'd made love, he thought maybe it had been an affirmation of what was good about life, and he was glad to sleep with her through the night. Maybe they were both too tired to dream, or have visions, or nightmares. He remembered holding her, stroking her hair — and then his alarm rang, announcing that it was seven-thirty.

He rose and showered and dressed, while Kelsey was still deeply asleep. He sat by her and tousled her hair, trying to wake her gently. He was worried; he hadn't thought she'd be quite so upset by yesterday's events. Her guilt about Sandy, in particular, seemed to distress her. He hoped she'd gotten over it — or at least forgiven herself.

She opened her eyes and groaned. "This was supposed to be vacation time while I decided about taking the job," she said. She closed her eyes again and opened just one. "You didn't happen to make coffee yet, did you?"

"I did. But you don't get any until you've had your shower," he told her.

That brought her to her feet, pushing him out of the way and flying for the bathroom. He returned to the kitchen; she was soon there, neatly and professional dressed in one of her dark pantsuits.

"Where are we going? The office?" she asked.

He nodded. "We'll keep getting information. Ned Bixby confessed to all the murders, but we know he was lying. I don't think he murdered his wife — that's in his mind. He believes it's his fault she's dead and he wants to be punished."

Kelsey got cream from the refrigerator for their coffee. "But . . . I thought you agreed the drowning victim — Cynthia Bixby — was the victim of a different killer."

"When we learned who she was and what her marriage had been like, I wanted to believe we'd found the killer. But when we sat with Bixby . . . Kelsey, he cried so hard over the pictures of his wife. I just don't know."

"You don't think he killed her in a fit of passion and anger? Or that maybe he *is* crazy and did kill the others?"

Logan shook his head. "I just don't feel it," he said.

Kelsey hesitated, running her fingers over the rim of her coffee cup. "Logan, I went back to the Longhorn yesterday because I'd talked to various people who helped us get IDs on two of the dead women. Both of them thought they had psychic powers. Whether they did or not, we'll never truly know. But I think you're right about the diamond. In whatever way this man is managing to drug the women, making them pliable — just as in a date-rape situation.

But he doesn't want to rape anyone. He wants to find someone who'll communicate with Rose Langley and have her reveal where the Galveston diamond is hidden. But . . ."

"But?"

"Rose doesn't know."

Logan studied her. "You asked Rose's spirit, I take it?"

She nodded. "I wonder so much about what we *see*, and what we can't see. I thought maybe she'd gone on, because what I saw in visions or dreams was what everyone calls a residual haunting. But yesterday, she was there. And what's . . . nice, I suppose, is that Rose and Sierra know each other. And maybe they're in that room together because of the diamond. Or . . . who knows why Rose is still here? Whether he really died fighting for Texas or not, Matt Meyer is certainly long gone."

"But Sierra's killer isn't — and men are apparently still prepared to kill for a diamond."

"We're back to square one," Kelsey said.

"No, we're not. Now we can safely assume that Sierra was a victim, just like the others. And even as a ghost or spirit or residing soul, she can't tell us anything because she must have been taken in the same way. The roofie in the drug cocktail keeps the women from remembering. But it does help to know that Sierra obviously met the same fate. Because we can start looking harder and closer at the people who were involved with the Longhorn at the time she died. Okay, not the old owner since he was never around and he's dead, anyway."

"We'll have to bring Sandy in and query her on everything from the day she made her down payment on the place."

"I'm afraid so," Logan said. "Let's get on in."

They'd started the drive to the station, both thoughtful, when Kelsey suddenly turned to him. "Why don't we stop at the Alamo for a bit? I want to see if Zachary Chase is around."

"All right," he said slowly.

As he parked, he noticed that there was a Ranger car in front of the Longhorn farther down the street.

Well, maybe Jackson had decided that when the forensic crew had finished, the inn — or the crime scene — was going to be in need of some protection.

They went to their usual bench. It was early, but already the plaza was busy.

"I wonder if Zachary will expect us at this hour," Logan said.

He needn't have worried. They'd only been there a few minutes when Kelsey nudged him. He saw Zachary excusing himself, unheard, as he made his way through a sea of tourists.

Kelsey and Logan moved apart, as they usually did, so Zachary could sit between them.

"I'm surprised to see you two," he said. "And I'm sorry, but I have nothing to tell you. I suppose that's good?"

"Actually," Kelsey began, "I've come to tell *you* something. Rose is still here."

Zachary Chase was silent. There was hope on his face, and sorrow. "My poor Rose. Her life became so wretched, and now she lingers in death."

"Maybe she needs a friend," Kelsey said.

Zachary was silent again, and neither of them broke the silence. Then he turned to Kelsey, puzzled. "Why don't you just ask Rose about the diamond? If the wretched gem is found, then —"

"She doesn't know where it is, Zachary. She died — and it disappeared," Kelsey told him.

He nodded. "It's terrible, isn't it?" he mused. "That people could kill, and die, for a stone."

"A stone, a hunk of glittering rock . . .

greed," Logan said. "Zachary, none of this is your fault, and what happened at the Alamo certainly wasn't."

"Perhaps I've been waiting. . . ." Zachary shrugged. "Could you . . . Maybe you could suggest to Rose, if you see her, that she take a stroll. That she walk by the Alamo. That she . . . well, perhaps you could tell her I'm here."

Kelsey smiled. "The Longhorn welcomes guests, Zachary."

"But it can't hold good memories for her," he said, his voice hoarse. "I don't want to be part of the memories she must have of being used and sold . . . and murdered."

"I'll see what I can do," Kelsey promised him.

"And I am ever vigilant," he promised in return.

Logan rose. "We'd better get going," he said to Kelsey. Zachary got up when she did, and he gave a slight bow.

"I'll remain vigilant," he vowed.

They watched as he walked away and disappeared into the crowd. Then they headed for Logan's car. Kelsey paused, looking at the Longhorn down the street and the vehicle parked in front of it.

"It's a Ranger car," she said.

"Yes."

"Is it a friend?" she asked.

He grinned. "There aren't that many of us, so most likely."

"Did you arrange it?"

He shook his head. "No, I assume Jackson did."

"Just one car," she murmured. "One Ranger?"

"I guess you haven't heard all our stories," he said. "In the early 1900s, the mayor of Dallas called on the Rangers because he was about to deal with an angry mob. When Ranger Captain W. J. McDonald stepped off the train, the mayor asked him, 'Where are the others?' To which McDonald replied, 'One riot, one Ranger,' or words to that effect. Trust me, Kelsey. One Ranger can keep a curious crowd from making Sandy crazy."

"Sandy is going to be crazy, no matter what," Kelsey said. "Trust *me.*"

He sighed, climbed into the car and revved the engine, then drove to the station. An exhausted Kat Sokolov was just leaving.

"I brought my findings in," she said. "The body was little more than a skeleton. There was some soft tissue left, but because of the situation, it became almost mummified. She was stabbed to death — no surprise there. I was able to tell she'd also been drugged, with the same cocktail used on the others.

What I haven't been able to find yet is any puncture mark on any of the victims. Not even Vanessa Johnston. I don't know how this man is managing to get the drugs into their systems. Possibly a patch, as I mentioned before, but . . ."

"You'll figure it out," Logan said. "Now it's your turn to get some rest."

She nodded and smiled wearily.

Sean was in the office when they arrived, working industriously at a computer. "We've got you for the day?" Kelsey asked him.

"Work on the documentary has been suspended."

"I hadn't realized Ned Bixby had that big a role in it. He doesn't really look like a Mexican," Logan said.

Sean raised one shoulder in a shrug. "He was playing a bunch of different roles. Word just came down from the producer, perhaps out of respect for the situation, that we'd resume next week." He looked at them both for a moment. "I think I've found something you'll want to see."

Logan and Kelsey walked around to stand behind him. Sean had a series of emails up on the screen.

"This showed up at eight," he said, indicating the computer. "It belonged to Linsey Applewood, and her landlord had it in storage. I hacked her code and brought up her emails. She was corresponding with someone called *Mr.Alamo.*"

"Were you able to trace it back to a name?" Logan asked.

Sean's expression was sheepish. "If I'd traced a name, I'd be dancing a jig. No, no name, but I did find out that the emails were all coming and going from an internet café a few blocks from the Longhorn. The thing is, you need to read the email correspondence."

Sean stood and allowed Logan to take his place. "Go to the first one. They start about two years ago, and become more . . . evocative, I guess you could say."

Linsey Applewood's screen name had been *seeitgirl.* The first email had been sent by *Mr.Alamo.*

Hey. Heard you have a gift. I have a gift. Maybe we could get together and explore options.

Seeitgirl had written back:

I'm the real deal. I don't play games.

Then you should come here. The area is full of legends, mysteries — and riches.

More emails followed in a teasing vein, including some that questioned *seeitgirl*'s abilities.

I talk to the dead, she'd written at last.

And *Mr.Alamo* had responded:

That's what is needed. Only the dead can tell the tale. When you come, I will prove that I am everything I claim. And then you must prove that you are all that you claim. If so, we can share fame and treasure.

"Where's the internet café?" Logan asked.

Sean gave him the exact address.

"I'll need to bring photos of the woman," Logan murmured. "Do we have a list yet of people working at the Longhorn at the time Sierra was murdered?"

"We have what I could pull off IRS logs," Sean said.

"I guess being federal is good." Logan grinned. "Very helpful. But we still need to interview Sandy, see what she remembers about any staff who were there a year ago."

He looked at Kelsey. She groaned. "I think that someone other than me should call her right now."

Logan nodded. "I'll do it."

"No, wait," Kelsey said, heading for one

of the other desks. "I'll get her down here. I can't believe she's still that upset with me, or that she'll refuse to help with an ongoing murder investigation."

She sat down and dialed the Longhorn. Logan watched as she got an answer, as she waited and then frowned. Finally, she hung up.

"Logan, Sandy is gone."

"What do you mean, gone?"

Kelsey's face was taut with tension. "I spoke with Ricky. He got the customers out at about four in the morning. He didn't see Sandy then, but he assumed she'd gone to bed. He went to wake her when she didn't show up this morning and he found that her bed hadn't been slept in. Her handbag's there, none of her clothing is gone, but he can't find her. Oh, God, Logan, do you think the killer was there last night? That . . . he's taken Sandy?"

CHAPTER 15

Kelsey felt dizzy for a moment, worried sick, afraid that her affiliation with the case and her relationship with Sandy might have put her friend at risk. She was going to stand, but she didn't. She couldn't allow trembling knees in front of her coworkers. And a U.S. Marshal didn't burst into tears. Neither did an FBI agent. She had strength. She knew it, and she knew her work. However, she'd had no idea what it would feel like when someone she cared about might be in a deadly position because of *her.*

Sean looked at her from behind the computer desk. She saw the concern in his eyes. Logan, too, wore an expression of concern; he moved closer to her. "She has a crush on Chasson, right? Let's find out if she went home with him." He glanced at Sean. "Try to get him on the phone, and try everyone you know until you find him. Sandy's probably with him, but even if she's not, we'll want to question him." He looked back at Kelsey. "Sandy could be walking around the city, just needing a break from the Longhorn. I'm not going to say you shouldn't worry, but the last day's been traumatic for her."

Kelsey nodded. Before panicking, there were a dozen intelligent avenues she could follow. "Under normal circumstances, she wouldn't even be considered missing yet."

"Let's go. While Sean tracks down Jeff Chasson, we'll start at the Longhorn and try to retrace Sandy's steps," Logan said. "Meanwhile, Sean can get a list of addresses for everyone we know was in the saloon last night, and we'll pay calls on them while we keep trying to reach Sandy. Sean, could you send someone to the evidence locker to see if they had a computer for Sierra Monte? You might check where Sheryl Higgins was last seen, too, and if there's a possibility she had a computer, iPhone, iPad, whatever. We'll stay in close contact."

Just as they were leaving, Jackson walked in. Logan briefed him on the latest developments, and Jackson listened gravely, then handed Logan the newspaper he'd been carrying.

"Have you seen this?" he asked.

Logan stopped and read the front page.

Ted Murphy had been at it again.

Missing Dead Woman Found in Walls of Historic Longhorn. Below that, Actor in Custody for Murder. Citizens Question Guilt as Body Count Rises.

The article went on to describe the discovery of Sierra Monte's body as disorganized and chaotic. The team assembled to seek out answers was compared to the Keystone Kops. While the sketches of local artist Jane Everett were helping identify the unknown victims, Texas law enforcement seemed to be working with so-called psychics. Women in San Antonio should bolt their doors. Apparently, the killer was using a drug cocktail, and no one was safe.

Logan didn't read the article word for word, but he noticed that Ted Murphy was promising an exclusive interview with accused murder suspect Ned Bixby the next day.

"I can make sure that doesn't happen. We can transfer him to a federal facility. Since he says his wife went to New Mexico, I could play the federal card," Jackson told him.

"If Murphy interviews Ned Bixby and gets something from him that we didn't, it'll be a good thing," Logan said. "Actually, I'd like to have Ted Murphy brought in for questioning. He has details in this article that we haven't released."

"We can have him brought in, but he'll be out in a flash. He'll claim his right as a journalist to protect his sources," Jackson muttered.

"Well, we can hold him for twenty-four hours," Logan said.

Kelsey was standing silently at his side, and he knew she was anxious to leave. Jackson didn't delay them any longer.

Kelsey continued her silence as they drove. He glanced at her and saw the same sick feeling that must have shown in his face three years ago. He reached out a hand for hers. "We'll find Sandy," he said.

"We saw a Ranger's car in front of the inn this morning. If someone was there through the night, how could this have happened?"

"Rangers don't tell people what they can and can't do," he said patiently. "If Sandy chose to go somewhere, walk out of the inn, there would've been no way he could stop her. Right now, we should think about Jeff Chasson. We both know she was hoping to hook up with him."

Kelsey let out a breath. "I'm sorry," she said. "It's just that every time a woman disappears around here, we seem to find her dead."

He didn't speak again. They got to the Longhorn and quickly parked on the street. As they started to head inside, Logan noticed that the Ranger car parked outside belonged to a good friend of his, Tyler Montague.

When they walked in, there were only a few stragglers in the saloon. Ricky was sitting at a table with Tyler, who was taking notes. Both men rose when he and Kelsey entered, and Logan set a hand on her back, leading her toward them. As they all sat, he introduced Tyler to Kelsey. Tyler made a perfect Ranger; tall, lean and muscled, he practiced martial arts during his off hours. Even better, he was smart and methodical.

Ricky was a mess. He looked tired and frantic, dark hair pushed back from his forehead in disarray. His eyes were red-rimmed.

He tried to smile at Kelsey. "The morning's been insane. The news is out about Sierra Monte's body, there's all kinds of stuff going on at the rodeo fairgrounds today and people have been rushing in from the street to gawk."

"Ricky, could Sandy have left with Jeff Chasson?" Kelsey asked. She looked over at Tyler Montague. "You would've seen them, right?"

"Marshal," Tyler said, "I didn't arrive until about two this morning, so anything that went on before then, I wouldn't have seen. Ricky's been giving me a description of everyone here last night and trying to recall everything that happened, and it doesn't seem to me that Ms. Holly could've been forced out by anyone. There were still a few people when I showed up, and part of what I was told to do was clear the bar. The assumption was that Ms. Holly had been upset and left the cleanup to her staff. We didn't know she never went to bed until Ricky tried to find her when it was time to start cooking and serving breakfast."

"I didn't see her leave," Ricky said. "But I didn't see Chasson leave, either," he said, brightening.

"Ricky, is her room locked?" Kelsey asked.

Ricky shrugged. "I don't remember if I locked it or not after Ranger Montague and I went in there. We saw her purse on the dresser . . . her keys were by it. I checked the closets — it didn't look like she'd taken anything with her."

"Has anyone contacted Chasson yet?" Tyler asked.

"They're trying from the station," Logan said.

Kelsey got up. "I want to go into her

room," she announced.

"You know where it is. Right behind the kitchen," Ricky told her.

"Of course," Kelsey said.

As Logan stood with her, Tyler said, "I'll hang here with Ricky and keep an eye on the place. Special Agent Crow wants someone watching the stairs and the gallery."

Logan nodded. He and Kelsey made their way to the kitchen and the room that branched off it.

"The kitchen was detached when the Longhorn was built," she said. "By the time Sandy bought it, though, the pantry hall had been built to connect the kitchen to the saloon and the smokehouse, which is now Sandy's room."

Logan studied the simple architecture. He noted that there was a private door leading to the grounds in back, which had probably been extensive once. Now, there was only the broad lower porch, some trellises, plants and little fountains. The back of the property was set off from its neighbors by a high whitewashed wooden fence, allowing guests privacy.

Logan walked to the door that led outside as Kelsey searched the room for any sign of where Sandy might have gone. Ricky hadn't lied; there was absolutely no evidence of distress. The bed was neatly made, Sandy's toiletries arranged in an orderly fashion on her dressing table, and there didn't seem to be a speck of dust on the hardwood floor. As he reached the outer door, Kelsey was peering beneath the bed.

The lock was just a push-button type that could be locked from either side. Logan stepped out and stood on the rear porch. From here, Sandy could take a pathway straight to the street, or she could turn to her right and go through the gate to the backyard. He looked for footprints, but the porch was swept clean. He headed toward the backyard, entered and glanced around. He saw a pretty little toolshed in the far corner. His eyes followed the lawn to where there was access from a door at the rear of the saloon. It led to the side of the stage.

As Logan surveyed the area, his phone rang.

"Raintree."

"Logan, it's Sean. So far, we haven't been able to get hold of Jeff Chasson. He's not answering his home phone or his cell. I've contacted Bernie Firestone and other people associated with the documentary, and they haven't been able to reach him, either. I had a patrol car go by his house, and his car *is* parked in front. Should we enter?"

"Give me the address. I'll go in," Logan said. "Get me a warrant while I'm on the way."

"Logan, the woman's been missing for only a few hours. I think you should hear some kind of noise and go for probable cause."

"If he proves to be our man, we can't have evidence thrown out in court."

"That's such a long shot, Logan."

"And we're worried about a woman's life," Logan agreed. "All right. I'm going in."

Kelsey knew Logan was watching her, and she started to worry that she'd be taken off the case, since she was personally involved. She had to act like a law enforcement officer and not a terrified relative.

"We may get more IDs on the other women today," she said, both to distract herself and to emphasize her professionalism. "At first, I thought the killer was going after women who were interested in or knew something about gems. Now, while that may be part of it, we also know he was looking for psychics. That would suggest the killer's aware that there are people who can really contact the dead, so I'm going to assume we're adding several aspects to our profile.

First, he's someone who's local, or frequently local, with a good understanding of the geography, history and legends of the area. And while the business was in transition — before Sandy officially took over — there could have been an endless throng of people in and out."

"Jackson has officers hunting down everyone who worked here," Logan told her.

"So . . . a local, with an avid interest in history, with access to costumes and to drugs. But drugs are easily available on the street, and still . . ." She turned to look at him. "It has to be someone with some basic chemistry in his background to be able to mix up the right cocktail. And administer it. How could you be so focused on a diamond that you'd go through all of that and kill over and over again?" she asked.

"The kind of money it would bring in today's market is astronomical," he reminded her.

"But wouldn't people out there — dedicated gemologists — know about the diamond?"

"Yes, but come on. You can buy body parts on the black market. Selling a diamond would be nothing." Logan slowed down. "That's Chasson's house," he said.

He pulled up behind a deputy's car. The

two officers who'd been watching the house emerged from it and approached them. They all introduced themselves, then the older officer said, "We've knocked, we've banged, we've walked all around the house. There's no response."

"Logan!" Kelsey gripped his arm.

The birds were back. They'd suddenly swooped in, hundreds of them perching atop the roof and the eaves, on utility wires nearby and the garden trellises in front.

"I heard a scream," she told Logan and the two local officers.

"It might've been those dratted birds," the older one said.

"And it might not have," Kelsey insisted. "We've got to go in."

"Cover the back," Logan said tersely. The officers moved around the side of the house, while he and Kelsey hurried toward the front door.

They didn't have to break in; it was open. When they walked inside, they discovered a sunken living room with white and brown furniture, chrome and glass tables, and the finest in ultramodern luxury. There were two filled wineglasses on the coffee table, neither of them touched. Logan headed toward the kitchen and family room, and Kelsey hurried down the hallway toward the bedrooms.

She found Jeff Chasson's room easily enough. It was filled with pictures of him posing with various actors, many of them stars. She didn't focus on the pictures, but on the bed.

It was wildly rumpled, sheets half on the floor, pillows scattered.

A moment's relief swept through her.

Well, she was pretty sure she knew where Sandy had spent most of the night.

Logan came up behind her. "I think we know where Sandy was, and what she was doing," he said lightly, echoing her own thought.

"Still, she left the inn with *nothing?* No purse, no keys, no overnight bag . . ."

"Maybe she thought she was just going out for a while," Logan said.

"So where is she now?"

"Where's Jeff Chasson? Neither of them are answering their cells. Maybe they decided on a romantic interlude."

"Sandy wouldn't just walk off. She would've told me, or if she's angry with me because of what I started, she certainly would have told Ricky. She stuck him with a real mess," Kelsey said.

Logan listened to her, but then shook his head. "We're already on dangerous ground,

Kelsey. Sandy is an adult and she hasn't been missing twenty-four hours. Jeff Chasson's an adult, too — chronologically speaking — and at the moment, we're guilty of breaking and entering. They might've had such a magnificent, tumultuous night that they went somewhere for a few days. And maybe Sandy's angrier at you than you think."

"We don't *know* that Sandy was the one who shared this bed with Chasson," Kelsey said. "And no matter how angry she might be with me, she loves the Longhorn. She would never just walk away from it. Besides," she added, "the front door was open!"

"But there's no sign of foul play here," Logan said.

"Yes, there is."

"What?"

"The birds," she said. "The birds are everywhere. Something definitely happened here."

Logan looked across the table at Ned Bixby. He sat with his attorney, who appeared to be frustrated. The guy was young, a civil servant, and Logan was sure that nothing in law school had prepared him for a client who wanted to confess to everything.

Since Logan was now convinced that Bixby hadn't even killed his own wife, he knew that he had to trip the man up. "Tell me about the way you stabbed your wife, Ned. It's important that we get the details."

Bixby stared back at him. "I don't remember."

"Sure you do. She was your wife. You loved her. Were you angry? Furious that she wanted to leave you and sleep with other men? I mean, that's what you believed, right?"

"She didn't want me," he said quietly. He looked down at his hands. "I drove her away."

"You drove her away because you wanted to control her with your love?"

"I . . . I expected too much. Please, I said I did it. I don't need a trial. I did it. I killed her. I killed them all."

Logan leaned forward. "If you make a confession like that, Ned, and law enforcement is pulled off the case, more women could die. Do you want that to happen?"

"Okay, I didn't kill them all. But I killed Cynthia."

"So tell me about the knife."

Bixby was crying again, tears streaming down his cheeks. "What's to tell? It was a knife. A carving knife, I guess. I grabbed it out of the holder in the kitchen. I thrust it into her heart."

"Ned," Logan said wearily, "we're going to release you."

Ned Bixby gaped at him. "But . . . I just confessed to killing my wife!"

"You didn't kill her, Ned. Cynthia wasn't stabbed. She drowned."

"What do the details matter? She was in the bathtub. I was so angry, I forced her head under the water," Bixby said.

The young attorney shook his head and lifted his hands. "He *wants* to be convicted."

Logan eased back in his chair, looking at Bixby. "Ned," he began, "you didn't kill your wife, but you feel responsible. You believe that if you hadn't been so possessive and dictatorial, she wouldn't have left you, and if she hadn't left you, she wouldn't be dead. But what you're doing is wrong. You didn't kill Cynthia, and what you don't see is that now her killer could get away with it."

Bixby's face contorted with anger. "I did it. I *am* responsible," he said. He frowned at Logan. "I thought I was fine. I thought I could live without her. But then you showed me . . . her body."

Logan rose. He walked around and set a hand on Bixby's shoulder. "She's gone, and you didn't do it. Get angry again because she was someone you loved, and she's dead, murdered." He pulled a chair closer to Bixby. "Tell me about her, Ned. Did she like the Congregational church a lot? Did she like music? Was she a dancer? Did she like jewelry? Did she prefer romantic comedies or horror movies or what? Help me out here."

Bixby inhaled on a deep, rattling breath. "She was full of light. She sang around the house." He paused. "She loved being in San Antonio. She'd go to the Alamo and just sit in the plaza and stare at the old chapel. She told me she could see them — that she could see the ghosts there. I'd laugh at her, and she'd be indignant and tell me that there could be a plane somewhere between this life and the next one, and I shouldn't be such a skeptic. She was happy about the ghosts she saw. She said it meant there was another world, one where everyone was happy." He winced. "I didn't make her happy."

"Ned, she did leave you, right? You saw her leave, as in take her things and walk out of your home, right?" Logan asked.

He nodded. "But she didn't take much. She just wanted out."

"Did you two have a computer?"

Bixby nodded.

"May I have it?"

Again, Bixby nodded.

Logan straightened and turned to the young attorney. "I'll see about getting all the charges against him dismissed."

The attorney looked as if he was about to kiss him. Logan stepped away.

Kelsey stood with Sean at the rear of the internet café. The business offered dozens of computers as well as coffee, sandwiches and pastries. The manager, Shelby Horton, was a harried man in a full apron and a hair snood who wanted to be helpful, but also wanted to get them out as quickly as possible.

"As many as a hundred people come in here on a typical day," he said. "Tall, short, men, women . . . so many of the hotels still charge for internet, and guests don't want to pay. I have strangers and locals and —"

"How about Jeff Chasson?" Kelsey asked. "Do you know who he is?"

Horton arched his eyebrows. "Actually, he has been here. He sometimes comes in when he's working on local shoots. He acts like he's afraid he's being followed or fans are going to come screaming after him. Frankly, not that many people even notice him. He's not *that* big a celebrity."

"But he comes in regularly?"

Horton nodded.

"What about the newspaper guy — Ted Murphy?" Sean asked.

"He's always in here. I guess he thinks he'll hear something, pick up some gossip and scoop the wire services, but he's crazy. Moms come in to connect with their kids. My computers all have Skype. Soldiers come in — we're not far from several bases and major military hospitals. Yeah, maybe Murphy thinks he's going to overhear some national secrets. Oh, and we get the cowboys. Now, that's funny. The guys in their rodeo getups pecking away at the keyboards. We get all kinds here."

"We're looking for someone who logs in as *Mr.Alamo*," Sean told him.

"I have no idea what people log in as," Horton said. "Did you trace it?"

"The name is on a free service. The address is fake, the phone number's fake, everything about it is fake."

Kelsey produced her badge. "Mr. Horton, someone is logging in from here to contact women and lure them to the Alamo — and their deaths. We need your help."

The man froze. He turned white. "Oh, my God. You're talking about all the murders . . . the women who had their pictures in the paper."

"I'm afraid I am. What I need is for Sean to spend the day here, searching through your computers."

"I can be discreet," Sean promised.

"I'm figuring you could get a warrant if you wanted, anyway, except . . . Oh, God, I'd never make you do that. I . . . oh. Oh, God," Horton said.

"I'll leave the two of you together then." Kelsey flashed Sean a smile and headed out, then paused and turned back. "Mr. Horton, what about interpreters? Actors in costume, say, from the time of the Alamo?"

Horton waved a hand in the air. "Sure!" he said. "Those guys and gals are stranger than the cowboys. They're pretty funny-looking in their period clothing, hunched over computers."

"Thank you."

Hurrying out of the internet café, Kelsey walked back to the Longhorn.

Tyler Montague was still on guard, and Kelsey noticed that he was making a point of talking to the men at the bar.

Among them was Bernie Firestone. As Kelsey walked over to join them, Firestone looked at her and took a long swig of his beer. "Any word from Chasson yet?"

"No." She caught Tyler's eye; he shook his head. There had been no change at the Longhorn. Ricky was doing his best to keep things running smoothly, but the bar was busy that afternoon.

"Gawkers," Bernie said.

"Yeah, you know how folks like to slow down at the scene of an accident," Ricky agreed.

"Anyone seen Corey Simmons today?" Kelsey asked.

"Corey's at the rodeo," Ricky answered. "Bull riding."

She nodded and glanced at her phone. She hadn't heard back from Logan yet, but she didn't want to bother him. She knew he was trying to ascertain the truth behind Bixby's confession. Sean was working the computer angle, and Jane, Jackson and Jake Mallory were at the station, following phone leads. There was still a guard on Chasson's house, but as yet, neither he nor Sandy had been found.

Restless and worried, Kelsey looked up the stairway to the gallery. "I'm going upstairs," she told Ricky. "Can you see that I'm not disturbed?" she asked Tyler.

"Of course," he said.

She walked up the stairs. The crime-scene tape had been removed from the stairway, but still covered the door to Room 207. She slid by it carefully.

No one had been in to repair any of the damage yet. There was plaster dust over everything and, now, a gaping hole in the wall. The body of Sierra Monte had, of course, been taken away.

Kelsey sat on the foot of the bed and said softly, "Are you here?"

But no one answered; no shadows appeared. She knew she needed patience, so she waited, but she'd disturbed the past yesterday, and even if it had been the right thing to do, she was now terribly afraid of the consequences.

She started when her phone rang and answered it quickly. Sean. "You found something?" she asked.

"Locals and regulars, people who work in the area and come in often. God knows, we may be barking up the wrong tree totally, but I spoke with a woman who was here one day and sat next to a man in costume. She's the friendly sort. I guess she tried to talk to him, and she said he was rude to her — he didn't want her to really see his face. He had a mustache and beard, but she was sure his hair was a wig. She also said there was something familiar about him. I'm trying to get her to remember what it might have been. When we were talking I suggested she might know him and that he was trying to hide his identity, and she agreed. Anyway, her name is Alice White, and I have her number. She couldn't stay because she has small children and has to pick them up, but she'll be happy to meet with you tomorrow."

"Thanks, Sean!" Kelsey told him.

She waited again, staring at the wall. Today, her ghosts had failed her.

She didn't know how long she'd been in the room when Logan quietly entered.

"You haven't found Sandy or Chasson yet, right?" she asked.

"No, but I did talk with Sean, and he's doing his best to trace anything he can on the computers, and Kat's doing more tests. I know we're close, Kelsey, and that we will find her."

Kelsey nodded. "The woman at the internet café, Alice White, told Sean that she encountered a man who was heavily costumed, trying to hide himself, and very rude. She also said he seemed sort of familiar. He has to be someone fairly well-known. Like Jeff Chasson."

Logan stretched out a hand to her.

"Where are we going?"

"My house. You have to eat. And sleep."

"I can't sleep. Sandy is out there."

"And there's going to be a whole city full of people looking for her. We brought Ted Murphy down to the station for questioning. He said he got all the information he had just by eavesdropping at the bar, but he did get a lot nicer. He's put Sandy's picture on their internet site and it'll be in the morning paper. There's nothing else you can do now, Kelsey. Come on. You'll be worthless when Sandy does need you if don't eat and get some sleep."

She took his hand, and they left the Longhorn. Kelsey was starved by the time they put together a meal of tuna sandwiches, chips and salad, and when she'd downed two beers, she was also exhausted. She meant to lie down and rest a little, but in minutes, she was sound asleep. She kept seeing Jeff Chasson as she slept, saw him reaching out for Sandy as they stood in Room 207, talking about the blood and Sierra Monte.

In her dreams Chasson turned to her and smiled bitterly. "You," he said. "You brought it all to life. You'll pay a price."

When she woke in the morning, she felt oddly refreshed — and furious. Logan was already up and in the kitchen; she showered, dressed and joined him there.

"It's Chasson. I *know* it's Chasson, and he has Sandy, and we're going to track the bastard down before he can hurt her!"

Logan looked back at her. "Kelsey, they found Jeff Chasson last night."

"He's guilty, I know he's guilty!"

"They found him dead, Kelsey. In his own neighborhood, beneath a massive pile of mulch at the end of the street. His throat was slit."

Kelsey's heart seemed to stop.

"And Sandy?" she whispered.

CHAPTER 16

"There's no sign of Sandy yet, but I'm sure she's alive and well," Logan said, trying to reassure Kelsey, which was probably ridiculous. The situation didn't look good.

Kelsey sank into a chair at the dining room table.

"Listen," Logan said, sitting across from her and taking her hands. "I'm going to talk to Jackson and get you taken off this case, because I know how much you must be suffering. That way —"

"No! No!" she said, standing and jerking her hands from his. "I am staying on this case, Logan. I know Sandy better than almost anyone. I know the Longhorn. I *have* to stay on this case. I need to talk to Alice White today. And we need to get Sean or Kat or someone researching files to figure out who's had chemical or pharmaceutical training. We're close on this — so close. And there's a chance we'll find Sandy alive," she said urgently.

She was passionate, and he understood how she felt.

There was no way in hell they could've sent him home once Alana had been taken.

This was different, of course . . . and yet not so different.

"All right. I'm going to drop you at the internet café with Sean. Then I'll stop by the morgue and see what Kat's learned. I'll check with the group at the station and find out how our research is going on the actors, construction workers, Ted Murphy, Bernie Firestone — and everyone who was then or is now at the Longhorn. They'll pull up everything, even on Ricky and the maids. When you've finished your interview with Alice, keep working with Sean, read any emails he's gotten. He can connect them with whatever correspondence he found in Cynthia Bixby's computer, as well. He'll need your help. And we'll meet up later at the Longhorn."

Kelsey nodded her agreement.

Logan noted that she appeared strong and determined as they drove, and he reminded himself again that she belonged in the fray as much as he did.

He also knew the kind of toll emotion could take on the human mind and body.

Sean greeted them at the front of the café. He'd apparently become friends with Shelby Horton, the manager; coffee was on Shelby.

Logan left the two of them to work and headed over to the morgue.

The body of Jeff Chasson was laid out on a table. He didn't look real anymore, Logan thought, and then again, he looked too real. Kat had performed the Y incision, but she hadn't gotten to the brain. Chasson's face, void of the animation of life, was sunk into his neck. Logan experienced a moment of guilt for disliking the man so much and then knew he didn't need to chastise himself — he would never have wished this on anyone, regardless of his own feelings.

"Cause of death?" Logan asked, although he'd already heard and it was obvious from the bright red necklace around the man's throat.

"Extremely sharp knife, at the jugular."

"Looks like someone was trying to take his head off," Logan commented.

"This killer wasn't trying to do that, but he did know that if you got the vein or artery, death would come quickly."

"He wasn't killed in his house," Logan said. "There wasn't a drop of blood."

"No. Here's what's odd. He was killed on that mulch pile. There's no sign of any struggle on his body, so he wasn't forced there. The incision is left to right. He could have taken his own right hand and slit his throat. But also . . ." Kat stood behind him; she was tiny, but he knew exactly what she was demonstrating. "Someone directly behind him could have done this, and the blood spray — there was a spray — went straight ahead. Chasson would've gone weak almost instantly, and then crashed forward into the mulch. The killer covered him with it, but Chasson's neighborhood is pretty swanky, and they have a neighborhood watch, so he was found. If there hadn't been a 'patrol' — two retired residents who get together and walk their dogs — Chasson could've lain there undiscovered for a month. That's when the mulch company does a pick-up."

"Do you have test results yet? Sounds like he was hit with the same cocktail the women were," Logan said.

"I don't have the results, but I do have something. Look here."

Kat lifted Chasson's head and held back his hair. There was a very faint circular impression near the hairline.

"What is it?" Logan asked.

"It looks like there was a transdermal patch here. I've taken a skin sample — you can see my biopsy mark — to assure us that this is indeed the method if it proves to be our fentanyl-roofie mix. You've seen nicotine patches for smokers trying to quit. And of course, fentanyl is given that way for extreme chronic pain."

"We're dealing with a brazen killer who planned this very well," Logan said.

"He got sloppy, though. Not enough mulch over the corpse, which was left in a place the killer hadn't really known all that well. We found hairs, but judging by the color, I'm thinking they'll be consistent with Sandy Holly's. We're pretty sure it was the two of them who had sex — the lab is testing the sheets now."

"Thanks, Kat."

"I'll keep you informed."

When he started out, she called him back. "Logan?"

"Yes?"

"Are you going to join the unit?"

"Are you?"

"Oh, yes! Are you kidding me? I'll get to run the show. I'll have funds I never dreamed of. Definitely. But then, I worked for some real good old boys before. You've been a respected Ranger."

Logan paused and then nodded. "I have to admit I like having the power to call the shots. I like the way we keep moving and pool different resources. Yeah, I'll probably take it."

He left the morgue and drove to the station, anxious to hear about further developments.

Alice White was an attractive woman in her mid-thirties. She was cordial when she met Kelsey, and they sat at one of the café tables, sipping coffee.

"I don't know if this means anything at all," she told Kelsey apologetically. "It's just that the man was behaving so strangely. We were at the little desks next to each other, and although he didn't exactly hide the screen with his body, it seemed like he was *trying* to. And I wasn't the slightest bit interested in reading his email! I was being polite."

"What did he look like?" Kelsey asked.

"A buffoon," Alice said. "So much makeup — fake hair, beard, mustache. I wondered how he made a living as an actor or reenactor, or tour guide. I mean, if he was giving ghost tours, a crowd of four-year-olds would've thought he was hokey."

"Do you remember anything else? Eye color, anything like that?" Kelsey asked.

Alice frowned, trying to remember. "I

think he wore contact lenses."

"Colored contacts?"

"Yes. You know how contacts can catch the light in a funny way? And the color was kind of murky. Maybe it was meant to be . . . or it might've been like blue over brown or something. I'm not sure." She paused, frowning again.

"Height? Weight?" Kelsey asked.

"Um, medium," Alice said, adjusting a bangle bracelet on her arm. "Not too tall, not too heavy. I'm sorry, I'm not a very good witness. Once when I was here, he came in and when I sat down near him, he got up and walked out. It was hard not to notice him. Like I said — a buffoon."

"What was he wearing?"

"He had on some kind of trousers made out of hide, or fake hide." Alice paused. "I wish I could tell you more."

"I'm sure the information you've given us is going to be very helpful," Kelsey said.

"There was just something so odd about him, and I'm not the only one who noticed it," Alice told her. "Yet he seemed sort of familiar, too."

"In what way?"

"I'm not sure. . . . Just an impression, you know? But there was a young man who passed through here. One day, when old creepy-actor gave me one of his scowls, the young guy looked at me and said, 'That dude's a freak. Something's not right.' "

"If I bring a sketch artist in, could you give us a description?" Kelsey asked.

"I'll do my best," Alice said. "There's a little office back there that Shelby will let us use."

Kelsey called Jane, who came over from the station immediately and sat down with Alice in Shelby's private office. Kelsey marveled at the dexterity in Jane's fingers as she quickly sketched and an image appeared.

"It looks like Blackbeard meets frontier-man," Jane said.

"The cheekbones should be a little higher, and the eyes a little farther apart," Alice told her.

Jane erased and changed, and showed Alice the picture again.

"Yes, yes, that's very close," Alice said.

When they'd finished the sketch, Kelsey could see that Alice White was growing restless, glancing at her watch; she needed to pick up her children. Kelsey thanked her, and let her go. Jane went back to the station with the sketch so the others could see it. When she'd gone, Sean came over to where

Kelsey was standing, saying goodbye to Jane.

"I've got something I want to show you," he said. "We might have found one of our other girls. Log-in name is *psychicchic*. She had a similar line of correspondence going with our suspect, *Mr.Alamo,* on a social network."

Kelsey followed him to the computer and read the messages between the two. *Psychicchic* had posted about a séance she'd attended and how the medium had turned to her for help. She bragged about the ghosts she'd contacted. *Mr.Alamo* started out by doubting her, then pressing her about proving she had real ability. She could stretch her talents, he said, by coming to the Alamo.

"There's her picture," Sean pointed out. "I'll run it off and see what kind of matchup we can get. And I'll try to trace her — find out if she's missing. The only picture of *Mr.Alamo* is right there." He pointed at a small image on the screen.

"That's Davy Crockett," Kelsey said.

"That's what it is," Sean agreed. "Okay, I'm going to the station now. Do you want to drive in with me?"

Kelsey shook her head. "I'm going to the Longhorn. I'll wait for Logan there. Call me if you come up with anything else."

"Kelsey . . ." Sean started to speak, but his voice drifted off. There wasn't much to say.

"She's been gone overnight now, Sean. And Jeff Chasson's dead. I'm really afraid it's not looking good."

"Yeah, but keep the faith," he said. "I can drop you at the inn."

"No, that's okay. I like the walk."

When Sean left, she thanked the manager for all his assistance — and his coffee. He assured her he'd be there if she needed anything else.

She walked to the Longhorn and looked over at the Alamo and the plaza, struck by how beautiful the city could be.

When she entered the saloon, some of the cowboys were there, and Bernie Firestone and Earl Candy might as well have been fixtures on their stools.

Ricky, meanwhile, was looking lost and forlorn, wiping a glass as he stood behind the bar.

Kelsey went over to greet them. All three were glum.

"Anything new, Kelsey? *Anything?*" Ricky asked.

"As you've probably heard, they found Jeff Chasson's body, but no trace of Sandy, so there's still hope," Kelsey said.

"Jeez." Earl stared into his beer. "I hated that bastard. He was a royal pain to work with, but . . ."

"Looks like we're all done filming," Bernie said. He raised his glass. "To Jeff. May there be a big audience to greet him in the sky!"

"I guess the documentary is . . ." Kelsey began.

"Dead?" Bernie asked her dryly. "No, we have enough to put together a film. And, trust me, it'll sell."

"Well, that's good," Kelsey said. "For everyone who's invested time and money in it. And it'll be a way of honoring Jeff."

Bernie nodded. "Who would've thought he'd die like that?" He shivered. "You know," he said quietly. "It seemed to be just women in danger. But now, no one's safe. I hope you catch the bastard."

"Me, too," Kelsey murmured, glancing around the bar. A number of men from the rodeo were at various tables, including Corey Simmons, who sat alone. He saw her watching him, and lifted his glass, his eyes grave.

She made her way over to him. "Corey, you okay?"

"I was. But I just heard about Chasson. And that Sandy's disappeared into thin air."

He grimaced. "This place isn't just haunted. It's cursed. I've got two more days to make some money bull riding, and then I'm out of here."

She patted his shoulder. "I don't believe a place can be cursed, Corey. People bring their own grief and guilt, but a *place* isn't cursed."

As she talked to him, the doors swung open and she saw that Ted Murphy had returned. He headed straight for the bar to take the seat next to Bernie Firestone and ordered a beer. He met Kelsey's eyes. "I've been doing anything you all have asked me to get those pictures out there. I'm doing whatever I can to get the public involved," he said defensively.

"I wasn't going to attack you, Ted."

"I'm ready to do whatever will help. The whole community is in a state of shock," he said. "Everyone's scared."

"That includes me. I'll be closing up early," Ricky told her. He leaned on the bar and whispered, "I gave Jackson Crow the names of our overnight guests. He ran them through some computer — goes all over the country — and at least we don't have anyone with anything worse than a parking ticket!"

"I'm sure we're safe here. I noticed there's

a police car outside."

"I wish they'd left Tyler, but this is a new guy. I felt safer with Ranger Montague. The one out there, well, he seems to be dozing with his hat on. Wish he'd come in and stare people down the way Montague did."

"Well, I'm here, Ricky, if you need me."

"Thanks," he murmured. "What the hell made Sandy go off with that guy?" he demanded loudly.

"Sex," Ted Murphy answered. "Chasson always told me he could pick up a woman and get laid any night he wanted." He cleared his throat, realizing he was talking to close friends of the missing woman. "Ms. Holly is very attractive, and Jeff Chasson could be extremely . . . seductive."

"Well, I'm going to my room for a while," Kelsey said. "Ricky, if something comes up or if anyone wants to see me, call me, okay?"

He nodded gravely.

Kelsey walked up the stairs, wondering why she was so convinced that the answers had to be somewhere in Room 207. But now, when she went in, it seemed empty, as if all life — and death — had left it. She was in the midst of well-tended period furniture and plaster dust.

The bed was in bad shape. She dusted the quilt, kicked off her heels and lay back.

Kelsey closed her eyes and tried to reconstruct everything she'd seen, willing herself to view the image of the residual haunting again. In a few minutes, she opened her eyes slightly, and a silvery mist seemed to pervade the air. Then it dissipated and the residual haunting began.

Rose and Matt. She, with her stunning dark hair piled atop her head, in her usual half-dressed state, the rest of her garments strewn about. Matt in his dark suit, a tall hat, dapper but still rough around the edges.

He strode furiously across the room and seized hold of Rose, saying, "You won't hold out on me! I want it, and I want it now."

"I don't have it," she said.

The rest of the scene played out as she knew it would. Just like he had before, he reached out for Rose and his fingers curled around her neck. He strangled her, ignoring her pleas. Then Rose went limp, dead, and Matt picked her up and threw her on the bed and the scene faded. But this time, when it was gone, Kelsey kept seeing the death in her mind, and she tried to figure out what bothered her about it.

Don't think too hard. Let it come.

She got up and walked to the broken wall. How had Sierra's killer had managed to do it all — kill her so viciously and disappear, right in the middle of the inn's sale and renovation?

A moment later, she went to her window and looked at the small yard. She caught sight of the old toolshed. It was just used by the gardeners now, Kelsey assumed, but she was suddenly tempted to check it out. She hesitated. She didn't want to go through the gauntlet of men in the bar again; she wasn't up to dealing with their questions and fears. But she wondered, if in the search for Sierra, anyone had inspected the toolshed. She couldn't imagine that Jackson Crow or Logan hadn't looked there.

Kelsey leaned out the window. There was a sturdy branch reaching up from an old oak; its leaves actually touched the outside wall. Reflecting that she hadn't been a tomboy for nothing, Kelsey climbed onto the sill and stretched out, swinging herself over, testing her weight. It was absurdly easy to grab the branch, go hand over hand to the trunk, drop to a lower branch and then down to the ground.

She started across the manicured grounds and toward the toolshed.

The door opened smoothly on well-oiled hinges. Inside, the small shed was dark, but she could see neat rows of gardening sup-plies and tools. She entered cautiously —

and heard something, or thought she did. She paused, listening. She studied the space in which she stood. It was about twelve by twelve, and with the lawn mower, the shelves and more, she didn't see anything that could make a noise.

But then she heard it again, and it seemed to come from beneath her.

The inn had a basement, of course, and she knew that Sandy stored things down there, in the various rooms created by the foundations. But would a toolshed have a basement? She wished she'd asked her more about the building itself.

The noise came again. And this time, it sounded like a word. A single word.

"Help."

"Sandy?" Kelsey cried anxiously. She fell to her knees, studying the floor. There was nothing, no hint of cellar door or opening.

She moved the lawn mower and still saw nothing. She ran her hands over the floor and felt a line, a slight ridge. Following the line, she realized it was a flat three-sided door. Probably the entrance to some kind of tornado shelter.

She opened the door and peered in. Pitch dark. She'd have to go back to the house and get a flashlight.

But she heard her name, called out in a

soft, barely discernible whisper. "Kelsey? Kelsey, please hurry!"

"Sandy, I can't see you."

"Just jump. It's low . . . there's sawdust, oh, please, please, before . . ."

Sandy's voice trailed off. Desperate, Kelsey angled herself around, gripped the edge of the flooring, dangled for a minute and then let herself drop.

She didn't fall far. She landed on a pile of old clothes or bedding and struggled to sit up.

A light began to glow and she felt something touch the back of her neck. She heard the sound of hoarse, throaty laughter. She felt a calm sweep through her body, a strange sense not of paralysis, but of almost lazy pleasure, and as her Glock was slipped from her holster, she knew she'd been hit with the drug cocktail.

"Welcome," came a voice. "Now we'll find the diamond!"

CHAPTER 17

When Logan reached the station, he was advised of the strides the team had made in the past few hours. He sat with Sean, who was reading emails and trying to match up Facebook pages with missing women. They were dejected when they realized that *psychicchic* was a missing eighteen-year-old from Nebraska who'd hitchhiked down to Oklahoma with friends and was then never heard from again.

Logan said grimly that he'd contact the family and they'd get a DNA sample.

"Where are we on looking up anyone who might have had a medical, chemical or pharmaceutical background?" he asked.

"Pretty much nowhere," Sean told him. "Most of the potential suspects went to Texas schools, and no one studied medicine, but they all had to take a pretty tough course in chemistry in order to graduate from high school. Our Ted Murphy recently took a course called 'Street Drugs and Slang for Journalists.' Cowboy Corey did some classes in animal husbandry. Ricky took a number of cooking classes. It doesn't matter about Jeff Chasson anymore, does it?" He paused. "Ironically, our latest victim — or likely victim — Sandy Holly went to a seminar called 'Young Woman on the Street, Beware.' "

As they spoke, there was a tap at the door. Logan answered it to find the desk sergeant with a tall, bald man who looked like he might have stepped out of a Mr. Clean commercial.

He offered his hand. "I'm Bobby Moore. I was the contractor on the Longhorn just before the murder took place. I was fired afterward when the old owner stepped back in and Ms. Holly was in a financial mess. I'm here to help you any way I can."

Logan invited him in. They arranged a chair for him in the center of the room and grouped around him.

"How could Sierra Monte's body have been walled in like that, without anyone knowing?" Logan began.

"When I heard, I asked myself that question. But I guess it wasn't that hard. We'd been working on some pipes and the electricity, so there was fresh drywall and plaster in a lot of areas. From what I understand, the room was covered in blood, but I guess even when there's blood everywhere and a massive search, if there's no body, there's no murder?" he asked, looking at each of them.

"That's changed a bit, but it's difficult to prosecute without a body, yes."

"Anyone going into that room would know some work had been done recently — but there'd been work done all over the inn, mostly on things necessary to get the building up to code. And the inspectors had been in just a few days before that blood was found, so there seemed to be no reason to start knocking down walls." He grimaced. "I got to admit, it gave me the chills when I heard, and I knew they'd have to investigate my team, but we were already out of there. We'd been out since the inspection. I was working an old mansion in Louisiana, and my men were scattered. I brought you a list of workers here in San Antonio — most of 'em day jobbers — and I also have a blueprint of the place, with the work we did, just in case you need it." He reached into his pocket and produced a sheaf of neatly folded papers. "My God, that this could happen . . ."

Logan opened the blueprint. He stared at

it, but he already knew the inn so well. He hadn't been to the basement, though, and was intrigued to see the original foundation lines of the old saloon, along with the modern additions.

"What's this?" he asked Moore, pointing at a line.

"Oh, that. There used to be a well out back. When city water came through, it wasn't needed, but there was an old walkway that led from the house to the well, so the whole thing was incorporated into an underground tunnel. It was walled off for years. The old well was destroyed and a carriage house stood there at one time. Then that was destroyed and a toolshed was put out there, oh, probably sometime back in the early twentieth century."

"I think I'll do some exploring there tonight," he told Moore. "Thank you for bringing this in, and for coming to speak with us."

Moore rose and shook hands all around. "I'm a phone call away," he said, "and happy to help."

Logan was planning to head straight out to the Longhorn, but Jane tapped him on the shoulder. "You haven't seen the sketches of the man who may be our culprit."

He sat with her as she showed him the

latest sketch she'd made; she'd entered it in the computer so she could alter hair, eyes and facial features at will.

There was something about the image that disturbed him. He felt he should have figured out what it was but couldn't quite pinpoint it.

"Since Kelsey spoke with Alice White, who gave me the description, maybe she'll have an idea," Jane suggested.

He tried Kelsey's number, but she didn't answer. Then he called the bar and got Ricky, who assured him that Kelsey was fine and up in Room 207.

Logan decided to go there and talk to her before he did any exploring. Checking out the property again, with the asistance of Bobby Moore's blueprint, was a last-ditch effort, but maybe they'd missed Sandy somehow.

"Jackson, there was a thorough search of the grounds, not just the house, after Sandy went missing, right?" Logan asked. "I'm not sure I gave this toolshed much attention."

Jackson nodded. "I went inside it myself."

"Okay, call me if —"

"There's a massive team out there looking for Ms. Holly," Jackson said quietly.

"I know . . ."

He'd gotten in his car and was halfway to

406

the Longhorn when his phone rang. He answered it immediately, assuming Kelsey was returning his call.

"Raintree."

There was silence. He almost hung up.

Then he heard the voice. It was altered, he thought, sounding like the voice of a murderous puppet in a horror movie. He'd heard speech that had been distorted by voice-altering devices before, the kind that could be bought at any place that sold "Nanny Cams" and amateur sleuth paraphernalia.

"Raintree. Yes, you are."

"Who is this, and what do you want?"

There was laughter. "Tough Texas Ranger! Well, you're not stupid. I want the usual. Don't try to trace this call. I'm not stupid, either. The phone is an unregistered pay-as-you-go. And don't go calling your buddies. You're getting a second chance here."

"At what?"

"At saving a woman you love."

He practically drove off the road.

Kelsey hadn't answered her phone. Ricky had said she was fine, up in Room 207. But Sandy Holly had disappeared just as easily, as if into thin air.

"Yes, tough boy, Lone Ranger, that's what you are right now. On your own. *If* you want

407

to play, of course. This is your chance. Yes, I have Kelsey O'Brien. Indeed, I do."

He and Kelsey had been professional. They hadn't run around holding hands or kissing in public. Not surprisingly, the team seemed to know, but respected their privacy. And maybe some of the people at the inn had guessed, too.

"I thought you'd enjoy this, Logan," the caller said. "A second chance. You had a first chance once, didn't you? And you blew it. So try number two. Kelsey's still alive, I promise you — at this moment, she's still alive. I'm hoping she'll do what I need her to do, but I know you have the power, too. Kelsey tells me she doesn't have any idea where the diamond is. *Get the diamond, Logan.* Get me the Galveston diamond, and you can have Kelsey back. You can also try to find me." The horrible laughter sounded again. "Find me, Logan. But scare me and Kelsey dies. One of you comes up with the diamond, or you both die. But her first, of course. I wouldn't want you to miss it."

"There, that's done!"

Prone on the pile of bedding, aware that she had no strength or will to fight, Kelsey pretended not to stir.

But she knew.

She had to get the patch off her neck and do it without being seen.

Now.

"That's done," she parroted.

She shifted, as if she was completely comfortable on her makeshift bed on the floor. She smoothed back her hair and felt the patch against her fingers — and she had it off. She noticed, however, that down here, there were more tools and lock boxes, and she was pretty sure the lock boxes were filled with the drugs that had been used on the women.

Her captor hunkered down beside her. "I know you can see ghosts, Kelsey. I know you can talk to them. Even when we were kids, you were seeing stuff, and people made fun of you, so you never said anything. You'd turn your visions or whatever they were into the most fantastic stories!"

"I see ghosts," Kelsey said, looking into Sandy Holly's eyes and wondering how she could have missed the fact that her dear friend, her hostess, the woman she'd known for so many years, was a psychopath.

"And you've seen the ghost of Rose Langley, haven't you, Kelsey?" Sandy said.

She was so weak. Her mind was still fogged.

She saw a row of tools that dangled from

a rafter above her. There was a large machete there, along with garden hoes and edgers. All Sandy had to do was reach up and grab the machete. One strike and —

She forced herself to stare into Sandy's eyes and giggle. "I thought you liked Jeff Chasson. Instead, you cut his balls off."

"I didn't cut his balls off!"

"Well, since he's dead, it doesn't really matter."

Sandy sighed. "Look, I did have a thing for Chasson. But he was a snoop, so I was trying to distract him, keep him in line. He was learning too much. Kelsey, listen, I don't really want to kill you. You're my friend . . ."

"Then don't!"

"What I can do is give you a little dose and leave you here. They'll find you sooner or later. All I want is the diamond, Kelsey."

"Why?"

Sandy sounded impatient. "I just do! I just want what it can buy. I want the power it can give me. It belonged to royalty, and it would mean a whole new life. I've heard about it since I was a kid. When my grandfather first told me the story, I could see it, imagine it — I almost felt like I could touch it. I've watched this place. I've worked so hard to get this place so I could have the diamond. It's my right!"

"What am I supposed to do?"

"Rose Langley had that diamond when she died. She hid it somewhere. You can talk to Rose Langley — you've probably already done it. So get her to tell you where the diamond is. I've already disappeared. You won't remember any of this once I give you a bit more, and the world will think I was the killer's last victim."

She didn't know how long she could keep it up, but Kelsey decided to stick with the stupid smile. "Why did you invite a U.S. Marshal to stay with you when you were killing people? Wasn't that kind of . . . dumb?"

"I wanted *you* here. All the other idiots who claimed to be great psychics were useless. I really just stumbled on Sierra Monte — and her belief that she was a psychic and could find the diamond. After that . . . after Sierra, I was sure there was a *real* psychic out there somewhere who could talk to Rose's ghost and ask her. But, as you know now," she added dryly, "I've been trying for a while. I figured I'd get to you eventually. And then I eavesdropped on you and Logan Raintree. Everyone in Texas knows about him and what happened to his wife." She patted Kelsey's head. "So, you find it, he finds it — I don't care. I just want it."

"You're good," Kelsey said. "So good . . . But I'm curious. Did you kill Cynthia Bixby? Was she coming around here? Had you contacted her?"

"Actually, no. I didn't kill her. I heard about her from Ricky and I did contact her, yes. She had some fantasy about being a psychic. But that was one messed-up woman. She had a hard time at home and claimed she heard voices. It might've been for real, who can tell? I'm willing to bet, though, that she looked at that water and just threw herself in. Drowned herself. I never had a chance to really get to know her — or to find out if she could locate the diamond. She was just . . . collateral damage. But you're right — I *am* good. I didn't let myself become a suspect."

Sandy shrugged. "You did give me a jolt when you dug Sierra Monte out of the wall. That bitch told me she was going to find the diamond and she was going to keep it. I was livid. That night was a mess, I can tell you! I had to put a sheet over my head to go after her, and she kept running, and I had to keep stabbing her. . . . Thank God there were drunkards down in the bar, a bunch of losers who couldn't hear an air-raid siren if it went off right next to them!

But I couldn't figure out what to do with the body. So I walled it up. Everything was all repainted later, after the room was cleaned, and no one was any the wiser. Anyway, when I was done, I went out the window and down the tree. When they told me about it, I cried, Kelsey. I cried real tears. I kept crying whenever I checked on the clean-up crew."

"What about the smell?"

"I used cinnamon bark — not just cinnamon, it has to be cinnamon bark — and spices. I put it inside the wall. And, of course, I made sure everything was airtight when I did my little home repair. Remember history? How people used potpourri sachets to hide smells? Cinnamon was the base for those, and believe you me, I had to think of that quickly after she wound up dead! She was my first, Kelsey. I was just learning, you see."

"Like I said, Sandy, you're good."

"I got good, that's for sure. I knew the bodies would be discovered at some point, but I was pretty careful about promising fame and fortune only if they came alone, without anyone knowing. Oh, Kelsey, you'd be stunned at how naive women are! I took a course on what to watch out for, but those little fools are the ones who really should have taken it. They were so gullible!"

"Why did you kill them?" Kelsey asked.

"I wasn't planning on sharing the diamond," Sandy said. She spoke in a chiding voice, as if Kelsey should have understood this.

"So you killed Jeff Chasson for getting too close to the truth." Kelsey made an effort to keep her tone merely curious.

"I told you that," Sandy said, pursing her lips.

"There's more to it."

"He was a prick!" Sandy leaned closer to her. "Do you know what he had the audacity to say to me?"

"What?"

"That he was interested in *you*." Sandy giggled. "Well, pretty soon, unless you get me that diamond, he *will* get to know you. The two of you can haunt San Antonio happily together. Oh, oh . . . it'll be a threesome. When the Lone Ranger shows up — minus any of his Tontos — one of you had better get me the diamond."

"Oh, Sandy!" Kelsey said, using a voice she might have when they were kids. "You're going to kill us, anyway!"

"I really don't want to," Sandy said earnestly. "I mean that. I just do what needs to be done."

"Dress up like a hairy frontiersman?" Kelsey asked.

"That was fun. I wore a costume and did the computer invites at the internet café. But down at the plaza? That wasn't me." She moved her lips close to Kelsey's ear, and Kelsey prayed she wouldn't notice that the patch was gone. "That was my partner. No one manages this kind of operation alone. You know what? He's a great actor. But he's going to die tonight, too. The diamond is *mine*." She moved away suddenly. "I want that diamond, Kelsey. And I want it now."

"You called Logan. He might come with the whole FBI. Then you can kill me, but they'll get you, and you won't get the diamond."

"Logan won't let you die. He'll come alone. You watch. Now, while we're waiting, why don't you see if you can conjure up Rose Langley for me?"

The voice didn't give it away. Whatever cheap little device Sandy Holly had bought, it was doing the job. No, it hadn't been the voice that had given her away.

It had been the sketches. There'd been something about the eyes, and when they'd spoken, he'd suddenly seen her face, and seen it with the beard, the mustache, the hair.

It made a shocking kind of sense.

Who knew the Longhorn better?

And who'd been around when the inn was changing hands?

He kept driving, trying to determine his course of action. So far, Sandy probably didn't realize that he knew about the basement — and the tunnel, supposedly walled up, that led to the toolshed. He was almost positive she'd found a way to get Kelsey down there. And Kelsey was tough and smart, but who would expect the enemy to be a friend? A friend who seemed to be in desperate trouble.

And, he thought, Sandy wasn't working alone.

If he called in the troops, if they came en masse, they'd be able to corral Sandy Holly and her partner.

But Kelsey would die.

He pulled onto the side of the road, and for a minute the pain that surged through him was so intense he couldn't bear it. Then he breathed, slowly and deeply, and considered what they'd learned about the men who hung around the Longhorn Saloon.

Finally, he thought he knew the truth. He kept breathing and put his plan into action.

He pulled back onto the road and drove to the Longhorn.

"Is he here yet?" Sandy asked.

Kelsey had heard the false wall between the basement and the cellar beneath it slide open, but she couldn't twist around to see who'd come. The voice was hoarse and low, and hard to recognize.

"No, not yet. I'm just down here to bring up some bottles of rum. The Ranger needs to come soon. The longer this takes . . ."

"Don't worry about it. We've kept captives down here for days when we've had to."

"They don't make any noise when they're dead. How's this one doing? Did we really have to call the Ranger?"

"Yes. One of them's the real deal. I know that for a fact," Sandy said. "And I'm pretty sure the other is, too. I want insurance. It's time to put an end to this."

The drug was wearing off; Kelsey had gotten to the patch quickly enough. But with both of them down there — Sandy and her partner — she didn't really stand a chance. She was afraid to try moving yet.

"Go back upstairs. Watch for the Ranger."

"Yeah, yeah. She must be another fake," he said, kicking the bedding where Kelsey

417

lay, "or she would've called them for you by now."

Kelsey forced a giggle. "I can call them. Do you want to play ghost?"

At last he stepped around in front of her. She wasn't surprised. It had all been an act from the moment she'd arrived at the Longhorn Saloon.

"Yeah, let's play ghost," he muttered.

Kelsey prayed for help, from the living — or the dead.

"Rose, Rose? Please. I know you're usually in the house. But can you come here? Now? Please, Rose, these people want to talk to you about the diamond."

There was no way on earth that Kelsey could have known she was performing on cue.

Logan had parked the car down the street and around the corner. He'd come in through the exit they'd taken from Sandy's room the night before. So far, easy. Too easy.

But what kind of shape was Kelsey in? How did he get to her without alerting the others? He'd studied the blueprints up and down and inside out, and there was no entrance other than the basement stairs — off the main bar — or through the false floor of the toolshed.

So, drop in, guns blazing? Would they be able to kill Kelsey that fast? She'd be drugged; she wouldn't be capable of defending herself. They'd surely have taken her Glock by now.

As he reached the house, he saw the birds. He'd never seen so many flocked in one place before, not even that day at his house.

"Hey, help me out tonight, brothers!" he said softly.

Logan was afraid of making any noise as he opened the back gate. He politely asked the birds to shift so he could hop over the fence. He approached the shed from the back.

And then he paused. The birds flew madly before him as he drew closer to the shed. They were like a cloud of bees, they moved so quickly.

And then . . .

The movement ceased, and the birds took shape, and there in the dusk and the moonlight stood Rose Langley.

Please.

He wasn't sure if he spoke the word aloud or if he thought it, and he wasn't sure if Rose was really there, or if she was an illusion he'd created.

But illusion or real, she understood. She brought a finger to her lips and walked toward the shed, opening the door so quietly he didn't hear it himself.

But he did hear Kelsey's voice. It seemed far away and distant, but the trapdoor in the shed was still open, and he moved close to it, and listened as she said again, "Rose, please, Rose, they want your diamond. Could you get it for them?"

"Nothing's happening," Corey said crossly. "And I've got to go back up and lure that cop down here."

Let him go. Let me save Kelsey, and then deal with him, Logan prayed.

His luck wasn't going to be that good.

"Stay here. The stupid cop'll go up to 207."

He heard Kelsey speak again, stalling for time, obviously determined to get the truth — before she died. He was astonished that she was conscious, that she could speak, but maybe he shouldn't be. It was Kelsey, after all. She had known about the patches, and must have somehow gotten hers off.

"So, Corey, are you really a cowboy?" she asked.

"You bet."

"But somehow Sandy got you to be a lackey for her. She teased you, and then slept with you, right? But she made you keep it a secret. You liked what the two of you did, though — didn't you? Kidnapping women and then killing them. But she tried to make you jealous, keep you in line. Didn't that piss you off sometimes?"

"Stop it, Kelsey," Sandy said.

"Seriously, I'd be pissed off. She slept with that poor producer and then flirted with the newspaper guy — like a true whore!"

"Hey, we had to shut him up!" Sandy said. "Corey, ignore her. She's doing this on purpose. Ignore her, okay?"

"I gotta go back to the bar," Corey mumbled.

Let him go. Let me save Kelsey . . .

He felt a gossamer touch on his arm. Rose. She looked at him with sorrowful, questioning eyes. *Should I?* she seemed to ask.

Logan nodded.

"Rose?" Kelsey's voice pleaded.

Rose preceded Logan to the drop. Like a feather through air, she stepped into nothingness and floated down.

He heard Corey Simmons's hoarse cry of astonishment as the ghost joined them. Logan leaped down and rolled with his gun cocked. Corey Simmons stared as if he were a ghost, too, but Logan aimed directly at him and shouted a warning when Corey went for his gun. "Drop it! I'll shoot to kill."

"*You* drop it!" Sandy demanded, flying toward Kelsey. "I've got another patch. This one is loaded with fentanyl. A hundred times more powerful than morphine. She'll be dead in seconds with this one, cowboy."

He had to shoot; he had to. He couldn't aim the gun at Sandy because Corey would shoot him, but whatever he did, he had only seconds.

There was a burst of noise in the room, and a burst of blackness. The ghost of Rose Langley had become a flock of furious flapping birds once again, and they were blinding everyone. Corey Simmons shot wildly. Logan turned his gun on Sandy and shot her through the forehead. Simmons had a bead on him, but to his astonishment, Kelsey suddenly scrambled up from the bedding and tackled him around the ankles. Corey went down, and his second shot went wild as he dropped his gun. He threw off Kelsey, then reached for his gun, but Logan had learned never to take chances. When Corey grabbed his Colt and turned to aim, Logan was above him, his finger on the trigger. He'd aimed true; Corey died swiftly, a bullet hole smoking between his eyes.

Kelsey staggered to her feet and fell against him.

"How?" he asked her.

"I got the patch off," she whispered. "Oh, Logan . . . Rose saved us."

"Even without knowing where the Galveston diamond is." Logan held her up, held her tight.

"I know where the diamond is," Kelsey said.

"You do, and Rose didn't?"

"I went to the room, Logan. I willed myself to see the residual haunting again, and I watched her closely. I saw something glitter in her hair. That's where she kept it. In her hair. Matt Meyer was a bastard who would've searched her body, but she could have slipped it into her hair and he would never have thought to look. When she died, she was a saloon-hall whore, and Texans were about to be massacred. There was no real justice for her, Logan. And there was probably no funeral. She was thrown in a pine box and buried, and if she was lucky, someone said a few words for her. If we find out where she's buried, we'll find the diamond."

By then, footsteps were tramping down the basement stairs. Ted Murphy came in, smashing the false closure to the walled-in tunnel. Ricky came after him, and then Bernie and Earl, and right behind him were the other members of the unit. Jackson pushed through, anxious to see what had happened. He looked from the dead on the floor to the living before him.

"You pulled it off, Logan," he said.

"*We* pulled it off. Kelsey was the first woman who managed to remove the patch. And she managed to keep Sandy talking. We pulled it off," he repeated. "By the way, your timing was perfect." He smiled apologetically at Kelsey. "Even if they'd killed us both, we had to stop them."

She nodded. "That's what we do."

"Sandy?" Ricky said brokenly. He turned to Kelsey. "Sandy?"

"Yes. I'm sorry, Ricky."

There were tears in his eyes. Ricky had really cared about Sandy. But then so had she, Kelsey thought. Sandy had been her friend, her childhood companion, a woman she'd loved. A woman she hadn't actually known. Whose depths of evil — there was no other word — she hadn't understood. The grief she felt now was for the Sandy who had never truly existed. . . .

Bernie Firestone was waving his hands in the air. "What the hell is it with all the birds?" he muttered. "Shoo, shoo . . . let's get them out of here!"

"I rather like birds," Logan said. "In fact, I'm very fond of them!"

EPILOGUE

Kelsey left the Longhorn, aware that Rose Langley was at her side. She smiled to herself as she walked.

They reached the Alamo plaza, and she saw Logan immediately — just as she saw Zachary Chase.

Both men stood as they approached. Kelsey nodded at Logan, but then gave her attention to Zachary and Rose.

At first, they simply stared at each other. Zachary took off his hat, and worked the brim anxiously between his fingers as he watched Rose, adoration in his eyes. Rose hesitated.

"Come on, he's waiting for you," Kelsey whispered.

"It's been so long, and . . . I don't know how he ever loved me," Rose said.

"Because your soul is beautiful," Kelsey told her. "Rose, you forgot how worthy you were of love. How worthy you *are*. Go to

Zachary now. Go to him. He still loves you."

Rose stepped ahead of her, until she stood in front of Zachary Chase. He took her hands and gazed down into her eyes. His voice was choked as he said, "Rose."

She stroked his cheek. "Zachary."

"Oh, Rose!"

Neither of them noticed as Kelsey joined Logan. Still gazing at each other, Rose and Zachary turned and walked toward the Alamo.

"Have they gone off into the light, do you think?" Kelsey asked.

"Maybe, and maybe they'll stay around for a while." He glanced down at her. "Rose was very happy, you know. You found her grave, and the diamond, and you saw that she was given a fine funeral and buried next to Zachary. It was really lovely."

"It was, wasn't it? And Kat was so respectful when she opened the box of Rose's bones and took out the diamond. It'll do wonders for the children in Haiti."

They'd all had quite a discussion about the diamond. At first they'd thought they should leave it with Rose, but then decided there might be other fortune hunters who'd kill for the stone. So they'd decided it had to come out, and that it needed to go to a good cause. They'd all agreed it should be donated to a charity.

"Sierra has moved on," Kelsey said. "She said goodbye to me that night, and she smiled, and I think I saw her wave. Then she was gone."

Logan looked in the direction of Zachary and Rose. "That's good," he said. "Zachary and Rose, they might stay on for a bit. They've just found each other after a very long time. I don't have all the answers." He smiled at her. "Neither of us does."

"But we have some of them," she said.

He nodded, still smiling. "Yes, we have some of them. And by the way, ma'am, there's far more to San Antonio than you've seen so far. I thought we could do a little sightseeing here, and then you could show me around Key West."

"Oh?"

"We'll have to head to Virginia for some training soon, and exchange our old badges for new ones. But I figured that since we'll have a few days — now that it's settled and the second Krewe will be Sean, Kat, Tyler, Jane and the two of us — we should enjoy some time in the sun, near the sea. . . . I want to go to Key West and see your home. What do you think?"

They were professionals, of course, and they always acted like professionals. They were standing in front of the Alamo, one of the most sacred shrines in the country. But she had a feeling that all the ghosts of the Alamo and every one of her professional associates would approve.

She stepped closer and rose on tiptoe and kissed him.

"Sounds like a plan," she said lightly. "And I can't begin to tell you how many truly beautiful birds we have in the Keys."

"I do love birds," he told her, and hand in hand, much like Rose and Zachary before them, they ambled along the plaza, eyes only for each other.

TEXAS RECIPES

To eat in Texas!
Chili con carne is the official dish of Texas.
This isn't just talk — it's official. As designated by the House Concurrent Resolution
Number 18 of the 65th Texas legislature
during its regular session in 1977, chili con
carne is it.

For Texas, chili is as historic as its wild
frontiersmen and its fight for independence.
The main ingredients — beef, suet, chili
peppers and salt — were ground together
and formed into bricks to be carried by men
such as the Texas Rangers as they headed
out to guard their borders (as vague and
disputed as those borders often were!).

At the Columbian Exposition of 1893 in
Chicago, the San Antonio Chili Stand
brought chili to fairgoers from across the
country and beyond, and ever since, chili
has been an American staple, especially
loved throughout the South and West.

And of course people wrangle over the recipe! Any decent chili aficionado has his or her own approach to making the best chili around — so much so that when I asked friends about a chili recipe, my mind was reeling. But here, putting together what I'm told is the best of the best, is a sworn recipe for San Antonio's finest chili.

In all my conversations, I was told that true Texas chili does not have tomatoes — hey, could those frontiersmen find a bunch of fresh tomatoes out on the wild plains? I guess not. So while I have a real get-down-and-cook recipe here and a quickie one, neither contains tomatoes or beans.

THE BEST TRUE TEXAS CHILI

Ingredients

10 dried chili peppers, chopped *(There are many kinds of chili peppers. These include anchos, pasilla, costeñas, guajillos and habanero, chiles de arbol. Mixing and matching can make for great chili. Habanero are hotter, or more piquant.)*

Dollop of suet (About two tablespoons. Can be replaced with a touch of olive oil.)

1/2 cup of water
4 slices bacon
3 to 3 1/2 lbs boneless Grade A beef chuck
  roast — cut into 1-inch cubes
1 onion, chopped
5 cloves garlic, minced
1/2 cup coffee
1/2 cup beer
1 tbsp cumin
1/2 tsp cayenne pepper

Dash of cinnamon
1/2 tsp oregano
2 cans beef stock

In this recipe, the chili peppers themselves are king. In a skillet (cast iron, if possible) drop the chili peppers and then, as they start to heat, add just a touch of suet so they don't burn. (If suet isn't available or just doesn't do it for you, you can add two tablespoons of olive oil.) Then turn off the heat, cover the chili peppers with half a cup of water (make sure they are covered) and let them soak for about half an hour.

In another pan, fry up the bacon. (Bacon was a commodity fairly available to the frontiersmen and could be dried or smoked and carried on the trail.) Remove the bacon, but leave the grease in the pot. Brown the meat, the onion and the garlic in the bacon grease. (Gauge this carefully; if the bacon was too fatty, you'll have greasy chili. About three tablespoons of grease is about right.) Crumble the bacon into the mixture, add the coffee, the beer, the spices and the beef stock, except for a half a cup.

Remove the chili peppers from their skillet, and puree them in a blender with the last half cup of the beef stock. Add the puree to the chili mixture, bring it to a boil, lower the heat, and let it all simmer — stirring occasionally and adding more liquid when necessary — for five hours. Taste as you simmer — every cook will want a little more of this or that, and some Texans actually add just a touch of Mexican chocolate (or, hey, whatever is around) to their creation. Some add more onions, some a dash of chili powder in case they didn't choose their chili peppers just right! However you choose to play with it, your base is there, and you can flavor to taste and perhaps add in some allspice or, if your taste buds are adventurous, go for it with another teaspoon of cayenne.

Chili may be garnished in many ways — with shredded cheese, scallions, croutons, bite-size pieces of corn bread, corn chip strips and sour cream.

THE BEST TRUE TEXAS
QUICKIE CHILI

Ingredients

3 to 3 1/2 lbs boneless Grade A beef chuck
  roast — cut into 1-inch cubes

3 tbsp olive oil (Replaces suet here!)

5 cloves garlic, finely chopped

2 to 4 tbsp flour

3 to 4 tbsp chili powder (Do you like it hot?
  Not as great as real chili peppers, but puts
  the chili in the chili.)

2 tsp ground cumin

1 bay leaf

2 cans beef broth

1 tsp salt

1/4 tsp ground black pepper

Sauté the beef in the olive oil for a few
minutes (on medium to medium-high heat),
coating the beef rather than browning it.
Add in the garlic, more or less to taste. Mix
together the flour (if you like a thinner chili,
two tablespoons; for a thick dish, four), chili

powder and cumin; lower the heat to medium, or medium-low, and toss in the bay leaf for some flavor. (You can also add a sprinkle of oregano.) Add a can and a half of the beef broth, bring all to a boil, lower the heat, let simmer and add the salt and pepper. Let it all brew for about an hour and a half.

Or . . . leaving in the morning? Not home until night? Throw it into a Crock-Pot, and let all the ingredients simmer throughout the day. Do you like other flavors in your chili? Not quite the purist? Add one chopped tomato and one small chopped onion.

Everyone has his or her own version of the best Texas chili. And, of course, that's a great thing about chili — it's the kind of dish made to be customized, and goes well with sweet corn bread, fresh green salads and, of course, a margarita or a good Tex-Mex beer!

To Drink In Texas!

History may have decided some of the most popular culinary tastes in Texas, as they tend to mix Mexican with American, or Tejano with Texian. And along that line, one of the area's most popular drinks can certainly be found and enjoyed on either side of the border.

So, pull out the tequila and let's get to it. Texans are known to love margaritas!

Now, simple margarita mix can be found in any liquor store. Premixed cocktails with the liquor can be found, as well. But, hell, this is Texas! It's the place to become a margarita connoisseur.

Start with . . .

Two jiggers tequila. *(Good tequila is always better, and quite popular these days is the brand Patron. Then again, let's face it, we're mixing, so pull out whatever you have.)*

A half part Grand Marnier. *(According to Texas friends, this is the best. You may add triple sec, which is better known, but Grand Marnier makes the ultimate margarita.)*

A half jigger fresh lime juice.

A half jigger fresh lemon juice.

A half jigger simple syrup.

A half jigger Limoncello. *(Those in the know say that Limoncello — also very popular in Italy! — adds the desired fruity flavor to the drink without making it bitter.)*

Rim glasses with coarse salt.

Mix ingredients well with ice and serve straight up or on the rocks.

Popular now, too, is the designer margarita. Strawberry, banana, blueberry, raspberry, mango! Add and subtract ingredients where you will, and as long as you stick with some good tequila, you'll have yourself a refreshing drink. By the time you have a few refreshing drinks, you won't even be worried about the salt and the calories!

If Margaritas seem too complicated, go for a Lone Star beer or pop the top on a Dos Equis.